Also by John Scheck:

*La Frontera Saga*

*Nothing Personal*

*Criminal Code*

*Lives of Crimes*

*Twenty-Seven Calls* by John Scheck

Published by Leftbanker Press

Library of Congress Cataloging-in-Publication Data

Author: John Scheck

Title: Twenty-Seven Calls

Paperback Second Edition ISBN: 979-8-9885351-5-7

# Contents

# PART 1

## Corpus Delicti

*Latin for "body of the crime" referring to a principle that proof of a crime must be established before anyone can be convicted, or in layman's terms, no body, no crime.*

# CHAPTER 1 – WORST NIGHTMARE

Elizabeth Owens caught her first glimpse of him on a downtown Philadelphia sidewalk before she approached the crossing signal: late thirties, almost completely bald, a ridiculous mustache, nearing morbid obesity, and dressed like a low-level white-collar worker in a polyester white shirt and cheap tie. She knew he was staring at her, catching a glimpse of his lewd smirk reflected in a storefront window, as if his admiration of her female form in itself were some sort of high compliment.

"Wow," he said in a low voice before she could move away.

The light changed and he got in lock-step behind her on the sidewalk.

"You work around here? Let's stop for a drink," he called.

There were dozens of people on the sidewalk, yet this guy felt completely uninhibited about directing a steady stream of lewd comments at the woman as he walked a few steps behind. She stopped to wait for the next traffic light, standing beside a couple in their late twenties who listened in silence as the stalker continued his onslaught of suggestive proposals and vulgar remarks, considered flattery among his ilk.

"Let's have a quick drink. Come on, baby. It's early."

Not early enough, as darkness had moved over the neighborhood, not that this sort of animal was nocturnal. He obviously thought of himself as a hunter, an alpha, a red-blooded American male. If his breed had to be categorized, it would fall somewhere beneath scavengers.

"Those jeans you're wearing are really doing their magic on me, know what I mean?"

The young couple made an abrupt turn, wanting nothing to do with a situation deteriorating with every remark the man uttered. They weren't willing to offer even the slightest bit of support. She could practically hear the young couple sighing in relief as they put this ugly incident out of their minds. She gave the young man a look of deep contempt as she walked away.

How can you live with yourself, you total coward? She almost asked him, but not tonight. She remembered a case when a man was hitting his ex-girlfriend with a baseball bat on a Philadelphia street, and no one had the balls to do anything to stop him. They took pictures with their phones.

There wasn't a single person on the street ahead as she kept up her pace, not hurried, but determined. The man practically lunged at her when she paused to look at the street sign on the corner.

"Lost, little lady? Where ya going?"

The damsel in distress. Lost in the city. *Can I be of any assistance? Let me help. What can I do for you?*

False chivalry: a typical doorway to misogyny.

From that point, it was like they'd been shackled together. She didn't pay him the slightest attention, but she didn't do the things women were instructed to do when ambushed on the street. She didn't pretend to talk on her phone, didn't enter the first business establishment, and she didn't strike up a conversation with another person on the street. It was never that easy, as every woman knew. Men like this were the most annoying salesmen imaginable, but in his tone, he carried something sinister, something hovering just within the reach of violence, as if that were the next tool in his box.

The man was almost skipping behind her as he felt the freedom of fewer eyes on him. His tone darkened, revealing his true nature.

"I'd tear that fat ass up, just give me a chance."

Typical predatory behavior rooted in degradation and intimidation. The very last thing men like this were after was a connection with a woman. They certainly weren't looking for a date, or even sex, at least not consensual.

This pig wouldn't know what to do with a woman if someone gave him a map, she thought, making her way down the block while pulling along her creepy admirer as if on a short leash.

She hadn't said a single word to him, hadn't looked him in the eye during the entire six blocks of his pursuit. He obviously had nowhere to go, and his relentless harassment would serve his masturbatory fantasies at some point. His deposit in the spank bank, as it was called.

Huffing on a cigarette, he looked to suffer from a laundry list of medical issues typical of a man of his age with an obvious disregard for his own health. She could hear him panting behind her, and not out of lust. The fat slob was actually winded at this leisurely pace she'd set.

As his insults tapered off, she thought he was about to throw in the towel and leave her be.

She dropped something out of her handbag and bent over to retrieve it from the sidewalk.

"That ass is so good. You gotta give that up to me."

He still had a little life in him after all, and more sewage to unload on her.

He was a big man, at least 6'2", and he may even have been attractive at some point in his miserable existence. She doubted he'd ever possessed a shred of class and suspected he'd been even less charming in his youth, if that were possible. How he could be more vulgar and disgusting than at this moment was hard to imagine. She tried not to.

What happened in his life to make him think his behavior was anything less than criminal? Where did he learn to treat women this way? Did he have a mother? Sisters? How could any man who had women in his life feel compelled to treat them with such utter contempt? Had something gone horribly wrong in his upbringing, or was this considered normal behavior somewhere? It was hatred of women, nothing less.

There was an underlying cowardice and cruelty in misogyny. Only a coward felt empowered by the weakness of his opponent, and only a diseased man looked at women as adversaries.

These questions rolled through her mind as she walked, but the answers didn't really interest her, if there were answers. She wasn't after answers. At this point, she was only interested in solutions.

One solution at a time.

The hatred was pulsing out of the man with every disgusting suggestion. She wondered how often he acted out like this. How many times a day did this pig do something offensive to women? How often did a similar incident happen on the streets of Philadelphia every day? She only knew about the situations that would eventually become criminal cases, and those numbered in the thousands every year.

He moved a step closer behind her on a street completely devoid of pedestrians and traffic, like the urban equivalent of a secluded corner of a dark forest. As she crossed another empty street, there was no noise from the previous busy thoroughfare. There was no life at all on the block, a sleepy commercial district after hours.

"Just stop and talk to me. You like men, right?"

He chuckled and lost a step; her pace was rhythmically dictated as with a metronome, or one of those walking applications.

A panel van drove slowly down the street in her direction.

Now his fatigue angered him; his monologue became even darker, more menacing, even threatening.

"Fucking stop, bitch. I'm talking to you."

The panel van turned left in front of her and drove a few car lengths down the street. The driver did a quick three-point turn and drove back, blocking the crosswalk in front of her. She was only a few steps away, walking directly toward the van. The side cargo door began to open from the inside.

She turned around just as her admirer took two long steps forward, almost lunging at her.

"Do it!" the man inside the vehicle shouted.

# CHAPTER 2 – 31 BRAVO

Growing up in one of the worst areas of Philadelphia, Elizabeth Owens had never given her future even a moment's consideration until she was only a few months away from leaving high school. She was graduating, and on time—a minor miracle among her peers in her predominantly Black neighborhood. Her first thought was that she needed to get as far away from where she lived as soon as possible. She talked to an Army recruiter who promised that if his organization was good at anything, it had a special talent for moving people far from home.

She left the city of her birth for basic training two weeks after graduation. While in transit from Philadelphia, Owens was having severe doubts about the wisdom of her decision to sign her life away, but the moment she stepped off the bus, with a drill instructor screaming and spitting in her face, she decided that she was going to make it, no matter what.

I got this, she decided instantly. It was like turning on a light switch.

She'd taken her first step toward becoming a military police officer, an MP, but more commonly known in the Army by its military occupation specialty (MOS) code of 31-Bravo.

For basic and her specialty training, she spent twenty weeks at Fort Leonard Wood in the middle of nowhere in the Missouri Ozarks. It was the farthest she'd ever been from Philadelphia. She thought it was a good start.

She'd never been a good student, but this was mostly due to the fact that she was raised in an atmosphere of criminally low expectations. Had someone told her to study, she would have studied.

In the Army, they demanded that you excel. While the Army never asked recruits at the dinner table about what they did at school that day, they had a lot of sticks and carrots to get soldiers to apply themselves. The Army was the helicopter parent she never had.

She barely left the post during the entire training program. For that, she would have needed a car. Besides children, she'd learned that cars were another thing that dragged people down into poverty. An Army E-1 (the lowest enlisted pay grade) couldn't afford any sort of automobile, not that this kept many soldiers from diving in way over their financial heads with car payments. She'd never make that mistake, not in the Army and not in her police career that followed.

U.S. Army Military Police undergo an almost endless barrage of instruction, beginning with the initial course of twenty weeks which includes basic training. Entering the 31-Bravo career field required above average test scores, a background investigation leading to a security clearance, and this is before setting foot in the actual training facility. The five-month course is designed to train soldiers in hundreds of law enforcement scenarios from hostage negotiation to prisoner control.

Owens quickly realized in her first days of class that she was at a sharp disadvantage because of her sub-standard education, even though she did well among the underachievers at her Philadelphia high school. She spent what little free time she had reading per the advice of one of her instructors who also told her that being able to express yourself well was a crucial aspect of police work, and there was no better way to achieve that goal than reading.

A simple bit of advice, but Owens took it to heart and became a reader. She read everything she could get her hands on and kept a stack of books from the base library on the desk in her dormitory room. She wrote letters to her best friend back in Philadelphia, long, hand-written volumes describing every aspect of military life. She sold military life so well that two months into her training as an MP, her friend enlisted in the military.

At one point in training, she was obliged to learn how to type. This class was an hour-long addition to her already full eight-hour day of military police training. She'd rarely even touched a keyboard before joining the Army, but one of her first purchases was a used laptop computer. Before the typing class, she'd used the hunt-and-peck method which she found infuriatingly slow.

"This class has a very simple goal: you need to type twenty-five words a minute. When you think you're ready, you can take the test at the end of the hour. Until you test out of here, you will attend this class Monday through Friday," her instructor said.

Never before—or after—had an objective been laid out this plainly. Never before had the carrot and the stick been so clearly evident. Each day there was a fifteen-minute instructional video on the mechanics of touch typing, followed by forty-five minutes of practice. Never before had she wanted out of something more desperately than she wanted out of that one-hour prison cell tacked on to the end of an already grueling day that began with morning physical training.

It took her less than two weeks to test out of the class, giving her one more hour of the day to herself. It was one of the most illuminating educational and motivational episodes in her life. She often thought that if she'd been given this sort of inspiration and direction during her years in the Philadelphia public school system, she'd have gone to a top university instead of Army basic training.

Although the instruction she received in her course work as a 31-Bravo was excellent, the motivation seemed mostly a question of avoiding the stick. At least twenty-five percent of candidates washed out of the program. If there was any hint you flunked out of the course through indolence, you wouldn't be treated well in your next duty station. This stick was explained often to students at every step in their training. Not only were slackers threatened with the worst jobs the U.S. Army had to offer, and there were some truly godawful duties, but the Army also had some miserable places to assign soldiers they felt weren't applying themselves.

Years after Owens left the Army and was no longer subject to their jurisdiction, she still had the occasional nightmare about one of those duty stations Army instructors used as a means to torment soldiers, almost mythical places like Fort Wainwright, Alaska.

Fort Wainwright, Alaska. Jesus, Mary, and Joseph, Owens thought.

Talk about a big stick. For a girl from Philly who hated the winters there, Alaska seemed like…she couldn't even imagine. All she knew was she didn't want to go there, not in this life. Every service branch had its own idea of hell when it came to duty assignments, and as bad as Fort Wainwright was in Owens's thinking, she'd heard of worse places in the U.S. military's Gulag Archipelago, or at least that's how Owens viewed these distant outposts.

Diego Garcia in the middle of the Indian Ocean was the Navy's purgatory.

Another purgatory was Thule, Greenland. No further explanation necessary. Greenland!

She remembered this name used in the Air Force as a level of Dante's inferno for people who'd screwed up. To Owens, the Air Force seemed like it was for total wimps, but lord have mercy, did they ever know how to negatively motivate their people. There was an almost diabolical cruelty to this on a par with the horrors of the Soviet work camps in Siberia.

The carrot of her training? That was simply the honor of one day wearing the MP badge on her uniform, at least that was the standard line. In training, instructors made it sound as if this badge gave the wearer superpowers, like it was the most exclusive club on the planet. The philosophy of the training was to prepare soldiers for the absolute worst so that they'd never, could never experience anything in the field that they hadn't been trained to handle.

After a few weeks of a rocky academic performance, Owens learned how to study for the first time in her life. She woke up every morning at 05:00, much to the chagrin of her roommate on the bottom bunk. She sat down at her desk and studied until the mess hall opened at 07:00. She had breakfast and returned to her room to study until her first class at 08:30. Two weeks into this regimen, she began acing her exams.

She started to move up quickly in the class ranking and after her tenth week of training, she knew that she was going to make it—barring any sort of physical mishap that might set her back or eliminate her from the school—always a possibility in such a demanding assignment. Injured candidates would sometimes be recycled back into another class while others were sent off to other duty training. From what she'd gleaned from people she knew who'd washed out because of injuries, there wasn't much rhyme or reason to Army doctrine regarding how they'd treat you after you recovered from an injury.

The lesson to learn from this was easy: don't get injured. Getting recycled seemed on a par with being sent to Alaska. Of course, young people never, ever consider that they'll ever have a debilitating injury. When you're eighteen years old, you feel absolutely invincible. You could lose a hand in a sawmill accident, and you'd shrug it off. Fuck it, it'll grow back, right? This attitude will remain with you as long as you avoid any major injuries, but somewhere as you near middle age, vulnerability sets in, to the point where you feel the need to be euthanized over a mild hangover. Middle age was the very distant future for the young soldier, way beyond the horizon.

Already proficient with a semi-automatic pistol and the M16 rifle from Army basic training, Owens kept up a steady stream of weapons training in her 31-Bravo curriculum. Her best results on the range were with the Beretta M9 9mm pistol, the standard issue sidearm in the U.S. military. This went on to become her weapon of choice throughout her law enforcement career, a firearm she was as comfortable with as any piece of clothing she'd ever worn.

She'd never been goal-oriented before her enlistment, barely knew what that meant. The U.S. Army would either form you into this sort of person or break you at some point along the way. Beth Owens thrived on the constant torrent of challenges heaped upon her as a soldier and a 31-Bravo. The obstacle course was a favorite training tool in the Army, but the organization's entire education process was analogous to an obstacle course. Owens appreciated the fact that someone, anyone, was finally motivating her to achieve goals of any sort. She made a list of things that she wanted to accomplish in both the short and long term.

If a newly minted MP fresh out of training felt a need for advanced training, Green Zone security in Iraq was just the place, which turned out to be the first duty assignment for Specialist Owens out of Fort Leonard Wood. She was offered two weeks of leave before shipping out, but she left Philadelphia with the idea of never returning, and with nowhere else to go, she saved her money and leave time and stayed on the post until flying out to Iraq via Mannheim, Germany.

Owens could never understand why so many soldiers were in such a hurry to run back home the first chance they were given, considering that many of them were from places as grim and hopeless as her corner of Philly. This temporary duty was called "casual detail" and what sort of work you were assigned depended on the exigencies of the U.S. Army and your unit commander. Often, the officer or noncommissioned officer in charge felt pity on the soldiers stuck on base while others were on home leave and just told them to study for their classes.

She was as careful with her leave time as she was with her meager pay and planned to use it to go somewhere a bit more exotic than eastern Pennsylvania. She'd already begun planning a trip to Spain when she finished her one-year tour in Iraq. To this end, she started learning basic Spanish from a class offered to qualified students who were doing well in their military training.

Before any holidays in Spain, she'd have to make it through a year in a war zone where survival was anything but guaranteed, and Iraq was particularly dangerous for MPs doing security in Baghdad, especially troops patrolling the treacherous route to the airport. After spending three months on station checking for roadside Improvised Explosive Devices (IEDs) and screening Iraqi workers entering and leaving the Green Zone, Owens was called in for a talk with her commanding officer.

"Talk" really isn't the correct word when a soldier in the lower enlisted ranks speaks with a lieutenant colonel. He talked and she listened. He told her that she was to be the liaison between the U.S. Army MPs in Baghdad and the Iraqi police in matters of violent crimes against Iraqi women.

Her CO was African-American so he didn't feel the need to tiptoe around the fact that she was chosen partly because she was a woman of color who he felt would be more amenable to the Iraqis, although he also made it clear to her that she was an excellent soldier in every respect and had distinguished herself thus far in her military career.

"This is no damn diversity hire," the young lieutenant colonel said. "You just gotta back me up on my choice by kicking this job's ass. Got it?"

"Got it, sir," Owens sounded off.

Violent crimes against women? From what Owens had seen in her short time in country, the Iraq War after five years seemed like a violent crime against an entire nation, a crime against humanity. Other than being a woman, she felt that she didn't have any qualifications to lend to problems facing women in Iraq, but Owens welcomed the challenge and was determined to apply herself to the fullest. She spoke no Arabic, and few in the Iraqi police spoke English beyond basic greetings, but, as they say, you have to start somewhere.

The "somewhere" in her case could have been the very last place Owens would ever see.

On her first liaison meeting with the local police, she was part of a detail of three U.S. Army MPs: Owens, her company commander who was a very young and newly promoted captain, and a grizzled NCO with twelve years of experience on the job, three of those stationed in Iraq and two more in Afghanistan. He'd seen it all when it came to war zones.

The meeting was in a Baghdad police precinct outside of the Green Zone which would normally require U.S. personnel to be in platoon force, at the very minimum. This mission was approved for just three as per the request of the Iraqi police. No one among the U.S. delegation thought this was a prudent move, but someone signed off on it in the upper echelons and that was that. Three MPs would venture out of the Green Zone with the promised support of the highly unreliable Iraq local police.

"Well, we all gotta die of some damn thing," the sergeant said.

Their unarmored Humvee rolled out of the gates of the Green Zone behind a dilapidated Iraqi squad car with two officers who looked more like patients on their way to heart surgery than anything resembling a U.S. Army MP. The young American captain tried desperately to mask his concern-terror as they drove out of the gate and into what the soldiers called the "red zone" which was anything outside of the safety of the Green Zone. Owens was too young and innocent to see it as anything but an adventure. She was nineteen, an Army MP, and invincible in her mind.

Owens drove, with the captain to her right, and the sergeant in the back. Owens glanced at the sergeant in the back who carried the bored look of someone waiting in line to renew a driver's license.

Staff Sergeant Núñez may have looked bored, but Owens could see he had a very sure grip on his very heavily accessorized M4, a more compact version of the M16, ideal for urban warfare. The rumor in the unit was that Núñez could shoot skeet with the M203 grenade launcher now attached below the barrel of his rifle.

Owens followed the Baghdad police cruiser through bombed-out and poverty-stricken neighborhoods, a veritable two-kilometer obstacle course of manned roadblocks, cratered streets, and hulks of destroyed vehicles. As much as Owens hated her hometown, even her old Philadelphia neighborhood beat the hell out of war-ravaged Baghdad.

The two-vehicle convoy passed a group of four young boys playing soccer in the street with a ragged excuse for a ball. The boys stopped abruptly, stood at attention, smiled at the Americans, and saluted. It was the first time Owens had seen an Iraqi smile since she arrived in country four months earlier. Owens smiled and saluted in return.

The squad car came to a stop in front of a one-story building that looked like a cross between a high-security prison and an insane asylum. All of the windows were barred, and the front door looked like a bank vault. Owens backed the Humvee up to the front steps of the building.

The captain and Núñez got out of the vehicle. Owens stayed behind the wheel. The captain walked around to the driver's side.

"We all go in; that's the order," he said.

"No escort for the vehicle?" Owens asked.

Núñez was at least as incredulous of the order as Owens.

"Ain't we got other orders telling us *not* to leave a vehicle?" Núñez said, making it more of an accusation than a question.

"It's fucked up, but it is what it is," the young officer said in apology. "I suppose the idea is that we're supposed to trust the Iraqi police to keep our vehicle safe while we're in front of their own fucking police precinct."

"I guess we'll see about that," Núñez just couldn't help himself.

The two Iraqis and their three American guests stepped into the open entryway of the station where policemen in varied stages of uniformed dress and undress sat on folding metal chairs. Owens counted the surly police officers, inventoried their weapons, and noted parenthetically that all of them were smoking.

One of the Iraqis stood up and offered cigarettes to the Americans who all declined. Owens sensed that the entire room took this as an affront, and she guessed that her gender also didn't sit too well in the room. The young Army specialist was well past giving a shit what men or their conventions thought about the role of women.

The three Americans were escorted down a dark corridor by two of the men in the lobby area. The door to the office of the police commandant for the precinct was open. He sat behind a small desk in the large room.

The captain knocked on the door frame.

"Welcome," the commandant muttered in English and waved them in.

He didn't bother to stand as his guests entered.

Owens and Núñez would let the captain do the talking. The American officer was about to salute, but cut it short. The Iraqi officer didn't even bother to look up.

Not a good first impression given to the visiting team, and the commandant's complete lack of respect was palpable.

"Maybe we need to teach them a little respect along with the police training," Núñez offered under his breath but loud enough for everyone to hear.

The captain gave Núñez a look that said he agreed but this wasn't the time to lecture the locals on protocol. The three U.S. Army soldiers stood at ease.

"I'm Captain Stephanos from the Eighteenth Military Police Brigade."

"I am Commandant Marzawi, Baghdad Police."

"As you've been informed, we have come to inspect your facilities, especially the lockups to assess security and prisoner treatment," Captain Stephanos said.

17

Stephanos had voiced his concern about the effectiveness of this mission, making it known that he felt the Iraqis would not present an honest view of their jail facilities and would whitewash any traces of prisoner abuse. His objections were duly noted, filed away, and ignored. The brigade commander felt that any contact with the Iraqis was better than nothing. The Abu Ghraib prison scandal had abrogated any high ground the Americans could hope to enjoy concerning the treatment of detainees.

Commandant Marzawi finished his cigarette and stood up. He grabbed a ring of keys off his desk and walked to the door.

"We shall to take look. OK?" the commandant said in his heavily accented English.

The commandant walked down the corridor with the three Americans a few paces behind. Two Iraqis with AK47s walked several steps to the rear. Núñez slowed down until he was between the two Iraqi escorts and looked at one, then the other as if to say, "We're all friends here."

The commandant opened a heavy metal gate that led to the cell block of the precinct.

Owens was almost overcome with the stench of the place, mostly shit and piss, but other, even more toxic odors. She wondered if there were any prisoners in the block as she couldn't hear a single voice, unusual in her experience. Jails were normally exceedingly noisy places where inmates only communicated in shouts. This wasn't true of American military prison facilities, but as an MP cadet, she'd visited civilian penitentiaries and was almost overwhelmed by the noise.

The captain seemed to notice as well.

"It's quiet in here," he remarked to the commandant.

"Because fucking prisoners know not talk when officer enter."

The Americans could only imagine what methods the police used to instill this discipline in their prisoners.

There were three windowless cells on each side of the corridor, each about five meters by five meters. The pens were nothing but bare concrete floors with a hole in the back corner that served as a toilet, with a tap above the hole presumably as a means to flush, wash up, and serve as a drinking fountain. Three of the cells were empty and two of them held five men each, from adolescents to old men. In the final cell, there were two naked girls who looked to be no older than thirteen.

Upon seeing the naked children, Stephanos threw up his arms in disbelief.

"What in the fuck is this?"

The commandant didn't seem to register the outrage and wasn't the least concerned with how the Americans perceived this tableau.

"They are Shiite terrorists. Scum. They kill Iraqi police."

Owens had stepped back in line with Núñez to keep an eye on the Iraqi escorts. She'd seen a lot of bullshit in Iraq, but this touched a nerve.

Captain Stephanos seemed frozen in his confusion as his mind raced between deciding between his orders, his career, his duty, and doing the right thing in this situation.

Owens and Núñez had far fewer things clouding their judgment.

19

Owens took two steps forward and spoke into her captain's ear, but loud enough for everyone to hear.

"Sir, I need to make myself perfectly clear right now, but if the commandant doesn't get these naked children out of this torture chamber immediately, we will."

"They are terrorists," the commandant shouted.

"He lets them out now or I'll put a round in his skull, take the keys, and let them out myself, and I don't give a shit about the consequences."

"Captain, you allow this *sharmuta* talk me like this?" the commandant asked, his English deteriorating even further with his anger.

"She wasn't talking to you," Núñez said. "I concur with Specialist Owens, sir, and you need to advise the commandant that he calls one of my soldiers a whore at his fucking peril."

The two Iraqi escorts didn't appear to speak a word of English and were unaware of the shit-storm that was brewing in front of them. They had their AK47s slung casually over their shoulders while all three of the Americans had their M4s in frontal slings for quick access. The Americans gripped their weapons.

About one meter after leaving the Green Zone, Núñez had advised them to take the safeties off their weapons. The captain had pointed out that this was against protocol but deferred to the far more experienced NCO. With rounds chambered, the three were ready to go from zero to rock-and-roll in a split second.

This was not a drill.

The potential for bloodshed cleared Captain Stephanos's thinking. His training kicked in and trumped his misgivings about confronting the Iraqi commandant.

"Captain, you allow this..." the Iraqi commandant paused and reconsidered his words. "You allow her talk me in this manner of disrespect, here in my precinct? I could call my men and all of you dead."

Núñez stepped up to the Commandant Marzawi.

"You see this on the bottom of my barrel? It's an M203 grenade launcher with a round in the chamber. I could fire this down that hall, smash through the door, and turn those nine pedophiles out there you call your men into hamburger."

Núñez wasn't completely sure if the M203 round would explode on impact with the glass door to the lobby area, or if he could shoot between the bars on the gate before that door, and he was positive the round wouldn't kill everyone in the lobby, but he was also sure the Iraqi commandant didn't know anything about the limitations of American military hardware.

The commandant obviously wasn't accustomed to enlisted rank personnel speaking to him with this kind of total disrespect. He wasn't used to being in such a potentially perilous situation. They were only three, but the Americans were intimidating in their high-tech military gear and all three had the physiques of professional athletes. The three Americans had more firepower than any Iraqi infantry platoon.

"Commandant, if you want our cooperation, and by cooperation, I mean millions of dollars in cash, you need to get these children the fuck out of this cell, get them dressed, and we'll take them out of here when we leave."

21

As arrogant as the commandant tried to appear to his American guests, Captain Stephanos knew enough about the Iraqi military to know that even the high-ranking officers lived in constant fear of being executed at the whim of anyone a step above them in Saddam Hussein's Iraq where paranoia and terror were the primary tools of leadership. It was a system that didn't encourage or reward valor, crushed any hint of dissent, and instilled blind loyalty.

The commandant made a quick assessment of his situation and decided that his chances of survival were infinitely higher if he deferred to these three American warriors. He ordered his escorts to free the two naked children and covered them with military tunics.

With Sgt. Núñez taking the lead, the Americans walked out the front door of the precinct with the two children and drove off without a word spoken between them until reaching the Green Zone.

As they drove through the checkpoint, Núñez finally broke the silence.

"Sir, permission to unpucker my asshole now?"

Owens almost lost control of the vehicle after bursting into hysterical laughter along with her captain.

They dropped the girls off at the Army medical station.

"The first rule of police work?" Núñez asked the young woman from Philadelphia.

"Don't take the job home with you," Owens said, wondering if she'd ever stop thinking about the two severely traumatized children.

After they'd checked the Humvee at the motor pool, Captain Stephanos turned to his two co-conspirators.

"I'll file a full report, but I want your word that you'll never talk about this incident to anyone," he pleaded. "I may have over-stepped a few boundaries."

"Copy that, sir. Never want to think about this again," Owens said.

Captain Stephanos looked at Núñez for his consent.

"The fuck you talking about, sir?"

The captain remembered that the staff sergeant was the most tight-lipped, hard-ass he'd met in his six years in the U.S. Army.

"Sorry, Staff Sergeant Núñez. I must sound like such a fucking punk for even saying that."

"Naw, captain. You done good back there. I'm fucking proud of you."

"Thanks, that means a lot to me."

The three were about to go their separate ways when Núñez had a brilliant idea.

"If, hypothetically speaking, seeing how it's completely against Army policy in this dry-as-fuck wasteland, a certain soldier were in possession of a bottle of Courvoisier VSOP, would anyone care to join this recalcitrant enlisted man for a well-deserved cup or two?"

Captain Stephanos looked over at his sergeant with a grimace.

"Armando, I've been fighting with these feelings for a long time now, but I have to say, I think I love you."

The two now looked at Owens for her response.

23

"I really hope I don't have to, but I'd fuck both of you ugly bastards for a drink right now."

***

Owens went on to distinguish herself again and again in her Army service, but she learned that military rank wasn't based on merit. Any further advancement would be due to dumb luck and the exigencies of the U.S. Army, whatever that meant. After her enlistment was up, she took her experience and knocked on the door of the Philadelphia Police Department.

She had about a year of college credit for her military experience and several university extension classes she managed to finish during her enlistment. Her plan was to complete her Bachelor of Arts degree at night, or whenever she wasn't being a cop. The first few years she pulled a lot of night shifts which threw a wrench into any plans of being a model student. Her GPA suffered slightly, but she made it through the irregular shifts and after six years on the force, she got her degree in sociology at Temple University.

Making rank was just as much of a mystery in the PPD as it was in the Army, but as a single woman without children, she managed well on her salary. She looked around at her friends, both on and off the force, and kids were what really turned normal people into poor people. Her own mess of a family soured her on having children, and she later decided that she couldn't ever afford kids. How could anyone afford children, she often wondered.

Her own mother was a shining example of how not to live your life. Pregnant for the first time at fifteen, she went on to have five children with three different men, none of whom contributed much of anything. Beth never even met her father, had no idea who he was. She was way beyond caring except she wouldn't mind giving him a beat down if she met him in a dark alley.

Her siblings were all train wrecks who she'd given up on years ago. Whenever anyone asked, she said she was an only child, parents deceased. It was a lot easier and less painful than the truth, and she was tired of being ashamed of her family. They didn't deserve to have that sort of control over her since she'd become a self-supporting adult.

If anyone thought this was heartless on her part, they didn't know her at all. She became a cop because she saw it as the quickest path to power for a woman. The Army and the Iraq War may have been completely ludicrous concepts, but from them Beth gained something that other women would call empowerment, although the over-use and misuse of that word made her cringe. With all skepticism aside, give a girl a gun and a badge that says she can use it, and you have empowerment.

After growing up in one of the poorest, most violent urban neighborhoods in Philadelphia, hell, in all of America, and after barely making it out alive, Beth was thriving.

# CHAPTER 3 – THE BIG BOOK

The Philadelphia Police Department's Domestic Violence Unit had a list of over seven hundred men—they were almost always men—suspected of or already convicted of committing violent acts, with women and children the primary victims. In theory, the unit had at its disposal every police officer on the streets of the city, but the fact was the unit consisted of only four officers: three women and one man, all of the rank of detective except the unit's chief, Sergeant Marcia Welling. In an average year, the unit reviewed over five thousand cases ranging from stalking to aggravated assault to murder.

The Domestic Violence Unit was part of the investigations branch in the Philadelphia Police Department requiring all officers to be of detective rank, although it seemed to everyone involved that all of the investigative work and all the good policing in the world didn't seem to stem the rising tide of violence against women in the city. Domestic abuse calls made up a sizeable part of every patrol officer's watch, whether it was days (08:00-16:00), swings (16:00-24:00), or mids (00:00-08:00).

During her years in a squad car, Beth Owens knew that the worst time was 22:00, ten p.m. when the wife-beating pieces of shit who had tied on a good one after work—if they had a job—and came home looking for someone, anyone to take out the frustrations of their pathetic lives. This sort of trash thoroughly resented female officers stepping between their fists and their wives or children, as if female authority gave further evidence of their impotence and failures as men.

She'd been attacked on seven separate calls, resulting in five convictions for assault on a police officer. She'd received various cuts and bruises, some separated rib cartilage, and a broken finger in her run-ins with disgruntled lovers. By anyone's calculations, she'd dished out more damage: a few concussions, a broken hand, and three very hyper-extended elbows. In each altercation, her partner was present, but Owens had waved them off.

She let her various partners know that if anyone came at her, unarmed, they weren't to intervene unless she asked for their assistance. She never had to call for backup or ask for partner intervention. Her thinking was that after dealing with Beth Owens, the abusers she sent to the emergency room might think twice before ever laying their hands on a woman again.

For many of the men on the unit's list of serial abusers, fear of being arrested and imprisoned didn't often weigh heavily on them, especially when they were intoxicated, and almost all of them qualified as alcoholics or drug addicts. As a cop, she also didn't consider herself to be anyone's idea of a substance abuse counselor. She never wanted that job; she already had one.

Police officers had always been reluctant to stand between couples in domestic disputes. Unless the wife pressed charges, or the responding officers witnessed an attack, it was difficult to make cases against the abusers that would stand up in court. Even when women did file charges against partners, they were far from slam-dunk convictions.

For serial abusers, women could file a restraining order against the suspect. In Philadelphia, they called it a Protection from Abuse (PFA) order, an almost tragic overstatement of the power of this flimsy tool of law enforcement. The consequences for violating a restraining order ranged from a misdemeanor to different felony counts, but it was often difficult to make a case. More often than not, all it came down to were fines against the suspects.

In spite of several high-profile cases in which women with restraining orders were further abused and even killed by their tormentors, this legal action wasn't completely ineffective at stemming some of the violence against women. Unfortunately, as a cop, all Owens had seen were the failures. The success stories never called the abuse hotline, and they weren't the subject of stories in the metro section of the *Philadelphia Inquirer*. In the same manner, the victories in the Domestic Violence Unit in the PPD were rarely heralded while their failures had often made national news stories.

One of the worst nights Officer Owens had back on patrol happened on a domestic abuse call. Under other circumstances, it would've never happened. She would've never been so off her guard as to allow anyone in a domestic abuse call to be in a position to strike her. That was the night she learned that domestic abuse crossed all ethnic, racial, and economic lines. In her many years of experience on the streets of Philadelphia as a cop, she'd learned the boundaries of the violent neighborhoods, down to the exact block where they began. If you crossed a street in a war zone neighborhood, you could find yourself in an upwardly-mobile, gentrified area of shiny, happy people where life was significantly less violent.

She and her partner were called to a Center City high-rise with a twenty-four-hour doorman who buzzed them in just after midnight on a Sunday morning. A resident had called the concierge complaining about noise and possible violence next door. Owens thought rich people didn't call the police, not in her experience, so this must have been one loud domestic squabble.

Owens noticed the building had three elevators. All she could deduce from this was that rich people hated waiting and were willing to pay a heavy premium to avoid standing around doing nothing. So much of what they valued revolved around not having to wait—or making someone else wait for them.

The two Philly beat cops could hear the agonized screams of a woman and a man shouting as soon as they got out of the elevator on the fifteenth floor. Owens was the senior officer on this call and stood in front of the door as she rang the bell. She could barely hear the doorbell over the shouting inside, but she thought she recognized the ringer as Pachelbel's Canon. Good Christ, they even have to install elite doorbells, she thought. A polite interval after ringing twice, she took out her nightstick and rapped firmly on the heavy door.

No answer and the shouting continued.

This time, Owens laid into the door like she was trying to break her stick or the door.

She learned quickly that police work rarely rewarded subtlety.

Another thing about the rich was they loved their heavy doors. She doubted the battering ram they'd left downstairs in the cruiser would even make a dent in this fortress gate. It would've been easier to smash through the wall.

More shouting and no answer.

This time, Owens wasn't being polite at all and beat the door like the proverbial ugly step-child and kept it up until the noise drowned out the shouting inside, damage to the door be damned.

There was a moment of silence.

"What do you want?" a voice inside bellowed.

"Philadelphia police, sir. We've had several noise complaints. Would you please open the door?" Owens said in her straightest White voice.

She turned out to be a talented linguist, as she'd learned when she began studying Spanish in the Army. She also learned she was good at imitating accents. She figured that if she could successfully imitate a Spanish accent, she could mimic the voice of a White suburban housewife.

"Fuck off, this is between two adults."

"We need you to open the door, sir. We heard what sounded like a violent argument and we need to see if everyone is doing OK."

"I said, fuck off. You can't come in without a search warrant," he said, his White privilege coming through even louder than his voice.

OK, one of *these* kinds of assholes, Owens thought, not a lawyer himself, but thinks he knows the law.

"We have probable cause to enter without a warrant, sir. We suspect violent activity has been going on. We heard calls for help. We can either break down the door, or you can open it. Your choice. You have exactly twenty seconds to decide which way this goes."

It pissed Owens off to no end to think that in a poor neighborhood cops would have already torn the fucking door off the hinges. Class and money have their privileges, mostly because police are fearful of the legal repercussions of infringing on the rights of the wealthy.

A full minute later, Owens heard the locks opening. Locks. Plural. Yet another thing about rich folks: their need for security trumped their complete lack of patience.

At 5'10", Beth Owens was above average height for women, but the man who opened the door towered over her at almost 6'3," and he was fit, very fit for his age which she guessed to be early fifties. She calculated that his haircut cost more than her best pair of running shoes. Even in the early hours of a weekend, he was dressed in one of the GQ uniforms of the elite: khaki slacks, a heavily-starched white shirt, blue blazer, and loafers.

"We don't need the goddamned police," he screamed.

The guy had "asshole" written all over him, Owens thought.

"Sir, we've had noise complaints, and we heard a woman screaming for help when we got off the elevator," Owens said in her calmest, Whitest voice.

"Everything is fine, I said."

He tried to close the door, but Owens had stepped in and blocked it open with her left foot.

"We need to speak with the other party. She can either step out here, or I can go in. Up to you."

Owens's partner was directly behind her in the hallway, a skinny Italian kid from South Philly who was a lot tougher than he looked. Owens had put away her nightstick, but her partner still had his in his right hand.

Mr. GQ made no effort to allow Owens through into the apartment.

"Ma'am," Owens called inside the apartment. "We need to speak to you. Can you come out into the hallway?"

No answer.

"Ma'am, are you OK? We need to speak to you."

Mr. GQ tried again to close the door. This was an act of aggression, and Owens should have known better. She was off her game in these opulent surroundings. Had a husband pulled that in one of the city's poor neighborhoods, she would've been on her guard, she would've pulled out her nightstick. It probably had something to do with the fact that what the guy was wearing represented about three weeks of her salary, not including the watch.

"Ma'am, we need…" Owens was craning her neck around Mr. GQ and calling inside the apartment to the woman who had yet to show herself.

Mr. GQ punched Owens square in the face.

The punch was a lot more of a surprise than painful. She'd taken a lot of punches to the face in MP training where recruits boxed, grappled, and fought in every fighting style ever invented—and beating the hell out of each other was how they spent much of their free time.

Mr. GQ made another attempt to close the door, but this time Owens grabbed both his sleeves along with a handful of the body of the jacket, pinning her assailant's arms to his side, a judo trick learned in her martial arts education. He took a step toward her trying to raise his hands. As his right foot came off the ground, Owens swept it with her left foot as she pulled him violently toward her, falling backward at the same time. Unable to balance himself with his arms which were pinned to his sides by her grip, his right foot spun around. He came down hard, with Owens guiding him toward his left side, crashing his head into the base of the doorframe.

*Ippon*!

Or that's what a referee would have called in a judo match. Point and match.

Owens's partner was right there to assist if needed, but it was all over. Mr. GQ was out cold.

Between assaulting an officer and the woman, Mr. GQ should have ended up doing at least a few months in jail, something that would've been at least two years for anyone without expensive legal counsel.

Mr. GQ happened to be James McMillan, a scion of one of Philadelphia's oldest families. Even after beating his concubine senseless and assaulting a police officer, James McMillan was furious with the young police officer, at least he was weeks later after leaving the hospital and meeting with his lawyer. He threatened a lawsuit against the city and Officer Elizabeth Owens in particular.

Both in the Army and on the Philadelphia force, her performance reports were immaculate. Her only blemish now, if you could call it that, was sending a billionaire to the hospital with a severe concussion. Fortunately for her, the man had broken her nose, something witnessed by another on-duty Philadelphia police officer. The incident went before a review. She was completely exonerated after the brief inquiry which had come about simply as a way for the department to stem a lawsuit by Mr. McMillan's lawyers. Lawyers. Plural.

Her broken nose required only bags of ice to reduce the swelling, but McMillan spent several days in the emergency care unit in an induced coma to reduce intracranial pressure.

Owens was encouraged to keep her mouth shut when a deal was made to drop the charges against the Philadelphia socialite, but even with her silence, the matter wasn't enough to prevent McMillan from working behind the scenes to hobble her career in the department, all without her knowledge, of course. It took her a couple of years to figure out that McMillan had enough power in the city to have some top people in the department deny her duty requests. She remained on patrol far longer than any officer with her exemplary record, test scores, arrests, and conviction rates.

After her successful promotion to detective rank, the only duty assignment made available to Owens other than patrol was her last choice: The Domestic Violence Unit—not exactly the path for an upwardly mobile police officer. For Owens, it was the equivalent of Fort Wainwright, Alaska.

It was the Philadelphia Police Department version of Thule, Greenland.

Three years after she had smashed James McMillan's perfectly-coiffed head into the doorframe of his mistress, Elizabeth Owens was moved to the DVU. To say that she wasn't overjoyed would have been a huge understatement, but she was determined to make the best of the post. At every job she ever had in her adult life, she'd done her utmost to set the example for excellence. She was going to make her mark in the DVU. She figured that the bar couldn't be very high since no one wanted to be there.

After a rash of domestic violence homicides in 2009 in which twenty-one of the thirty-five homicide victims had made almost two hundred previous calls for help, Philadelphia Police adopted a new protocol for answering domestic violence calls so that officers would know if there had been previous complaints from the address.

On her very first day with the unit, an outgoing officer was showing her the ropes which consisted of paging through a book the unit kept on every suspect they had on file for any sort of crimes against women.

"If I could somehow make every asshole in this book disappear..." the outgoing officer said.

Then she snapped her fingers as if to illustrate how little these men rated as human beings.

"A less politically correct cop would call this book a kill list."

There were hundreds of names in the book, updated every six months.

"There aren't two sides to most of these stories. There's no 'he-said-she said.' Not when some guy comes at a woman with a baseball bat or a hammer, or shoots her in front of their kids," she told Owens.

"My advice to you, Detective Elizabeth Owens, is to do your best here for no more than three years, then move on to something less soul-crushing."

I don't want to be here in the first damn place, Owens wanted to shout. Three years seemed like a lifetime in this hellhole of a unit.

It was a tough first day on the new job. The outgoing cop hadn't been the least bit cynical; she was just telling the newbie how it was. Owens wasn't anyone's idea of a dreamer, not even much of an optimist, but she did think that if she couldn't do something to help the women of her hometown, no one could. She'd received some of the finest training in the world to make it possible.

The Domestic Violence Unit was an investigative branch of the PPD. They weren't the people responding to abuse calls. They did the follow-up investigations and made sure that the abusers were put into the data bank so that if another call was made, the cops knew what to expect when they arrived. It wasn't as hands-on as responding on patrol, but Owens appreciated the fact that she was able to spend a lot of time talking with the victims. At least, this was her first impression of the job.

She'd begun a master's program at Temple in sociology with no area of study in mind other than it would relate to police work of some kind. She'd never considered domestic abuse as her emphasis, but once assigned, the unit seemed like a logical choice. However, for PPD career advancement, homicide was the ticket. Owens was furious that she was passed over for less qualified candidates.

On the bright side, her professors at Temple couldn't contain their joy at having someone who was truly involved in the process of giving aid to women, as opposed to their own entirely theoretical approach to the issue. The greater interest her professors showed in her work as a cop working in the field of domestic violence, the more Owens decided to make the most of her new assignment.

"I'm going to kick this job's ass," Owens told her faculty advisor.

Her initial interest in academia was merely to advance her police career. Once embedded in the DVU, her old opinion was evolving away from, "those who can, do, those who can't…write scholarly texts on the subject that few people read, and no one gives a shit about." She immediately saw the value in documentation and study.

Still, she was more interested in direct action.

Owens learned soon enough that direct action wasn't really the focus or purpose of the DVU. They were an investigative unit tasked with making cases against offenders and providing officers in the field with as much information as possible when they responded to calls involving repeat offenders. They were also responsible for training officers on the most effective techniques for defusing potentially violent situations.

The department had hundreds of hours of body-cam film footage from PPD officers involved in domestic violence calls. It was one of the unit's primary functions to sort through every call and try to come up with the best approach for officers on the scene. There were new tapes to scan almost daily. In addition to the raw video footage, the unit had to sift through every word of the reports made by the responding officers.

"It would help if any of these ignorant humps could write a decent English sentence," Owens moaned as she read through a stack of reports.

"Tell me about it," Captain Welling agreed. "I can almost excuse the ones who speak another language, but is it so hard to write in your native English?"

"Check this one out," Owens said as she read from a page. "'Individual entered individual's domicile through before-mentioned broken window in last paragraph and waited until individual entered via front door.' Why do they all sound like cops from really bad TV shows?"

"It's a vicious cycle. It's impossible to know where it began, a chicken or egg thing. Did cops start talking like this after learning it from TV, or did the TV writers simply parrot what they heard cops say?" Welling asked.

"Someone needs to end the cycle. It's driving me batty. Take away a rookie's service weapon and give them a copy of Strunk & White's *Elements of Style* until they can form a coherent thought on paper."

Welling and Owens were both critical of new cops carrying firearms. Police recruits had little training and zero experience yet were armed with lethal firepower, then released into the streets of a dangerous city. A firearm wasn't a tool new cops needed, not before they'd learned how to carry themselves in stressful situations and deal with citizens in a broad range of encounters. Even with her military police experience, Owens felt that it had taken her two years on patrol in Philadelphia to get a good feel for the job. Now she was tasked with instructing other officers on how to respond to highly volatile domestic calls.

No matter how many hours Owens pored over the video clips of domestic calls, they would never come up with a perfect, one-size-fits-all approach for cops stepping in between family members or lovers. The most dangerous factor in these confrontations was that many of the abusers suffered from some form of mental illness which removes predictability from many of the equations. And often there was drug and alcohol abuse thrown into the mix. Drunk and crazy was a cop's worst scenario.

As self-serving as it sounded, officer well-being was of prime importance in domestic violence calls. Owens's own injuries were nothing compared to the deluge of assaults against Philly cops arriving in the middle of knock-down, drag-out family feuds. Two police officers in the past three years had been shot dead at the scene while trying to get between husbands and wives intent on harming each other. Add to those tragedies a couple dozen stabbings and other various assaults against law enforcement.

On her first day in the unit, Owens saw the book. The Big Book of Shitbags was the unofficial title, although it was clearly posted on the cover. The people working in the Domestic Violence Unit, mostly women, weren't even slightly interested in trying to be politically correct on the subject of wife beaters.

The book contained the names and info of hundreds of the city's worst sexual offenders, wife beaters, and abusers of children. They were walking around and free to act on any and all of their worst impulses. Law enforcement could do nothing but wait and hope someone would testify against them in court, then they'd be the problem of the courts, and hopefully, the penitentiary system.

All police work was reactionary: someone committed a crime, and the police responded. Owens had a very hard time thinking that her job was waiting around for one of the shitbags in The Big Book to murder his wife so that she could make a case. How was that part of the "protect and serve" motto of the police?

And then there was the case of Alba Moreno.

# CHAPTER 4 – ALBA MORENO

Anyone who read a newspaper in Philadelphia knew the case of Alba Moreno was no different than that of millions of women across the nation who lived in cycles of abuse, all clearly defined by experts in domestic violence and criminal behavior. As well-documented and studied as the subject of violence against women was, it remained a significant concern for police, and severe outcomes like murder were on the rise. Life had become increasingly dangerous for intimate partners in relationships. Of course, most of the victims were women, eighty-five percent to be more precise.

A native of the Dominican Republic, Alba Moreno had emigrated to the United States with her parents when she was eighteen years old. She moved from New York City to Philadelphia after she married Anthony Martin from Queens, who took a job in a cousin's barber shop in South Philly. They had two children before Alba was twenty-four. They separated when she was twenty-eight.

Tony Martin spiraled into alcoholism and drug addiction. He abused his wife and two young children. He was arrested twice on battery charges and given suspended sentences on both counts. Alba had worked hard to establish her own career as a hair stylist and was mostly independent of her husband's income. By the time she finally filed for divorce, his attacks were a regular part of her life.

She lived through every phase of the abuse cycle with Tony Martin and many steps along the way were documented by social workers and the PPD. It began with emotional abuse: name-calling, constant criticism, jealousy, lack of trust, and threats. Then came the physical abuse. At first it was slapping and holding her down, followed by the guilt and apology phase in which Tony Martin swore he'd never do it again. The cycle continued with increasing levels of violence.

Then came the death threats.

The DVU logged over eighty calls from Alba to the police requesting protection over a two-year period. A restraining order did little to keep Tony Martin away from his ex. She ended up in the emergency room on three occasions. Alba was reluctant to press charges against the father of her children, and although Tony was arrested on three occasions, he was never charged with a crime.

Two Philadelphia police officers were called to her apartment at three-thirty in the morning by neighbors who reported screaming. One of the detectives responding to the triple homicide called Owens at four that morning after finding her card on the murdered woman's nightstand. Alba and her two children, ages eight and six, had been shot to death in the mother's bed. Tony Martin had surrendered to the patrol officers without a struggle.

Eighty-six calls. That's how many times Alba Moreno had begged the police to protect her from her husband and then ex-husband. Her case was only one of too many in the United States where at least three women are murdered every day by someone they know.

Tony Martin didn't choose to end his own life, as often happens in these cases. Owens could never understand why the murder-suicide losers didn't just kill themselves first and do the world a huge favor. The same was often true in the new American phenomenon of mass shootings in which the gunman often took his own life to end the pathetic drama of his existence (they were all men).

Owens thought one solution could be a campaign to reach out to anyone contemplating taking the life of his lover, or thinking of committing a mass killing, or doing harm against anyone. In Owens's plan, there would be television announcements encouraging these diseased and violent men to take their own lives and leave behind a letter explaining their darkest thoughts that they had abandoned in favor of suicide. They would be hailed as heroes, they would become

41

famous, or at least their names would be mentioned on one of these early morning televised announcements.

"You're a freaking loony," one of her coworkers told her after Owens had explained her plan.

"Maybe, but it's worth trying. Nothing else is working."

How do you change men? Owens believed that the law could only do so much to deter violence against women. The lot of women had fared much worse before modern times. In countries with a stable rule of law, there was no question that things had improved for women, but in recent times, things were getting worse, not better. Owens had a front-row seat to every crime and threat against women reported in the city. She was certain of one thing: she didn't need a government study or one of her university professors to tell her the current situation was totally unacceptable.

She'd been to Alba Moreno's house on several occasions. She knew her two children by name. Owens had visited Alba at her job and talked with her employer who had nothing but the highest praise for the young woman.

"Her personality was like a warm sunny day," or something to that effect, was how people described her. A hard worker, an attentive mother, a good friend, a loving daughter, kind, generous, blah, blah, blah.

"Now just another victim of some violent sociopath," Owens said over a beer with her unit, two days after the murders.

All four members of the unit were incensed at their own inability to make any difference in the Moreno case.

"If any asshole so much as hinted that he wanted to kill the president of the United States, he'd be in prison before he so much as finished his thought," said Detective Ed Batista.

Detective Batista was the only boy in the unit, and the other three referred to him as a boy because of his looks and the fact that he was the youngest member of the unit. He was also a former Army infantryman with combat experience, so he and Owens became unusually close almost immediately.

"Yet we have this guy Tony Martin making dozens of death threats against his ex-wife and we do fuck all about it. I don't know about the rest of you, but I'm totally ashamed of myself."

"You can't take it personally," Sgt. Welling said.

"Fuck that, I take all of this shit very personally. I'm furious, like I can't even see straight," Detective Owens said. "After he threatened to kill her for the fifth or sixth time, we should have taken little Tony Martin out and put him in a wheelchair for life."

Owens took a couple of deep breaths before going on.

"We've all met that total piece of shit. Tell me how the world wouldn't be a better place if he'd just disappeared forever about three days ago."

"Explain 'disappeared,' Owens," Batista said.

"You mean how would I do it?"

"We're all friends here, right?" Batista asked.

Owens gave her coworker a look.

43

*"Oye, Eduardo, hablamos."*

An hour later it was just Owens and Batista at the booth. Time to really talk.

What was taking shape in Owens's head hadn't occurred to her until Batista had asked her how she'd get rid of a scumbag like Tony Martin. She immediately knew that it wasn't something she wanted to share with her current supervisor and the other members of their unit, Rachel Laury, a dim officer with fourteen years on the force and almost nothing to show for it. She wouldn't confide in Rachel Laury about her favorite brand of gin (Tanqueray).

"Like you've never thought about this before?" Owens said, more an accusation than a question.

"Fucking of course I have," Batista said.

The young detective suffered from this common form of military-induced Tourette Syndrome in which profanity made up a good portion of his speech. If Batista gave up swearing entirely, people would describe him as the quiet type.

"We basically just sat back and watched it happen. We let that piece of shit end her life. I'm not at all OK with that."

"I told you I talked with little Tony last week. Went to his barber shop," Batista said.

"No, you didn't report it."

"Thought I told you. I didn't write it down because I like having a job."

"You put your hands on him?" Owens asked.

"Didn't touch the cocksucker. Totally regret it now."

"What'd you do?"

"I walked into the shop. He was alone, so I closed the door and put the 'closed' sign in the window."

"That's some Hollywood shit right there."

"That's what I thought, too. He didn't know who I was and started to give me shit about closing the door. I told him to sit the fuck down in the barber chair. He sat the fuck down like the little bitch he is."

"You do have a way of making yourself clear to people."

"I made myself very clear. I identified myself and told him we were watching him like a hawk…and then I fucked up."

"What?" Owens asked.

"I didn't follow through with what I went there to do."

"Fuck his shit up?"

"Exactly. I just mumbled the usual shit about the consequences of violating a restraining order, blah, blah, et cetera, et cetera. Jesus, I sounded like some asshole lawyer. I totally kept my cool. Then I left. Now Alba's dead because of that total piece of human filth."

Owens didn't say it, but they were both thinking it.

"And he gets to live," Batista said for the two of them.

"Didn't even have the guts to off himself like any decent piece of shit wife-murderer is supposed to do and spare us paying his room and

45

board for what I sincerely hope is the rest of his miserable life," Owens said.

"I knew it, too. I swear, I knew he was going to kill her," Batista confessed.

"Of course, you knew it. Everyone who knew the scumbag knew it."

"Yet we just sit back and let it happen, again and again."

"Since my first day in this unit when they showed me *The Big Book of Shitbags*, I haven't been able to get it out of my head that we have the names of hundreds of Tony Martins, guys who we know are going to do something awful, someday," Owens said.

"And we sit back and wait for it to happen. That's our job: waiting for these atrocities to happen," Batista said. "If it were any more cynical, we'd have a betting pool on who's next."

To avoid responding to this statement she agreed with completely, she took a long drink from her beer.

"That's why I went over to his shop that day; I was sick of waiting. I wanted to do something," Batista said. "He's such a coward. He about shit himself as I was talking to him."

"Is that why you didn't lay into him? Felt sorry?"

"Not because I felt sorry for him. I guess I'm just too much of a cop."

Batista paused.

"Right? Because that would be illegal?"

Owens laughed at his joke.

"This unit really drives home how little we can do. At least on patrol we could stop some shit before it got out of hand. Most of what we do here is look at crime scene photos and talk to witnesses after the fact, and by 'the fact' I mean the atrocity, the god damned disgrace," Owens said.

"Right? Most of the time it's not even a surprise. Tony Martin killing his wife? I mean, who wouldn't have guessed that was bound to happen sooner or later?" Batista asked rhetorically.

"It's the damn book that gets me. We know that a full seventy-two percent of the domestic homicides have called the police before..."

"Twenty-seven times," Batista said, giving the number of calls most domestic homicide victims had made to police.

"Twenty-seven fucking times. Women are begging us to step in and help them, hell, save them, and we sit back and take notes."

"I was just about to put Tony Martin in the emergency room after many more than twenty-seven calls, and I didn't do it. Coulda saved three lives."

"Nothing much would have come of it. You'd just say he came at you, and you ended it," Owens said.

"I'm just thinking out loud here, but there are better ways to do it," Batista said.

"We're just talking," Owens agreed.

"No need to involve the Philadelphia Police Department's internal investigation people."

"They got better things to do, like firing cops over stupid shit like taking a free meal in a restaurant or working the wrong second job to pay rent."

"I mean, I know we can't prevent all of these tragedies, but damn, just seems like we could stop some of them. There's gotta be some metric we could use to step in and just fucking do something," Batista said.

"We could decide on something according to the Big Book of Shitbags."

"There you go. We can't fuck all of them up, but there should be a limit, some line in the sand they cross. Then we act."

"Twenty-seven calls to the police sounds about right to me. That number could've saved Alba. We were way late with her."

"Twenty-sevens calls for help! Christ, if that doesn't set off an air raid siren that something desperately needs fixing..." Batista said, unable to articulate further. "Twenty-seven calls and we take out the next Tony Martin."

"Fuck Tony Martin," Owens said, raising her pint.

"Fuck Tony Martin and every other creep who inspires twenty-seven calls!" Batista said.

***

Poring through the data bank, Owens saw that twenty-seven calls weren't as highly unusual as she'd thought. There were also a lot of other victims who'd made far fewer calls but were in more desperate straits regarding their abusers. There were many cases with more than twenty-seven which seemed much less severe than what Alba Moreno suffered. Still, twenty-seven calls seemed like enough of a benchmark for flagging an abuser. In the greater Philadelphia area in which she had authority, there were forty-two men who made it on this list of inspiring twenty-seven distress calls.

Most of the cases involving this absurd number of pleas for help never made it on the nightly news, or in the pages of the newspapers. The case of the murder of Alba Moreno and her two children made it into the *Philadelphia Inquirer*, but back on page three. Irony would've been better served had it been printed on page twenty-seven, Owens thought.

Owens needed as many eyes going over the statistics as possible, so she showed her colleagues at Temple *The Big Book of Shitbags*. She thought it was like looking at hundreds of ticking time bombs and trying to determine which would go off next. The department needed help.

The main problem was the uneven amount of information. Some women were more likely to report abuse than others. Some women in the worst of circumstances never called, suffering through a lifetime of abuse. In the past two years alone, fifty-three women had been murdered by their partners, or former partners in many cases. All but five of the victims had called the police for protection against their aggressors, one of them had made more than fifty distress calls to local police.

Although well on her way to becoming a social scientist, Owens felt that it didn't take a professional to see cases that were heading in a sinister direction. In her mind, any man capable of striking a woman or a child with his fist was capable of murder. There were dozens of cases in which women were beaten so badly that it was only through the miracle of modern medicine that they didn't end up as homicide victims.

One of the great advantages about patrol work was that when she'd actually been on the scene to see a man strike his wife, it made for an easy conviction. The prosecutor didn't need the victim to testify; they had a professional witness in the form of a trained police officer to address the jury. Abused women often made unreliable witnesses in trials for a host of reasons as the deck was stacked against them in so many ways. This was among the reasons why Owens never once admonished a victim for not bringing charges against her aggressor.

With the help of her professors and fellow master's degree candidates, Owens attempted to construct something of an early warning system, something that could help predict the next atrocity, the next Alba Moreno.

It sounded fiendishly calculating, impersonal, and even cynical, but Owens wanted an algorithm to predict violence against women.

On the academics' first day of studying the names, they came up with thirty-eight men they deemed as high-risk candidates, and four who were extremely likely to act out violently. If Owens could've pushed a magic button to make all of them disappear forever, she'd have done it yesterday. Short of that impossibility, she didn't have much of a plan.

The unit's mission was purely investigative. They felt they shouldn't advise women beyond recommending other resources from other organizations. There wasn't anything in the unit's charter that allowed them to confront aggressors who were intent on harming their spouses. Yet, that was where Owens found herself with these four names from The Big Book of Shitbags, men whom she'd bet had a good chance of harming their spouses.

At the very least, she and Batista could go out and have a face-to-face with these men, the most likely candidates. Between the two highly-trained former Army MPs turned PPD detectives, they should be able to muster the self-control to keep the situation from devolving into a severe beat-down.

Owens could never stop thinking about what might've happened that day in the barber shop if Batista had kicked the living shit out of Tony Martin. His verbal threats were completely in vain. The legal system had done nothing to prevent the three homicides; Alba's restraining order was no match for the cheap pistol Tony Martin bought only two days before the killings.

After a week of studying the names in the book, Owens, her fellow graduate students, and four professors came up with eight candidates likely to harm their spouses.

Without sharing with her colleagues at Temple, Owens told Batista about one of the men, a complete shitbag named Arthur Simmons, thirty-eight years old, arrested three times for battery against two of his three wives. He and his current wife were separated. She'd called the police on thirty-two separate occasions but hadn't pressed charges. Arthur had never served more than a few days in lockup and somehow managed to plead his earlier charges down to misdemeanors, paying fines and forced into community service on exactly three weekends, this for physically abusing his two former wives on several occasions, sending one of them to the hospital with a broken arm.

Arthur was also suspected in the disappearance of a former live-in girlfriend. He claimed the woman moved out and gave no word where she was going. Simmons said she left him three months before police contacted him after family members of Susan Decker, from Ohio, called Philadelphia Police, reporting she hadn't been heard from in months, no exact date given. Her unemployment benefits had run out a month earlier and her bank account had been drained of every penny. In the last three months, her debit card had been making withdrawals from various bank machines in New Jersey.

51

Arthur told police she'd left him for a Black man—no name given—who lived in New Jersey, no further details offered. The police were unable to find a single friend of the woman in Philadelphia. Her last job was at a small convenience store that went out of business and left her unemployed. Police were unable to contact anyone from the failed thrift mart. They were also unwilling to speculate that Arthur was a killer as there was absolutely nothing to suggest foul play. Arthur would remain a person of interest in the matter, but nothing more.

Arthur's latest run-in with Philadelphia police officers was only three weeks previous when neighbors called in a complaint after they heard screaming coming from his wife's home—the couple were separated at the time. Owens had seen the body-cam video of the response. Simmons had opened the door to the two on patrol. A fat, shirt-less slob with a shoe brush mustache. The lead officer was absurdly polite to Simmons, who was extremely intoxicated and belligerent.

Off-camera, Owens had spoken with the officer who confessed that keeping his cool that day was one of the major challenges of his five years on the force.

"It was all I could do not to rip that mustache off of his fat face."

The wife didn't file a complaint. While not showing any visible injuries, both officers reported that she'd been physically assaulted. There wasn't a lot the police could do in that situation.

Arthur Simmons worked at a local franchise appliance center and was under investigation for sexual misconduct at the store. Two fellow employees complained about completely unwanted advances. Owens had talked to both women on the phone without giving her name or badge number, one was a sixty-two-year-old grandmother, and the other an eighteen-year-old still in high school. They both said the same thing regarding Arthur: he was a total creep, every woman's worst nightmare. He stared at them constantly, touched himself, and almost everything he said was completely inappropriate.

If Arthur Simmons had any value as a human being, it wasn't showing up in her investigation. He really was a shitbag. Textbook example. Classic case.

Maybe he could be rehabilitated, redeem himself, change his ways, turn things around, be a new man, but it was a lot more likely that he'd continue down his path of becoming progressively more violent and abusive. Owens and most police officers had little belief in the rehabilitative nature of the nation's penitentiary system. Prisons build better and more violent criminals. It's what they do best.

And what would it take to put Arthur Simmons behind bars for any meaningful period of time? Another black eye, another punch to the stomach, one more vulgar remark—the life of Arthur Simmons wasn't worth one more moment of suffering from another woman. He'd already done more than enough damage and may have murdered an ex-girlfriend. Owens didn't have all of the data on Simmons, but she knew that the women he'd abused in his life had made more than twenty-seven calls.

Arthur Simmons had run out of chances.

# CHAPTER 5 – WORST NIGHTMARE CONTINUED - ARTHUR SIMMONS (1983 – 2021)

Batista had the side door of the van open. Arthur Simmons had his hand on Owens's shoulder when he saw Batista inside the van only a couple steps in front of him. Owens turned around and grabbed Simmons by his mustache, catching him completely by surprise. He howled in agony as she pulled him forward by his upper lip. Simmons bent over and shuffled to alleviate the pain. Owens grabbed the middle of his back with her free hand and launched him into the open van door.

"You're under arrest, cocksucker," Owens said.

Batista kicked Simmons in the stomach before he fell face-down in the van.

"That's just so that you know that we aren't fucking around here, not even a little," Batista said.

The stalker landed hard, the edge of the doorway catching him mid-thigh. He was unable to resist after the vicious kick stunned him. Owens pushed him the rest of the way inside while Batista pulled on one of his arms.

When they had Simmons inside, Owens closed the cargo door from the outside, walked around to the driver's side, and got in. As she drove away, Batista was binding his hands behind his back with flexi-cuffs.

"Help!" Arthur screamed.

His desperate cry was met with another kick to his midsection.

"Shut the fuck up," Batista said.

Simmons obeyed. Batista then bound his ankles together with another flexi-cuff.

The red wig and Elton John sunglasses made Owens mostly unrecognizable. She had worn flat-heeled shoes in an attempt to downplay her above-average height. She was sure that no one on earth would note Arthur Simmons' absence enough to report it to the police, at least not for a few days, if then. There was always the possibility that someone on the street witnessed the abduction, although neither of the two cops had noticed any pedestrians. There could have been a witness in one of the buildings along the street, but they wouldn't have much to pass on to police if they bothered to report what they'd seen. The world was a cruel place, and no one would care about a fat, middle-aged man getting pushed into a panel van, a van with a stolen plate.

Owens drove away slowly and headed toward the Ben Franklin Bridge. The van posed a few problems. It belonged to Batista's uncle, but they had swapped out a license plate from a similar vehicle on the street that looked like it hadn't moved in months. Batista felt that using this vehicle posed less of a risk than stealing a van for the abduction. Owens had agreed as this meant one less chance of tipping off police.

His uncle's van was about as common as possible: seven years old, in fair shape but slightly dented, impossible to distinguish from hundreds, perhaps thousands of vans in the city and surrounding areas. What might attract attention would be an attractive Black woman behind the wheel. She switched with Batista at the first stop sign and moved to the back with Arthur.

Arthur was on his side. Owens grabbed him again by his mustache and raised his head. He whimpered in pain.

"You still feel like tearing up my ass, Arthur?"

He couldn't utter a word with his upper lip feeling like it was about to be ripped off his face.

"You like beating up women? You get off on it?"

Owens let go of her grip and his head bounced off the floor of the van.

"Ever killed a woman? Shit went too far?" she asked. "Ever thought about it?"

Arthur didn't dare move.

"Answer me, motherfucker."

Owens kicked him in the stomach.

"Have you ever killed a woman?"

"No," he whimpered.

"Seems like you tried a bunch of times. I bet you thought about it a lot."

Arthur only moaned.

"Where is Susan Decker?" Owens yelled.

Simmons fell into an even deeper panic.

"I've thought of killing you. Know why?"

Arthur looked up at Owens and knew she was waiting for an answer.

"No," he muttered.

"I want to kill you because I fucking hate you."

"I don't even know you. I've never seen you before," he whimpered.

"And yet you followed me down the street saying some completely repugnant shit. What did I do to deserve that?"

"I was just having some fun with you. I didn't mean…"

Owens kicked his right leg.

"Shut your fucking mouth, you filthy fucking pig."

He shut his mouth.

"Why'd you buy a pistol, Arthur? Planning on killing your wife?"

"How do you know my name?" Arthur stammered in confusion. "I got the pistol for safety…how'd you know I bought it?"

"What if I told you that you were never going to harm another woman ever again? How would that make you feel, Arthur?"

"I've never hur…"

Owens tore into him again with another kick.

"You've been convicted of hurting women. We call that a pattern of violence. Everyone knows that you killed Susan Decker, but we can't prove it."

"I didn't ki…"

Owens kicked him again.

"Guess what, Arthur. That needing to prove shit doesn't apply to this right here. We know you're guilty."

Arthur cried out in pain.

"You tell us what you did with Susan Decker and all we'll do is arrest you. Keep lying to us, and this'll be it for you. Understand?"

Arthur was so overcome with terror that he couldn't talk.

Owens covered his mouth with a length of duct tape with a small hole to let him breathe.

"We're done talking for now, Arthur Simmons. Think about what I said and decide if you want to go on living."

Camden, New Jersey, across the river from Philadelphia, is about as close as you can get to a failed state. It's like the Honduras of the United States. With the city's police budget drastically slashed by a collapse in tax revenues, two people in a nondescript van on a nefarious mission of disappearing a serial abuser had almost no chance of being stopped.

They weren't stopped.

Parts of the city were a hellscape of businesses dealing with the waste products of more prosperous communities: trash collection, scrap metal, chemicals, fluids, building debris, not to mention the toxic and contaminated refuse most citizens aren't even aware they're throwing away, week-in, week-out.

There were dozens of scrap yards filled with cars that looked like parking lots of the apocalypse. More than anything, there were abandoned properties and half-ruined buildings. It looked like where capitalism had come to die.

Camden, New Jersey, is the Valhalla of body disposal.

Driving along a block of warehouses with broken and whitewashed windows, Batista pulled up to a lot surrounded by a twelve-foot chain-link fence covered with green nylon webbing so that nothing inside was visible. He parked in front of the gate. The sign read:

*Hermanos Hernandez - Hernandez Brothers*

*Landscaping and Tree Service*

He got out and unlocked the gate as Owens took the wheel. Batista opened the gate, she drove through, then he shut it and locked it from the inside. Batista flagged her over to a large flatbed truck with a trailer attached. A pile of tree branches stacked next to the trailer. Owens parked next to the branches and opened the cargo door from the inside. Batista helped her haul Arthur Simmons off the floor of the van.

Batista fired up the tree shredder, which made a terrifying roar, but not nearly as loud as when he fed a tree limb as thick as his thigh into the machine, and then another.

"This is the end, Arthur," Owens said to the horrified heap of flesh on the ground. "Tell us what happened to Susan Decker or you're getting tossed in next."

"I don't know," Arthur said, sobbing.

Batista pulled Arthur Simmons off the ground and faced him directly in front of the maw of the malevolent machine made to rip trees into sawdust. Owens grabbed Arthur by his bound left arm, Batista gripping his right arm at the elbow.

"Up to you, Arthur," Batista said while they lifted the man up on his toes as the tree shredder screamed in idle mode waiting to be fed.

Owens threw in another large branch for dramatic effect.

"Arthur, this is it for you. Confess to your crimes and we'll arrest you. If you lie to me one more time, you're going in. No bullshit."

"I have rights," Arthur moaned.

"Is that what Susan Decker told you? Just tell us what you did with her. We can't use this confession against you, but we can lock you up for violating your restraining order. We can keep you for forty-eight hours in lockup. Think your shitty job will be cool with that?"

Arthur knew they wouldn't be cool with him missing two days. He knew they were begging him for another excuse to fire him without going through the hassle of letting him go for sexual misbehavior. No company wanted that on their record, especially when he should have been let go months ago.

Arthur Simmons gave his confession along with detailed instructions on where he buried her in the garden of a house they rented.

Of course, they weren't going to arrest Arthur Simmons for violating his restraining order. They disappeared him, sending him into the maw of the horrible machine. They sent a pile of tree limbs into the machine until no trace of Arthur remained in the pile of sawdust or in the tree shredder.

With the van now unburdened with the likes of Arthur Simmons, Batista pulled into an empty lot filled with weeds and trash in another shabby area of Camden to reinstall the legitimate license plate to the rear before they drove back over a different bridge into Philadelphia.

After leaving the van with its rightful owner, the cops grabbed bike-share bikes to ride to their respective homes. Pedaling home, and against their better judgment, the two co-conspirators decided to have a drink or two at a bar equidistant between their Philly addresses.

Owens and Batista had too much in common not to have hooked up, which they'd done on many occasions, but it was mostly physical. Batista let Owens know that his family expected him to marry a nice Latina from the neighborhood, or from back in Puerto Rico. They'd never understand if he dated a Black woman. Owens wasn't interested in a relationship and had no interest in meeting his folks, so their thing worked well for her.

"Any feelings of regret," Owens said after downing her first pint.

"Fucking hardly," Batista said without a thought. "You?"

"Hell no. After hearing what he said to me walking down that street, all I can think about is how many women he terrorized in his miserable life."

"Not sure how to handle what he told us about the woman he murdered and keep our part out of it. It may all be bullshit. People say all kinds of shit under duress," Batista said.

"Maybe, but it seemed very detailed to invent it on the spot like he did."

"If it is true, just knowing has to be better for the woman's family than not knowing what happened to her," Batista said.

"Too bad they'll never know what happened to Arthur."

They both finished their beers before talking again.

"We've never talked about it, but you ever kill anyone before?" Owens asked.

This was a subject they'd never even hinted at in all of their conversations together, instinctively avoiding the topic.

"You know I was combat infantry in Afghanistan and Iraq before coming back home to retrain as an MP, then returned to Iraq. I don't keep score, but if I did, Mister Wife Beater Arthur would be number 'I don't give a fuck.' Understand?"

"Roger that."

Owens completely understood. Fat, bald, and mustachioed was someone completely forgettable. She couldn't imagine a single human being who would lament his absence on this earth.

"It's messed up, but I still have nightmares about men I killed in combat, guys just doing what they were told. Pretty sure I'll forget all about this miserable bastard," Batista said.

"How can you say that? It just happened. Shit, you haven't even slept on it."

Batista waved the bartender to have another round brought to the table. Both of them only a short walk from home.

"This isn't my first 'Arthur Simmons' if you have to know."

"How's that?" Owens asked.

"I took out a motherfucker in Iraq. A noncombatant. A much bigger shitbag than Arthur or anyone in that damn book."

Batista went silent, paying more attention to the new pint placed in front of him by the waitress. When she walked away, Owens spoke.

"Naw, fuck that. You can't start that story and not end it," Owens demanded.

"My first time telling it, so excuse me."

"I'm flattered, just give it to me," Owens said.

"This was in my infantry days. We were doing these door-to-door sweeps in villages, small places with only a few thousand people, if that. If any occupying force had done that in my hometown, I'd've dedicated my life to killing them, but at the time, it seemed like what we needed to be doing.

"Our intelligence was for shit. Convoys were being picked off by IEDs left and right. Christ, to this day, I can't hear a car backfire without wanting to dive to the pavement."

"Same here."

"So, we're tagging all of these villages along the highway looking for bomb-building sites or just caches of the artillery rounds they used. For one of my first times in Iraq after months of combat, I felt I was doing something that was useful."

Owens had to interrupt.

"Don't get me started," Owens said.

"I mean, I thought we were really doing something positive without punishing the locals like with so many of our other missions. One night at about nineteen hundred, more or less, we knock on a door. We were a full platoon, with a lieutenant just out of ROTC—in my humble opinion, the worst officers they manufacture—along with our staff sergeant. The lieutenant was a good guy, just a bit clueless. He mostly led from inside an armored Humvee.

"So, I knock on the door and this guy answers and he's furious from the start, screaming at me about upsetting his cherished home or whatever. I look inside and see a crowd. Three women I guessed were his wives, or at least one of them was, and eight children. I tell him we need to enter the dwelling because we're looking for weapons—we didn't mention artillery rounds.

"He goes totally mental, screaming at the top of his lungs about how America doesn't respect the Muslim family and twenty other things. His English was pretty good, which was a miracle in these villages where most people spoke English like I speak their language.

"He doesn't want to let us in with his body blocking the door. I tell him that we have to enter, that we got orders to search every domicile because of the rash of IEDs in the area. Maybe I was the asshole in the situation, maybe I was just over my entire time in Iraq, but I grabbed him by the throat and threw him to the ground. I entered with two in my platoon covering.

"I'm really trying to be respectful, you know, about the women in the house, and I was. Didn't even look at them, trying to make sure they didn't have any artillery rounds under their dumpy clothes. Then I made my way to the back of the house and found a door that was padlocked. Why would anyone lock a door like that? My guy cut it.

"My question was answered as soon as I entered the room. There was a boy, ten, maybe younger, wearing a vest of explosives."

"Like ready to walk out and blow himself to hell?"

"I guess so."

"Was it the guy's own kid?" Owens asked.

"Don't think so, but who the fuck knows? The guy was some sort of religious leader in the village. There were about twenty people of all ages running around the house, more like a community center."

Batista stopped to take a sip of his beer, like he didn't really want to bring this up again, even to his partner.

"So, what'd you do?"

"What I did next was just a snap decision, or I snapped. I have to admit that I've thought more about the clothes I put on for the day. This isn't to justify and definitely not to apologize for what I did. I've never talked about this with anyone since, and I don't need you to accept…"

"We're on the same team, Ed," Owens said. "Now more than ever, obviously."

Batista considered this for a few seconds and continued.

"I got the vest off the kid who was terrified, as you'd imagine. It had a phone attached to it, so I figured that was the trigger. I'd had a bit of experience with bombs and was…" he paused, "…fairly positive that I could disarm it. You probably had your share of briefings on bomb protocol."

"Quite a bit," Owens said. "It's not like in the movies with the red and blue wires. You basically just rip off the wires and that's that."

"Exactly. So, I ripped off the phone and got the vest off the kid. Two guys from our platoon were keeping the sheik, or whatever he was, in the other room. I walked out with the kid's explosive vest in my hand. The guy didn't even bat an eye, like he was saying 'so what?' or some shit, like I had no right to even be there. He's screaming at me in Arabic with a few English words mixed in. We don't have a translator—almost never did—so I just grabbed him by his beard and walked him out of the house and threw him in the back of my Humvee and sat next to him."

Batista stopped like he didn't want to tell Owens everything. She gave him a "you can't stop now" look.

"While the rest of the platoon went through the house looking for more bomb materials, I told the lieutenant I was taking the sheik out for a little ride in the desert, and that me and my driver'd be back in twenty minutes. Tops. Took the vest with me. It was a simple affair of a couple hundred grams of Semtex and packed with nails and screws.

"We drove about two klicks out of the village and off the road if you could call it a road. Nothing in the way of agriculture, just ravines, like a moonscape. We came to a stop, and I pulled the sheik out and secured his hands behind his back and then fastened the vest around his neck. He wasn't taking it too well, but he was too petrified to even speak, which was fine with me because I didn't want to talk to him. I told my driver to hold tight and stay behind the wheel.

"I walked him up this little incline and up a rock face. At the top, there was a drop of about five meters, like a small cliff. I fastened an M67 grenade to the vest. Then it was just a matter of pulling the pin, pushing him over the edge, and ducking down for cover.

"Wasn't even sure the grenade would detonate the Semtex, but it did," Batista added parenthetically.

"The little cliff protected me, but it also did a great job of muffling the sound because it was facing away from the village. When we got back to the house, no one seemed to have heard anything."

"What'd the LT say?"

"He didn't want to know and didn't ask. I wasn't going to say anything, but felt bad for the LT. He was the one who'd have to answer for the sheik if anyone came asking. So, I told him he ran away while I was questioning him. Never heard another word about it—I don't think he was a popular guy for some reason."

"An M67 and Semtex? I doubt he was identifiable. Be lucky to find even one unshattered tooth. You didn't take a peek after, just to see for yourself?"

"Nope. Didn't care."

Batista took another sip of beer.

"That one, that one didn't bother me one little bit. I felt worse about guys I put down in firefights, soldiers trying their best to put me down. Some cocksucker wiring kids up with a heinous explosive device? Fuck that guy."

Owens raised her glass as did Batista.

"Fuck the sheik and the mustache man, too," Owens said as they clinked glasses.

A beer later, Owens interrupted the silence.

"This one we don't have much to worry about. No one's gonna give a shit, for starters, especially the women in his pathetic life," Owens said.

"I don't even care at this point. After Alba, shit, it's like *not* doing something is totally irresponsible, even criminal," Batista said. "No doubt in my mind that we saved someone's life today."

"The problem is that damn book. How many Mister Mustaches do we have in the fair city of brotherly love?" Owens asked.

"Today may have been easy, but you know we can't take out all of the trash in this city. We both know scumbags get caught mostly for two reasons…"

"Greed and stupidity," Owens finished. "Sometimes it's just bad luck, or whatever you call it. Fate? Destiny? Divine intervention?"

"Good for us that we don't believe in any of that."

Just as they were about to leave, Batista had another question.

"You ever kill anyone before?"

"That's going to have to be a topic for another day," Owens said.

# CHAPTER 6 – NEXT IN LINE

It was as if Arthur Simmons had simply never existed. No one reported him missing, not in Philadelphia or anywhere else, as far as Owens could discern. His employers were probably overwhelmed with relief he didn't show up for work for his next shift, meaning they no longer needed to go through the show trial of drumming him out of the company for sexual misconduct. No one in the Domestic Violence Unit mentioned his name, and more importantly, his wife never had to call the police to protect her.

Owens wasn't anxious for a repeat performance in vigilantism, or frontier justice, or whatever it was. She was still walking around in abject terror of being arrested, but Arthur Simmons had been such an easy problem to solve it became impossible not to consider how many other names in the book would be just as effortless to erase. Because that's how it seemed to Owens, like Mister Mustache had simply been erased.

Not only were the two police officers never interviewed about the disappearance of Arthur Simmons, but as far as they could tell without digging too deeply, except for a few bill collectors, no one seemed even slightly interested in his absence. He wasn't reported missing, which meant no one went looking.

"The messed up thing is that at this point, even if I confessed, no one would believe me, and they sure as shit couldn't prove it," Batista said. "Shit, I couldn't prove it."

Owens had some questions about the tree shredder and whether that could get back to them.

"They've probably run ten acres of forest through that shredder by now," Batista assured her. "Even if through some miracle they discovered some human DNA, Mustache Man isn't in the system."

They sprayed the shredder with some bleach after the crime, then ran a huge pile of cuttings through it.

Mulch.

That's what Arthur Simmons had amounted to in the end. Mulch. The landscaping crew dumped the cuttings the following morning at another Camden business that mixed the mulch thoroughly with topsoil which was then bagged and sold as commercial potting soil.

"I have to say, as far as the world is concerned, no crime was committed," she said.

"I don't see how that's going to change," Batista said. "Would've been the same with Tony Martin, except we fucked up and didn't do anything."

They were both very well-trained police officers. They knew exactly the sort of things that trip up criminals. They'd never shared a text message or a phone call about the affair, they'd never said a word about it on duty, never talked about it to anyone else.

"Now what?" Batista asked.

"What the hell do you mean?"

"I mean, what now?"

"Now? Now we do our jobs, just like we've always done," Owens said.

"I'm just saying, I got another name."

Owens knew exactly who he was talking about. Another top shitbag from the Big Book.

"You mean Alton, right?" Owens said.

"Ex-wife's made over thirty calls to police and various social agencies begging for help," Batista said.

Jeremy Alton was a real piece of work, by anyone's estimation. Two years earlier, he'd served six months in county lockup for a battery charge against his wife at the time, now divorced. They'd discussed him, both agreeing that sooner or later, Alton was going to harm his ex-wife again, and probably his two children. The emotional damage he'd already inflicted on his family wasn't a matter for the police to determine, but it didn't take a doctorate in a social science to know his negative impact on the world around him was considerable.

The elder of the mother's two children was from a former marriage. Alton had been particularly abusive to this daughter. Owens grew up in a similar predicament and was the target of abuse as a child from her mother's third husband, a mentally deranged loser who somehow couldn't resign himself to the fact he hadn't married a virgin, or some other macho mental poison.

Owens suffered through this violent patch in her childhood at about the same age as Alton's stepdaughter. Just reading about what Andrea Alton endured at the hands of her mother's second husband made her furious. More than anything, it made her fantasize about going back in time and confronting her own tormentor, Dwight Thomas, a sociopath who constantly insulted her for being a few pounds overweight, or for having skin a shade or two darker than his.

Not long after she became a Philadelphia cop, she looked up Dwight in the database. She was overjoyed to learn that he'd served a

71

seven-year sentence on a drug charge in New Jersey. Since then, he'd been released and thrown back in prison on a parole violation after only four months on the outside.

She wondered if at thirteen she would've felt better had she known the man who slapped her around and insulted her on a regular basis would end up locked in a cage for a good portion of his life. She often considered telling Andrea Alton that her worthless ex-stepfather was destined for a similar fate. As a young girl, Owens somehow always knew things would get better once she made it out into the world on her own. The problem for Andrea Alton, as was the case with many of the children she dealt with in the unit, was this kid might not make it out of her childhood in one piece.

She might survive physically, but at what price?

Jeremy Alton obviously had never considered the pain and suffering he'd left in his wake. If any of the men in the Big Book had anything resembling a conscience concerning their violence and sexual abuse, they didn't allow it to interfere with their criminal behavior.

Of course, none of her professors at Temple knew that the Domestic Violence Unit called their case book The Big Book of Shitbags; they would've been horrified if they'd known the cops called it that. Few of them had ever faced an abusive spouse at two in the morning in a dark hallway, the wife screaming in agony a few steps away. They'd never had to restrain a drunken maniac or talk someone out of shooting their own children. Most had only read the case reports of the worst sort of horrors that police dealt with all too often. Academics worked assiduously to see the problem from both sides. Owens knew this was bullshit. A fist only has one side.

The academics had never intervened directly to save a woman from being murdered by her ex-husband. Or worse, arrived just after a spouse had killed his wife and children.

None of them had ever thrown a convicted abuser into a tree shredder in a rundown part of Camden, New Jersey.

Not that Owens was proud of that brutal act, but she was surprised by how little she thought about it. Even the gruesome manner they'd chosen to disappear Arthur Simmons didn't keep her awake at night. Her only anxiety was about being arrested for the crime, and with every passing day, that became an impossibility.

Now Batista sat across from her with another target in his sights.

How would a scumbag like Jeremy Alton qualify as any more of a human being than Arthur? Would he go unnoticed?

"As I said, I felt more compassion for the guys I capped in Iraq," Batista repeated.

She was surprised at how little the thought of disappearing Jeremy Alton troubled her.

"Am I some kind of serial killer?" she asked.

"Hell no, you're a soldier. Mustache Man was the enemy of every decent human being on this planet, especially women."

"I guess that's the way I see it, too," Owens said. "I feel guilty about not feeling guilty."

"We should feel guilty about not taking care of little Tony Martin before he did what Arthur Simmons was going to do, sooner or later. Same thing for this maggot, Jeremy Alton."

Owens was quite certain the world would be better without Jeremy Alton, but it wasn't as if she didn't have reservations about taking such an incredible risk.

"I'm sure everyone's thought about committing a major crime, and what it'd take to push you to the point of doing it, cops probably more than normal people," Owens said.

"It's part of detective work; thinking up ways to circumvent everything we use to put people away," Batista said.

"To protect people I care about, I wouldn't think too long about doing something drastic. I suppose that I'd risk prison for money, but it'd have to be a lot of fucking money. Here I am doing this for free for complete strangers. What kind of strategy is that?"

"This is about standing up to a bully," Batista said. "Protect and serve."

"I came to that same conclusion myself. Still. When I thought about doing a job for money, my cut-off was a quarter million dollars, the absolute minimum," Owens said.

"We went over it a thousand times beforehand. There wasn't much in the way of risk. If we'd been stopped, we could've said we had him for questioning."

Batista obviously wasn't losing any sleep over Arthur Simmons.

"I hate to bring it up, but a second after he went through the shredder, it would take the entire forensic department months to piece together enough evidence to prove a crime had been committed."

"Let's not get too confident in our work," Owens said.

"Yeah, I get it, and I totally understand the part about there being nothing in this for us."

"We did something good for Simmons' family—a lot more than he ever did. I'm cool with that," Owens said.

"I kind of liked cutting out the middleman of the rest of the criminal justice system, but now we just go back to being cops?" Batista said.

"We need to be cool."

Batista shrugged saying that he was cool.

"Besides, now that we have a squad of professors and grad students sifting through all of our files, we need to ratchet up the discretion," Owens said. "None of these college people are down with capital punishment."

Batista laughed at this.

"That's the messed-up part of it; I'm totally against the death penalty," Owens said.

"Me, too."

"What we did, I don't see that as an execution. It was…"

"It was like curing an illness," Batista said. "Like cutting out a malignant tumor."

"Exactly. We didn't punish Simmons; we saved his wife."

Owens and Batista had similar conversations on the subject over the course of the next two months, or two months and six days, to be precise. On that day, Jeremy Alton paid another visit to his ex-wife and didn't leave before breaking her cheekbone with his fist and knocking his daughter unconscious when she came to her mother's defense. This was nothing that would shock or surprise a police officer in almost any municipality in America, and the two ex-Army MPs had seen much, much worse in their careers.

But they'd pegged this sociopath weeks earlier as a candidate for abuse, not that this was something akin to seeing into the future, just reading the writing on the wall.

Batista was on duty when the call was received at the unit. He immediately called Owens.

"Take a wild guess who's in the emergency room with her face split open?"

"The daughter OK?" Owens asked.

"She got smacked around good."

"What about Alton?"

"Still in the wind. We have units looking for him: work, home, hangs," Batista said. "Wife told people at the hospital he had a gun, threatened to kill her and the kid."

"Did that get out to patrols?"

"Just now," Batista answered.

Owens was so furious that she could no longer form words.

"See you at the station at five," she said and hung up.

A patrol car arrived at the townhouse in South Philly that Alton was sharing with two other men. No one answered the door. They looked in a few windows before walking back down the steps of the stoop.

On a whim, the two patrolmen left their cruiser parked in front of the townhouse and walked to the nearest bar, an old-school place called Southside Tavern. The two cops each had a little over two years on the force, had excellent performance reports, and thus far were a credit to the department. Both young, as fit as professional athletes, and smart, like two recruiting-poster examples of Philadelphia police. Both were only twenty-three years old.

Unfortunately, working on their hunch, they were at a distinct disadvantage when they entered the tavern. They were in uniform and had only a vague description of Jeremy Alton. They knew that he was dangerous, but they hadn't received the most recent bulletin saying he was armed. He was wanted for battery, which meant they'd proceed with caution, but not with guns drawn.

They walked into the dark, windowless tavern at four in the afternoon, the prime hour for day-drinking alcoholics and a few hipster dive bar aficionados. The bar had nine customers and the bartender. Two of the customers were at the pool table, five at the bar, and two more who reported later that they were in the toilet. The cops were looking for a forty-two-year-old White male, medium height and build.

Before their eyes had even adjusted to the poor light in the bar, two shots rang out, then two more. The first two shots struck both cops in the chest. Both were wearing body armor. The shock threw them both to the floor. Then another bullet struck one of them in the hip.

Miraculously, the cop with the hip wound managed from the ground to draw his service weapon. His vision somewhat acclimated to the darkness of the dive bar, he shot Alton twice, with both rounds hitting him squarely in the chest. Although the police body armor stopped the rounds from the .25-caliber semiautomatic handgun, the impact was still considerable, like taking a home-run swing from a ball bat to the chest. The shot to the hip wasn't life-threatening, but all bullet wounds are serious. Alton, who didn't have the benefit of body armor, bled out on the scene before emergency responders arrived.

At the unit office, Batista was waiting alone for Owens when she walked in.

"Just heard Alton was pronounced dead at the scene," Batista said. "One of the cops was released; the other is doing well and out of surgery."

"We should be betting on horses the way we picked Alton," Owens said.

"I'd put money on any shitbag with more than twenty-seven calls against him. And by 'put money on,' you know what I mean."

She did, and she cut Batista off with a hand gesture to her throat. Even in this sort of code, she was very uncomfortable having a conversation in the office. Cops have good reason to be paranoid, seeing that their job is to outthink criminals.

They left the police district and made their way to a bar three blocks away.

Before they took their first sip of beer, Batista was ready to talk.

"I could pull at least twenty names from our book we'll be cleaning up after in the next six months. So much for 'protect and serve.' It's more like 'sit back and wait for it to happen.' I feel fucking useless."

"I can't help thinking that if those cops knew what we knew about Jeremy Alton, things would've gone another way," Owens said. "This shit isn't on us, but I'm just saying."

"We didn't know he was armed. He was a convicted felon, so he couldn't have bought it himself, not legally."

"Still, we knew he was dangerous, more than the average wife-beating piece of shit, like a rabid animal," Owens said.

"He could've just as easily killed both cops," Batista said.

They both sat back to consider that ugly thought.

"It's just messed up that we have all these names, addresses, history, fucking everything about them written down, and we just sit back and do nothing," Batista said. "It's like watching ticking time bombs."

"And another one just went off," Owens said. "Who's next?"

# CHAPTER 7 – DEUS EX MACHINA

Work schedule permitting, Owens had classes at the university two days a week. Mondays were with her graduate advisor, Dr. Madeline O'Neill. After class, the two normally had a coffee together. O'Neill had twenty years on Owens, but they got on exceptionally well, and their relationship was much stronger than the usual professor-graduate student model. The truth was, Professor O'Neill was fascinated with the stories Owens told her of life on the job on the streets of a major metropolis and in one of America's most violent cities.

The two were about to take a seat at their usual café terrace when O'Neill couldn't contain herself any longer.

"Were you on duty Sunday afternoon?"

The story of the domestic abuse case was all over the media and had dominated conversations throughout the city. Most of the fervor surrounded Officer Warton's cool head and straight shooting after taking two rounds from Jeremy Alton. Owens knew O'Neill wasn't interested in the gunfight at the dive bar.

"I got called in as soon as we heard," Owens said, before adding, "It's not like this was a surprise to any of us. Just a miracle the shitbag didn't kill anyone."

O'Neill had cautioned Owens about getting too comfortable with using the term "shitbag" to describe the abusers in their book, warning that the term might slip out inadvertently at some inappropriate moment, like at a press conference or in court. Owens blamed her foul language on her work career in the military and the city police, two foul-mouthed organizations that probably invented a lot of profanity.

O'Neill spared Owens the sermon on this occasion. At this point, it would be impossible to defend the recently deceased against charges he was a shitbag.

"He was definitely at or near the top of my list of the men in your book," O'Neill said.

Owens shouldn't have been surprised her faculty advisor had come to the same conclusion as she and Batista. Still, this revelation from O'Neill made her feel exposed, transparent, like this algorithm could go both ways and implicate what she and Batista had done.

"He was definitely on the road to repeat offenses," Owens said, hoping to steer the conversation away from this idea of pulling likely suspects out of the book.

"And yet, as a society, we're unable to do anything but wait," O'Neill said.

"Warton's hip injury isn't too serious. Still, he'll be on medical leave for two months, at least," Owens said as a way of changing the subject.

"If I may ask, how did Alton get a gun? He's a convicted felon."

O'Neill didn't want to let this go.

"Are you joking? This is the United States. It's easier to buy an illegal firearm than it is for a twenty-year-old kid to buy a six-pack of beer."

Owens didn't expand on her answer in another vain attempt to stifle O'Neill's interest in the case.

"So, you obviously didn't know he was armed?"

She wasn't letting go.

"No, and we haven't been able to find out where he got the piece. Him being dead hinders the investigation somewhat," Owens quipped.

"I imagine it would. I just can't stop thinking about the fact this known…this convicted and violent abuser was just walking around like…like a ticking time bomb."

Owens was officially nervous at this point, nervous enough to think she needed a lawyer present to answer further questions.

"Think of the grief that could be spared by taking some sort of action before things go to hell, like in this situation," her professor said.

What the hell, Owens thought.

"Like what?" Owens asked.

"Like taking that guy out for a long ride and not bringing him back," O'Neill said.

Owens was waiting for the punchline, or some sign from O'Neill she was joking. None were coming. Owens felt her faculty advisor, mentor, and friend had loads of virtues, but a sense of humor wasn't among them.

"Like taking them out and putting a bullet in them?"

"I could think of plenty of worse things they deserve," O'Neill said.

How about throwing them in a tree shredder? It was all Owens could do not to verbalize this thought.

"He shot two cops, not to mention how he's tortured his family for years…and who the hell knows how many other women. Are you telling me this doesn't piss you off?"

Does it piss me off? Owens thought. You have no idea, professor. Or maybe she did? Owens had always seen her teacher as a highly clinical, rational person, to a fault. For the first time she sensed anger in her voice, even hatred.

"Getting 'pissed off' doesn't really factor into police work. If it did, absolutely everything we see in the course of a workday on the street would piss us off."

"I don't know how you can do it. How can you see this and not want to step in, like in an ancient Greek play, the *deus ex machina*? Change the…"

"What?"

Owens wasn't familiar with the concept.

"In the Greek plays, there was an actual machine that would lower and raise a character into a scene, a god, who would miraculously save the day," O'Neill explained.

"And you want cops to do this? Not our job, sister. We don't do Greek theater. Miracles? Nope. We got enough problems as it is just in case you don't read newspapers."

"We've talked about the Alba Moreno case. All I can say is if I'd known about this Tony Martin and his history, I'd've at least tried to do something to stop him," O'Neill said.

Had this discussion transpired over the course of several beers, Owens would've blamed her professor's aggression on the alcohol.

This was over coffee in the morning and represented a dark side Owens had never seen before in her mentor at the university. This wasn't a judgment on Owens's part, just an observation.

"I'd love to meet some of the people you work with," O'Neill said as they were leaving.

Owens couldn't wait to introduce her to Batista. The three of them had a lot in common.

***

Civilian clothes were required for most investigative work and follow-up calls for the members of the DVU. It was felt uniformed police arriving at a household caused more stress for the family. Detectives in civilian clothes attracted less attention from neighbors and were less disruptive. Owens wasn't so sure about this policy and thought a show of force by the police was often a lot more helpful than what she felt was sneaking around in disguise. Disruptive to the neighborhood or not, a patrol car with lights flashing sent a message, a warning to husbands, boyfriends, stalkers, or anyone else who may be lurking in the shadows.

Owens drove with Batista to South Seventh and McKean Street in an endless expanse of two-story residences in South Philly. They were doing a follow-up after Bree Hawkins had reported her husband had violated his restraining order by waiting for her to come home from work three days earlier. After a heated argument complete with death threats, her husband, Gerald Hawkins, had fled the area after a patrol car happened to drive down the street.

Police had been unable to contact the husband, although Owens knew no one had tried very hard. Running down restraining order violations was a thankless task and far from a PPD priority.

About the only positive thing Owens could say about this area of the city was parking wasn't the nightmare it was in most other parts of Philadelphia. This was due to the relatively low population density in South Philly, where two-story row houses were the rule.

"Lots of parking. Unfortunately, there's no reason to ever come here," Owens said as she slammed the door and walked up to the address.

The apartment was above a shuttered Asian restaurant, either for the day or forever. Batista rang the bell.

"Wha?" came the voice over the intercom.

"Detective Batista, Philadelphia PD, ma'am. We called."

The woman came to the door down the stairs from her upstairs apartment but didn't open the door all the way.

"Afternoon, we're here to talk about your complaint."

"You find that asshole?" Bree asked.

"People are on it right now. Can we come in?" Batista asked.

"Man, my place is a disaster. Can't we just talk here?"

Owens and Batista looked at each other and shrugged. They didn't have much to say—the doorway would work for them.

Owens did all of the talking. Batista got a call on his cell from the unit.

"Let me take this. I'll be right back."

He walked back to the car to talk to Welling.

Owens continued the questioning when the woman looked over Owens's shoulder and moved backward in panic. Owens turned around just as a man of about her height grabbed her by the hair from behind and punched her in the lower back.

This could only be the loving husband, Owens thought, wincing in pain.

"Batista," Owens shouted out to her partner, and then, remembering she wasn't in uniform, "Philadelphia police, motherfucker."

She spun around to her left with her right arm over her head, breaking the man's hold, although not without taking a clump of her scalp along with it as he still had a firm grip on her hair.

Gerald Hawkins was a construction day laborer, twenty-five years old, and strong as hell, something that wasn't in his file Owens had read. She had his right arm pinned under her right arm. He grabbed her around the waist with his left arm from behind and picked her up off the ground as if she were a toddler.

Owens pushed her head back as hard as she could and connected solidly on his nose. As he fell backward, Owens struck with both of her elbows into his chest while hooking one of his legs with her right foot. He fell on his back, and she could hear his head bounce off the sidewalk. He was barely conscious when she turned around and planted the toe of her black leather ankle-high boot into his ribs.

The savage kick seemed to revive Hawkins, and he gave out a moan like a slowly deflating tractor tire.

Batista had missed the whole thing and now stood over the crippled suspect lying on his back with his face covered in blood.

"Looks worse than it is," Owens reassured him. "I broke his nose with the back of my head. I got blood back there?"

She turned to show Batista her head.

"Some, more on the back of your jacket."

"God damn. I just bought this suit," Owens said.

A ruined suit would turn out to be the least of Owens's problems in the Gerald Hawkins matter. Batista hadn't seen any of it, and the wife refused to corroborate what Owens put in her statement. What investigators had to weigh were a few strands of hair from Owens against the complaints of Hawkins who'd suffered a concussion, a broken nose, and two broken ribs.

Hawkins was arrested and booked after his hospital visit, then promptly filed a civil suit against the PPD. It was pure rubbish, but unfortunately for Owens, the incident had come only three days after a highly-questionable police shooting of a fifteen-year-old boy in the city. The press and activist groups were out for blood, and Owens became a target.

Batista was totally willing to say whatever Owens needed him to say, but she ordered him to give an honest statement. His words in no way contradicted Owens's version of the events, and PPD was confident the matter would blow over with no consequences for the decorated officer. However, a certain James McMillan from the highly exclusive suburb of Gladwyne—the Loire Valley of Philadelphia—had news relayed to him of the current predicament of Detective Elizabeth Owens.

James McMillan was a lot of things: rich beyond reason, successful, greedy, petty, racist, and misogynistic, but more than any of these, he was vengeful. Owens would have been completely dumbfounded to learn this billionaire and world-class shitbag girlfriend-beater was still out to destroy her.

James McMillan had grown up fabulously wealthy, as had his father, and his father's father, and another generation of the family before that. When you're raised with so much privilege, you aren't accustomed to having anyone even argue with you. Everyone is either a minion, a servant, an employee, or some other lesser human being, or that's how they see it. James McMillan was never picked on as a child, never bullied—his father wouldn't have allowed it. The McMillans would do the bullying.

James McMillan's wife had been terrorized by the man. Although they were officially still married, they'd lived apart for several years. She accepted her role as the mother of his two children while sharing a few days a year with her husband just to keep up appearances. She didn't know and didn't care he had a string of mistresses he supported; she was just glad she was no longer one of his targets for aggression and abuse.

McMillan was among the wealthiest men in the city as well as a world-class prick who enjoyed firing employees and humiliating anyone beneath him on the social ladder, and most were beneath him. He wasn't the sort of man to forget a slight, no matter how veiled or indirect. To have someone slam his head into a doorway in his own home—or at least one he paid for—was simply too much for him to accept.

He'd spent two weeks in the hospital and now had to wonder about the future health of his damaged brain as severe concussions were extremely worrisome, especially for a man of his age (he'd been in his late fifties when it occurred). The true outrage for him was that it had come at the hands of a Philadelphia police officer, an organization he felt he'd already bought and paid for. And it was a woman. And she was Black. As much as he had tried to sabotage her career, evidently Elizabeth Owens was just too much of a shining star to bring down: a decorated war veteran, outstanding record with the PPD, and a native of the city. And she was Black and a woman, two qualities the department needed to promote.

Perhaps it was due to the severe concussion, but McMillan had a hard time accepting the fact that being African-American could somehow actually work in a person's favor, at least sometimes. He was among those elites who couldn't understand the advantages of promoting qualified minorities in a city with an almost equal number of Blacks and Whites, forgetting the careers of minorities had been stymied for most of Philadelphia's history.

McMillan hadn't forgotten about Owens, though in recent months he'd done little to undermine her career at PPD. Now he saw a new front opening with this recent arrest and the fact the accused had also suffered significant injuries at the hands of Owens.

Even without the eyewitness account of his wife, convicting Gerald Hawkins should have been a walk in the park for even the most inexperienced, thick-headed district attorney. However, the case seemed to have taken on a life of its own with advocacy groups taking up the cause of the construction day laborer who'd been thoroughly trounced by a cop. It didn't matter Hawkins had a record of spousal abuse and his adversary was a female police officer.

Why had the mob taken up this particular case with such savage fury?

A tax-deductible gift to the well-meaning citizens action group and an anonymous contribution to the defense fund of Gerald Hawkins by James McMillan certainly helped to get the smear campaign started against the young detective. Defending herself against an enemy as powerful as James McMillan would have been problematic for Owens, but especially so when he was completely in her blind spot.

McMillan was an incessant list-maker. He was also the type to make a perpetual habit of crossing things off his lists. He'd yet to decide just what it meant to cross Elizabeth Owens off his list, but once her name popped up again on his radar, he saw a way to destroy her career.

# CHAPTER 8 – THE WAYWARD CRUSADE

Gerald Hawkins was arrested at the scene for assaulting a police officer before Batista escorted him to the hospital. His injuries were consistent with what Owens filed in her report. His broken ribs were somewhat problematic for her, but she claimed she'd kicked him while he was sprawled on the sidewalk because she still felt in danger. Batista hadn't seen her kick the suspect on the ground, he missed the whole show. It would've been easy enough for him to back up what his partner reported, that's what cops did, it was expected of them.

Owens told him again to stick with the truth. She assured her partner this arrest wouldn't be a problem.

Unfortunately for Owens, her injuries weren't very obvious. Hawkins still had a clump of her hair in his left hand when Batista cuffed him, but this wasn't logged in as evidence. She had a bruise on her back where Hawkins had punched her, but it was barely visible against her dark skin. Just to cover her bases, she had a photograph taken at the station, but it wouldn't be very convincing if this arrest were challenged.

Owens wasn't worried in the least about the arrest. That was about to change two days later when she reviewed the case with her unit supervisor, a highly irregular occurrence for routine arrests.

Sgt. Welling passed the news on to Owens that Hawkins was filing a civil suit against her, claiming brutality and excessive force. This sort of ploy was typical ambulance chaser lawyer bullshit, but this had been presented by one of the top criminal defense attorneys in the city.

"Where does a shitbag like Gerald Hawkins come up with the loot to hire a lawyer?" Batista asked two days after the incident. "Guy's paid his child support exactly twice in the past year and a half."

91

"This isn't just a lawyer," Welling said. "It's Noah Gottlieb."

"The fuck? Noah Gottlieb is taking on this case?" Owens asked.

Noah Gottlieb had made a fortune defending many of the most notorious defendants who'd gone to trial in Philadelphia in the past decade. Most of them were guilty, and more importantly, they were all stratospherically wealthy. Cartel bosses, mafia dons, and the Brahmin class of Philadelphia who found themselves on the wrong side of the law in criminal cases. If your teenage son killed someone in a drunken hit-and-run, or maybe pop got caught screwing an under-aged babysitter, or you had any other rich White people type of felony arrest, Noah Gottlieb was your best chance to sweep it all under the rug.

In recent years, Noah Gottlieb's way of expunging his own record of defending the worst of the worst was to take on many of the more quixotic legal battles involving the poor, dispossessed, and the downtrodden.

He'd made his fortune defending the deplorable but became famous for successfully defending four Black teenagers accused of murdering a young woman in Rittenhouse Square. Had the victim been African-American, the story would've never made the local news, but this victim was White, attractive, and wealthy—qualities assuring media saturation in a murder investigation. It was yet another example of a racist police department following their initial instincts in the investigation after the four youths had been reported in the area of the crime without another shred of evidence against them.

After the boys had been described by two different people who'd been somewhere in the vicinity of the knifing, the case for the PPD was simply a matter of tracking them down. Of course, the police hadn't bothered to run down any other leads they found in the case because they'd gone all in on the four teens. They hadn't bothered to even investigate the young woman's romantic past, which became Gottlieb's first priority in his investigation.

Gottlieb all but made the case for the state by implicating a former lover of the victim who was charged, convicted, and sentenced to life for the murder. The lawyer went on to fame and notoriety by telling reporters his clients had been "Williams-ed" in reference to the soon-to-be-disgraced Philadelphia district attorney, Seth Williams, known for taking the path of least resistance in racially-volatile court cases.

"Gottlieb only takes cases for one of two reasons: money or a crusade. So why would he defend a creep like Gerald Hawkins?" Welling asked, a question no one present could answer.

Gottlieb was certainly treating the case like a crusade, even though the weakest and least experienced prosecutor in the D.A. office wouldn't have a hard time convicting Hawkins in the assault. The fact Batista hadn't corroborated his partner's account seemed to make the case even stronger for the state as the local press reported this as evidence of police not resorting to the usual tactics of circling the wagons to protect their own, with the implication Owens must have done nothing wrong.

Initially, it was the word of a decorated police officer and Iraq War veteran against a convicted wife abuser. Even a highly-talented litigator and crusader like Gottlieb wouldn't have gone to trial holding those cards. It seemed obvious to the PPD the defense attorney's role was to simply stir the pot in a city boiling with racial tension and anti-police sentiment.

Gottlieb had the best of both worlds with this case. In the press, he was the defender of a working-class guy (when Hawkins was employed) against a police department constantly under fire for the excessive use of force against the citizens of Philadelphia, and he was being paid his normal fee for taking on the case, what he collected from drug lords and the hyper-rich.

In this particularly un-Dickensian drama, Gerald Hawkins had a very wealthy benefactor whom he'd never met, or even heard of, and never would. The case of Gerald Hawkins mattered little to James McMillan. Hawkins was nothing more than a pawn in McMillan's obsession with harming Elizabeth Owens who was nothing but another pawn in his life, yet the longer she escaped his retribution, the more he felt compelled to continue his battle against her.

Owens was relieved no one had witnessed her *coup de grâce*: the savage kick to Hawkins' ribs. She didn't harbor a bit of remorse or regret for the blow; he more than had it coming, even after his broken nose and the concussion, which technically wasn't her fault. Blame the sidewalk and gravity.

"The wife'll come around; I'm just dumbfounded as to why Gottlieb would take on this case. Pretty far from his usual profile of the do-gooder crap he does to cover up the stench of keeping cartel assassins out of prison," Owens said.

Noah Gottlieb knew nothing of McMillan's secret war with the Philadelphia policewoman. He didn't know James McMillan was paying him to defend Gerald Hawkins and to file the civil suit against the arresting officer. The more Gottlieb looked into the case, the less confident he felt in pursuing the suit, but he'd defended much worse people than a wife-beating shitbag, as he'd heard Hawkins described by several police officers he had on his payroll.

Gottlieb had been called every sort of insult imaginable as a high-profile criminal defense lawyer. He'd inspired the creation of more than a few lawyer jokes during his brilliant career. He was known throughout every Philadelphia police district where these jokes were repeated and embellished. Cops mostly thought defense attorneys were the enemy, while Noah Gottlieb held a special position at the top of this list for his part in undoing some of the biggest criminal cases brought to trial in Philadelphia.

At almost sixty years old, recently divorced for the third time and a mostly-absentee father to two children, Noah Gottlieb's attitude of late had become increasingly reflective and self-critical. He liked how he felt when he was on one of his crusades and felt less compelled to take on other cases simply because they paid well.

Hardly a moment after his office had filed a civil suit against Elizabeth Owens, he realized he was on the wrong team. One of his bright young staffers had prepared a dossier on the young cop. It read like a modern-day fairy tale of a woman coming from one of the city's poorest and most violent neighborhoods to become a true inspiration.

"Born and raised in one of the grimmest areas of the city and a product of the ruined public school system, Owens prospered in the United States Army. A bona fide Iraq War hero who came home to serve her country again with the Philadelphia Police Department. While working full-time as a policewoman, she earned a B.A. at Temple and presently is pursuing a graduate degree there. Her record at PPD has been completely beyond reproach, as far as I could discover," Gottlieb's young assistant told him at a briefing on Owens.

Gottlieb looked over the eight-page document his staffer had prepared.

"Is this a joke? I don't know whether I want to adopt this cop or marry her," Gottlieb said. "Where's the dirt I asked for?"

"Sorry, boss," the young woman said. "In other terrible news, if you haven't seen her on the news, she's also tall, Black, and hot as hell."

Gottlieb groaned.

"And she beat the shit out of a wife-beating asshole," the woman added.

So why would someone want to do a hatchet job on Elizabeth Owens? To Gottlieb, that was obviously happening with the Hawkins case. This had zero to do with his usual *pro bono* work, and not just because he was receiving his top billing fees. He hadn't arrived at his current financial status by looking gift horses in the mouth, but at this point in his career, he'd trade his mansion in Cherry Hill, his beach house in the Bahamas, and his farmhouse in Spain for anything approaching the integrity of the current district attorney.

Gottlieb had an idea, something defense attorneys never did, something he'd certainly never considered and lectured young law students to avoid at all costs, but he wanted to meet this cop for a face-to-face. He had one of his minions set it up.

Owens was definitely disinclined to meet with a defense lawyer. Cops have an almost inherent hatred of lawyers in general, and especially those who defend the people they arrest. Owens most definitely didn't want anything to do with this particular attorney who seemed intent on dragging her through as much mud as he could find.

Owens didn't have a car, her condo was modest, and her wardrobe was slightly chic, but mostly second hand. However, she indulged herself on her Center City health club. She didn't go for all of the high-tech exercise equipment, most of it seemed geared toward computer geeks who barely broke a sweat in their exhaustively detailed programs. She stuck with the same routine she began in her high school days, mostly pull-ups and push-ups and whatever cardio she was in the mood for that day, or not.

What she loved about her club was its almost clinical cleanliness. She'd arrive at the desk and was handed a pristine white towel that always looked brand new. She'd throw her bag in a locker and begin her routine by washing her hands. That's how clean the whole club was, like you didn't want to defile it with your dirty hands from the street.

When she finished her gym routine, she spent about thirty minutes between the steam room and the sauna, then finished with a few laps in the pool. For Owens, the *pièce de résistance* was the shower. Even as much of a clean-freak as she'd become as an adult, over-compensating for a childhood spent mostly in squalor, the gym showers were cleaner than her own spotless bathroom at home which was like something out of an advertisement for cleaning products.

Who needed a beauty spa when you had the Center City Fitness Club?

Owens walked out to Chestnut and turned right, heading to the bike share station in the middle of the block. An older man wearing a fedora stepped toward her on the sidewalk.

"Detective Owens, could I have a quick word with you, please?"

Not a bad-looking guy for his age, was Owens's first thought, also thinking his impeccably tailored and expensive suit didn't take anything away from whatever natural appeal he had.

Owens didn't say anything, waiting for him to explain.

"My name's Noah Gottlieb. I'm a defense attorney."

Owens knew the name, of course, but didn't know what he looked like until now.

97

"I'm not looking for counsel, and if I were, I couldn't afford your ass."

"I'd just like to set up a time when we could talk, in private. Whenever you're available. I can arrange…"

"Right now's good."

"I was hoping you'd say that."

She walked with him to Eleventh Street where he invited her into a restaurant too expensive for her budget. They sat at a booth in the bar area.

Before their drinks had arrived, Gottlieb got directly to the point.

"As you may know, I've been retained to represent Gerald Hawkins…"

"By whom?" Owens demanded.

"I'm not quite sure, to be honest."

"Please be honest."

"At first, I thought it might have been a wealthy donor to one of the foundations I've done work for in the past," Gottlieb said.

"Like the Sinaloa Cartel?"

"Touché," Gottlieb laughed. "Maybe it was the Sinaloa Cartel. Tell me, detective, have you ever pissed them off?"

"Not that I know of. I've never worked in narcotics, never want to. I've had some dog shit assignments in my time at PPD, but I never wanted to land there."

Gottlieb thought on this.

"With your record? What have been some of the worst assignments for you so far?"

"Right where I am is pretty dog shit. Nobody sane would want to go to Domestic Violence."

"Why were you sent there?" Gottlieb asked.

"Like I fucking know."

"With your record?"

"Imagine that," Owens said.

Gottlieb pulled out a small leather notepad and flipped it open.

"Army MP. Purple Heart, Bronze Star," he said before halting. "Bronze Star?"

He looked at Owens, but she didn't respond.

"That has to count toward promotion, right?" Gottlieb asked.

Owens remained silent.

"OK, and then there's your record at PPD which seems not only pristine, but exceptional. I don't know much about the inner workings of the department, but I'd go as far as to say 'outstanding' wouldn't be an exaggeration to describe your career."

"Well, the bad news for me is no one gives a shit what a drug lawyer has to say when it comes to PPD politics and promotions," Owens said. "And why do you care about my career? You some long lost uncle?"

Gottlieb didn't respond.

"Maybe a drug lawyer with a heart of gold?"

"You're getting close. I'll let you know when I figure it out myself. All I can say now is instead of filing a civil suit, I'd rather be backing your play as chief of police, or congresswoman, or whatever."

"Slow down, drug lawyer…"

"Please, call me Noah."

Owens wasn't sure she wanted to call him anything except something with an expletive attached to it.

"Why'd you ambush me in front of my club, my one sanctuary in this city."

"Sorry about that, but it made more sense than in front of the district. I wanted to be as discreet as possible, for both our sakes, seeing how we're directly involved in a current case."

"We are, and one you're gonna lose."

"While I refuse to apologize for offering the finest legal counsel available to anyone wrapped up in the criminal justice system, there are a few things in this most recent case that don't sit well with me."

Gottlieb paused. Owens thought it was just some lawyer-drama nonsense.

"Let me say that this must be completely off the record. While no laws are being violated, it does violate my personal code…"

"You have a code?" Owens asked, her incredulity tangible at this point.

"More and more, yes. I do have a code, at least recently. Part of my code involves not shanghaiing the career of someone I feel is an exemplary cop."

"I'd thank you, but I have a civil suit you filed against me that says otherwise."

Owens was savvy enough about legal matters to understand Gottlieb was taking all of the risks at this meeting which leaned toward his sincerity. She couldn't see any other angle for him to come forward like this.

"I have no doubt the wife will come forward and corroborate your story, and that will be that. The broken rib… could be a bit of a problem for you, which is why you should have kicked him in the head."

What Gottlieb brought to the table for Owens was a promise to find out why his fee was being paid to defend a reprobate like Gerald Hawkins. Did she have an enemy, an enemy with deep pockets?

"Hungry?" Gottlieb asked.

"I could eat," Owens said, looking around at one of the city's top restaurants. "If you're paying, of course."

"Of course," Gottlieb answered. "Maybe you could tell me about your military service."

# CHAPTER 9 – BOMBS AND BRONZE STARS

By the time Owens was deployed to Iraq, the strategy of the U.S. forces didn't seem to go much further than hunkering down and trying not to get blown up. Firefights with enemy combatants were infrequent, but the dangers of IEDs (improvised explosive devices) had kept forces at a constant threat level. Neither U.S. troop surges nor reductions made much difference in the quality of life for the average Iraqi citizen. Most lived under a constant cloud of violence, poverty, and insecurity about their future.

One of the most dangerous pieces of real estate in the entire country of Iraq was the road linking the Green Zone in central Baghdad with the airport almost due west. After her initial indoctrination at the Army outpost, Owens was assigned to the airport escort detail. Most of these convoys used armored Humvees.

MP units soon labeled these vehicles "not-armored-enough" Humvees. Then again, any old grunt knew there was no amount of armor that could protect a vehicle if the enemy used enough explosives. The Iraqi insurgents had an almost limitless supply of field artillery rounds of various sizes due to the failure of U.S. invading troops to secure military bases in the country back in early 2003. Of course, that ship had sailed, and these abandoned armaments were taking a devastating toll on U.S. soldiers and Iraqi civilians.

Owens soon had three close brushes with IED detonations on airport runs. All of the attempts were captured on video which her brigade studied to help them find a strategy to defeat this new combat menace. As much as each incident was studied, there was only so much the patrols could do to defend themselves against devices detonated by pressure plates, mobile phones, radios, or by suicide bombers. The bombs could be buried under the street, placed along the roadside, hidden in a heap of trash, placed in a baby carriage, in parked cars, on the backs of donkeys, and in countless other delivery methods.

In Owens's fourth brush with an IED, she was two vehicles behind the blast that claimed the lives of four people in her regiment, people she considered friends. She brought her Humvee to a screeching halt, almost rear-ending the vehicle in front of her disabled by the explosion. The lead vehicle was thrown three meters off the road with nothing much left of it except a chassis landing upside down on top of a parked car.

They set up a defensive perimeter, but usually there was no follow-up to an IED attack. Why take the risk of engaging the enemy when this new type of warfare was proving to be very effective? In armed combat, the Iraqi insurgents were no match for the Americans who were better trained and armed.

Off-duty time in the Green Zone was about how Owens would have imagined prison life. She spent most of it between working out and reading. In the mind of many U.S. soldiers, the more the military tried to make life more livable and ordinary in Iraq for its people, the more absurd the occupation seemed.

"Why are they building Pizza Huts in this place?" Owens asked during a group physical training session.

"Just another way to take back the money they give us. It's just like the camp stores in the mining towns of the old West. The mining company ran the stores and bled the workers of everything they could," a soldier named Schmitt said.

Owens knew the guy, but not well. Intelligent, educated, and politically left-leaning to the point of being a bit of a socialist, or at least a far-left liberal for U.S. Army standards of the day.

"I'd rather eat MREs and leave one day sooner than have all of this America fast-food garbage available to me," Schmitt added. "The people who work in these places make bank while we get soldier's pay to protect them."

She liked him. From what she'd seen, he was at least as tough as anyone in the unit, a monster at PT, one of the top marksmen, but he didn't have the false self-confidence of the ex-high school sports stars and other loudmouthed macho morons.

And he read. A lot.

Owens had never seen that as a virtue in a man, but this guy Schmitt made it look sexy as hell. She didn't know his first name, not that anyone used first names in the Army. You either went by your last name or you had a nickname. Schmitt didn't look like the type who would allow a nickname assignment.

She heard he'd dropped out after a couple years at some college, USC or UCLA, one of those California elite schools. Two years of college was like royalty in the Army, double down on that for grunts in a battle area. Owens could hardly believe she felt shy around him. Shyness wasn't part of her nature, or at least not part of her act. This one made her feel like she was thirteen again.

Because she was an attractive woman in the military, Owens had to literally beat away suitors with her night stick. She wasn't the type to get off on that kind of power over men and ended up just feeling sorry for most of the poor fools who came on to her. Schmitt had never come on to her. She'd have to buck up and bring it to him. She decided to ambush him one day during his exercise routine.

For all his reading and two years at some semi-elite school in California, Schmitt was as much of a knucklehead fanatic as every other 31-Bravo when it came to martial arts. The brigade had a special area set aside where soldiers honed their fighting skills. It was nothing more than a sand pit about thirty meters in diameter, part sumo ring, part gladiator arena.

There was a printed sign on a wood stake, *"Ave Caesar morituri te salutant!"*

She asked six people before learning its meaning.

"Hail Caesar, those who are about to die salute you," Specialist Green told her. "Fucking Schmitt. What kind of faggot speaks Latin?"

Of course, it was Schmitt, and Owens thought it highly fucking unlikely this grunt would have insulted Schmitt to his face. Or maybe he would, knowing Schmitt had a sense of humor and would never use "faggot" as a pejorative.

Schmitt was wearing a judo gi and rolling with a much bigger guy wearing fatigues. The big guy looked twice Schmitt's size, and he was over six feet tall. The big guy had Schmitt on his back, yet he wasn't in control, not by a long shot. In ground fighting, being on top can mean something, or nothing at all. In this case, it meant the big guy was having his ass handed to him. As the big guy struggled to push Schmitt away so he could stand up, Schmitt grabbed the giant's right wrist with both hands and swung his right leg over it, locking the elbow. The big guy tapped out.

"Nice," Owens said when Schmitt was on his feet again and taking on water.

"The big muscles just wear you out on the ground," Schmitt said. "How're you doing?"

"It doesn't get any better than this," Owens said, using a line from a beer commercial adopted by soldiers to mock their life in the war zone.

The two sat down on a wood cable spool and watched the other gladiators in the pit. Schmitt apologized for having to leave soon for an Arabic class he was taking.

Of course, he's learning Arabic, Owens thought.

She told him she needed something to read.

"I just finished an amazing book. Maybe it isn't your cup of tea, and I admit the premise sounds ridiculous, but it was, without a fucking doubt, the most fun I've ever had reading."

Even Renaissance-man motherfuckers like Schmitt swore like pirates, Owens was relieved to hear.

"High praise," Owens said.

"I read it so fast, I thought my eyes were going to pop out of my head. I have it right here."

He reached into his gym bag and gave her the hardback copy with a slightly damaged dust jacket.

"Hardback. Nice," Owens said. "I promise to get it back to you soon."

"Pass the book on when you finish, but I'm looking forward to talking to you about it."

Schmitt apologized again for having to leave and told her once more how much he wanted to hear her opinion of the book. They shook hands.

Owens wanted to go take a shower with him right then and there, but they shook hands.

She looked at the book. *Memoirs of an Invisible Man* by H.F. Saint.

The next airport run the following morning was going to be a big deal. Some of President Obama's people were coming to town to sell the new president's plan for exiting the nightmare of the Iraqi occupation, then in its seventh year. Even a high-school educated grunt like Owens could see there was no way to "win" in Iraq. There never had been. No one had even planned for what victory would look like. It was way past the time to leave—assuming anyone believed they should have been there in the first place. Before U.S. forces could turn around and go home, the plan had to be sold to the Iraqis. These newcomers were assigned this task.

The MPs had swept the route a half-dozen times in the twenty-four-hour period leading up to the convoy. Everyone who knew any better was aware this meant exactly doodly squat as insurgents could have placed IEDs weeks ago, just waiting for the most opportune time to set them off, or they could lay charges out at a moment's notice or come at the convoy in a frontal assault. The total nihilism of the insurgents had never ceased to confound, frustrate, and terrify the American forces.

As much as intelligence analysts tried to mask the arrival of the VIP delegates, all it took was someone watching planes land and the increased American security response to determine a high-priority target was on the road to the Green Zone.

Owens saw the young politico-soldier Schmitt as they geared up for the convoy. She only managed a smile which the handsome boy returned. Not exactly the right time for chit-chat as they both strapped on their Kevlar helmets and checked their weapons one last time before piling into their vehicles. His would be directly in front of Owens and her crew. As they pulled out, she could see Schmitt up top on the M60 machine gun. She wished he'd duck inside.

I can't believe I'm worried about him; don't even know his first name, she thought.

She had other worries the moment her vehicle moved out. She was assigned to the SAW. The grunts called it an M4 on steroids, the pretty hate machine, the un-equalizer, and the population controller, among other pet names. Owens had been training on it extensively since deployed to Iraq. For fire practice, her unit would head out of the Green Zone in force to the outskirts of the city, its purpose being as much for intimidation as training for the soldiers. Any insurgent watching the MP drills out in the desert would think long and hard about challenging them face-to-face in combat. A highly-trained U.S. Army platoon is truly an intimidating presence on the battlefield.

The purpose of the M249 SAW in an actual firefight was to pin down an enemy using its higher cyclic firing rate of 850 rounds per minute, enabling riflemen with lighter M4 carbines to maneuver into position and outflank insurgent positions. It weighed more than the M4, especially when carrying extra barrels and 200-round cartridge boxes. But that was the whole point of the weapon: 200-round cartridge boxes. It was the personal firearm equivalent of turning it up to eleven, as yet another hillbilly arms instructor had put it, trying his best to imitate an English accent.

Owens often wondered if there was a single arms instructor in the Army who wasn't from Georgia.

As expected, there were no complications going out to the airport. Owens was impressed Obama's VIPs had come in from Kuwait on an ancient C-130 Hercules prop. No drink service on those, nothing but canvas jump seats and noise. The team of five advisors walked to the

Humvees, mostly thirty-somethings wearing L.L. Bean catalog clothes with desert boots. To their credit, they didn't seem to be too terrified.

If they only knew, was all Owens could think about as she checked out these newbies to Iraq. They'd learn sooner or later this place was mostly terrifying.

Unfortunately, their baptism of fire came less than thirty minutes after touchdown in country.

Owens ushered the five of them into the third in the line of four Humvees. She rode shotgun in the second vehicle, with Schmitt still in the turret of the lead.

"Fuck armored Humvees," Staff Sergeant Núñez said from the driver's seat of Owens's vehicle. "We should have Bradleys or fucking tanks."

If Núñez is worried, I should be shitting myself, Owens thought. Núñez was normally so cool you could only wonder about his mental health when he was under fire. He gave off an aura of invincibility. She normally felt safer just hearing his voice. Now he seemed concerned about their security, not that he sounded rattled, and she doubted it was possible to frighten him, but he just sensed danger, or at least more danger than usual.

Like the storied jeep in World War II, the Humvee became the iconic vehicle of the Iraq war. The problem was neither vehicle was designed to fight; they were designed for transport. While the Humvee had the capability for limited ground support of infantry, it often fought way above its weight class in Iraq.

The first explosion was triggered just as the lead vehicle entered beneath an overpass for the Rabi Skyway over the airport road. It was determined later the IED had gone off a bit early and if the lead Humvee had been four meters ahead, the explosion would have disintegrated the vehicle completely. As it happened, it was flipped up off the ground but did not somersault backward, finally coming to a halt beside the bomb crater on the far end of the overpass but still beneath it.

Núñez managed to halt his vehicle just before the underpass and quickly reversed, veering off to his left so as to avoid the two vehicles coming up from behind. He didn't want them to be sitting below the underpass—an ambusher's wet dream. As he was backing up furiously with their turret gunner scanning the top of the overpass for shooters, the second explosion erupted just behind the fourth and last vehicle in the convoy. It was disabled, but not badly damaged.

The third vehicle with the advisors slammed to a halt about ten meters to the left of Núñez.

"Owens, cover the tourists," Núñez shouted as he ordered the three other soldiers inside the Humvee to dismount.

The three sprinted toward the crippled and burning vehicle below the underpass. They carried their carbines as well as three fire extinguishers.

The turret gunner knew his job: cover the top of the overpass, the most likely place for an attack, if one were coming.

With her SAW and an extra 200-round box of belt-fed ammunition, Owens scanned the perimeter while eyeballing the VIP vehicle. In theory, the safest place for the advisors was in the back of their armored Humvee, something the Army specialist riding shotgun was explaining to them once again. He instructed them to cover themselves as best they could with Kevlar shields. The driver remained behind the wheel as he'd been instructed for just this scenario.

His orders came as soon as Núñez could see he was now in command of the convoy after the captain in the lead vehicle had not been heard from since the blast. Núñez radioed the driver of the VIP Humvee. The driver looked at Núñez to his right. He pointed forward with two fingers, signaling he was Charlie Mike, continuing the mission. He punched it and sped past the burning Humvee under the overpass, heading back to the Green Zone alone with the VIPs.

Owens knew an escort had already been dispatched from the Green Zone which would meet VIPs in less than twenty minutes. The fate of the three remaining Humvees, two of them disabled, was far less certain.

Her mission now was to repel any insurgent attack against the two crippled Humvees. Under normal procedure—if you can ever use the word "normal" in combat—the SAW gave support to riflemen. Unfortunately, those were in very short supply as the three soldiers from Owens's vehicle were in the process of rescuing any possible survivors from the burning lead Humvee.

The last vehicle was hit harder than it appeared because only one soldier dismounted out of the crew of six. The turret gunner lay dead or severely injured on top.

Before leaving in the morning, the weather report cancelled any chance of air support from Apaches. She hoped desperately it wouldn't, but this looked like it could get very interesting, very quickly. "Interesting" was the euphemism Núñez used as a synonym for a desperate firefight, AKA, the shit hitting the fan.

111

What seemed like two hours later, but couldn't have been more than two minutes after the first explosion, two shooters began firing from the top of the overpass. One of them was immediately taken out by the top gunner on the .50 cal. Owens barely looked in that direction as her job was to scan every other point on the compass.

As the turret gunner peppered the top of the overpass, Núñez maneuvered the vehicle beside the disabled fourth vehicle to see about casualties. It didn't look good. Everyone had been hit except the driver who was pulling out the wounded soldier in the passenger seat. Núñez got out and helped put the injured man in the back of his vehicle. He was only bleeding from the back of his shoulder, but the three in the back looked worse. Their turret gunner was definitely KIA.

The only relief in the flat area was the overpass and the build-up on both sides of it to make the bridge over the airport road. Owens set up the tripod of her SAW on the hood of the disabled fourth Humvee. Owens knew there was still one little bastard on the overpass behind the one-meter-high concrete wall on the bridge. The turret gunner fired rounds into the wall below the last spot where the gunner had popped up to fire.

The concrete was crumbling like stale bread against the onslaught of the .50 caliber rounds now firing on full-automatic.

"Chill the fuck out, dude!" Owens screamed above the deafening roar of the gun.

Owens knew there were times when full-auto was appropriate, and when it was prudent to be more judicious with your use of ammunition—exact words from one of her country boy instructors on the range back in 31-Bravo school. They were very often highly articulate when talking about their area of expertise although difficult to understand at times with their bottom lips jammed with dip.

Sure enough, the .50 cal jammed up like a toilet at a chili cook-off—another of that same Georgia instructor's many memorable quotes.

To his great credit, the turret gunner only needed a couple of seconds to determine his time would be better spent with his carbine outside the vehicle than being exposed for the two-minute minimum to clear his weapon. The good news in this mayhem was the shooter behind the wall had been torn to pieces by the rounds penetrating the poor-quality Iraqi concrete in the wall.

"Oh shit," Owens gasped. "Ten o'clock."

To their right on the top of the rise, seven armed insurgents appeared, firing wildly down toward the two exposed vehicles. Owens took a deep breath, then another before pulling the butt against her shoulder and letting go with a burst of about sixty rounds. Just as the former top gunner had time to point his carbine at his ten o'clock, he saw at least five of the insurgents fall face-first down the incline.

He was sighting his weapon when there was another furious eruption from the SAW. When the deafening roar of the SAW stopped after the 200-round ammo box had been drained in the fusillade, there was silence. Silence like the dawn of a new day.

Núñez, the top gunner, and the other driver all looked at Owens.

"Motherfucker!" they said in perfect unison.

They surveyed the slope now littered with seven dead insurgents.

"Owens, they prolly won't let me keep you on a leash, but I don't want you to ever be more than ten meters away until I'm back home in Texas," Núñez said.

Noah Gottlieb slid back in the booth of the chic Center City bistro. He'd asked Owens to give him her version of why she was awarded a Bronze Star.

"I think you're the first actual war hero I've ever met," he said.

"Whatever, on the range, the same shooting would have earned me a pat on the back from one of those instructors from the great state of Georgia. Don't put too much stock in that hero business. The VIPs made the medals happen. Five medals were awarded on that messed up mission. I'm forever embarrassed I got the Bronze Star and not Núñez, a guy whose boots I'm not fit to shine."

"What about the boy? Schmitt?"

"He made it, sort of. I just know he was airlifted to Ramstein as soon as he was stable. Like I said, I didn't even know him, just wanted to."

"You never heard anything else about him?" Gottlieb asked.

"Damn, I wasn't stalking him. I asked around. No one knew much. He must have made it, or I would have heard about it."

"How's that?"

"That's the screwed-up part of military life. If someone dies, you hear about it. If they survive, no one seems overly concerned about spreading the good news."

She hadn't really thought about Schmitt in years, or not much. She'd asked around about him with her military friends but with no luck. She never considered searching a little harder, like a detective would. This thought suddenly popped into her head. She was a cop, after all. She could find him.

"I just don't understand why someone's out to destroy you," Gottlieb said.

"What the hell are you talking about? Seems like you're the one doing the destroying around here."

"I'm just a lawyer doing what I get paid to do. Whoever is paying my fee went to a lot of trouble to remain anonymous. They've done a better job of layering their contribution than even the cartel folks who I know intimately."

"So I've heard," Owens said, not trying to mask her contempt.

"Do you have any enemies?"

"Are you fucking kidding? I'm a cop. I don't get a Christmas card from any of the scumbags I've locked up."

"Of course, I'm sorry. I meant do you have any enemies powerful enough for this sort of subterfuge?"

"Your current client is typical of the people I've been putting away. Mostly even bigger low-lifes when I was on patrol. Pretty sure Gerald Hawkins isn't my enemy."

Owens took a bite of her *salade niçoise*.

"I can't believe it's so tough to find out who's footing the bill to hire a lawyer of your caliber to go after some lowly cop on this ridiculous, not-shit case."

115

"I have someone looking into it, some financial whiz kid, but so far, he's telling me uncovering the source of the money isn't looking good. I just don't understand why anyone would go through the trouble," Gottlieb said. "There's nothing illegal about hiring a lawyer for someone else, Gerald Hawkins in this case."

She never once considered that her failure to get the preferred duty assignments was due to someone plotting behind her back. What Gottlieb revealed to her seemed to point toward a conspiracy.

# CHAPTER 10 – KNOW YOUR ENEMY

Under normal procedural rules in a case involving a civil countersuit filed against the arresting officer, any contact by the officer with a potential witness for the plaintiff would have been out of the question. At their meeting together, Noah Gottlieb had encouraged Owens to have another talk with Mrs. Hawkins to let her know that, without her sworn testimony, her husband could destroy the career of a police officer who'd always been on her side and might have prevented a tragedy the day Owens was attacked by her husband.

This time when Owens stopped by her apartment in South Philly, she made it clear they needed to talk inside. They walked upstairs to the modest, two-bedroom apartment. Owens accepted the beer she was offered, hoping to calm the woman down a bit. Owens recognized the characteristics of battered women who seemed to flinch when talking to anyone they perceived as dominant or in positions of authority.

When they were seated, Owens began immediately with her prepared sales pitch.

"Let me make it clear to you, Andrea," Owens said, using the woman's first name for the first time in an effort to lighten the mood. "It won't be easy convicting your husband without your testimony. Not only that, but he's also filed a civil suit against me claiming excessive force. He denies coming at me first. All I need from you is to tell the truth. You stand up and tell the court he attacked me from behind while the two of us were having a conversation, and he's done. You won't have to worry about him for at least two years."

Andrea Hawkins was too terrified to answer. Owens took a couple of drinks from her bottle of beer, hoping her rattled witness would do the same and relax just a little bit.

"Here's the really good news—besides Gerald getting what he deserves. If you give a statement about what you witnessed, I can promise you this will never go to court—got this direct from his attorney. He'll never take this to trial because he knows he doesn't have a damn prayer of winning. Gerald will plead guilty and the civil suit against me goes away, too."

Andrea took a long drink from her beer and then took an even longer breath.

"You won't even have to see him. He attacked a police officer, he shouldn't be on the street, and he won't be. I just need your statement."

Mrs. Hawkins didn't appear to be totally convinced.

"That motherfucker pulled out my damn hair and punched me in the back so hard I pissed blood."

While it had been a vicious blow, it hadn't caused internal bleeding—a nice bit of embellishment to her story.

"I know you're afraid of him, but if you don't stop him this time, there'll be another time, another time when I won't be here standing between the two of you. Then what? You'll be a lot more afraid then, I guarantee it."

Mrs. Hawkins responded to this part of Owens's speech by slouching down so low on the sofa it seemed she wanted to disappear into it. The officer could sense this woman never wanted to see her husband again.

"Andrea, I've got an officer coming by soon to take your statement. Just tell him everything. That's all I'm asking you. Tell the truth, and you'll be helping yourself."

Down on the street, Batista was waiting in the car. Owens got in the driver's seat.

"Up to you to bring this home, *compadre*," she said. "I did all the heavy lifting, as usual."

"What if she saw the part where you kicked the asshole and broke his ribs?" Batista asked.

"I don't think she did, but even so. It's like the old schoolyard rule goes: 'He started it,' is nine-tenths of the law."

Batista got out with his clipboard.

"I'll call you after she finishes and read it back to you before I leave."

Owens would have preferred a woman officer take the statement, just to put Hawkins more at ease, but Laury was too much of an idiot and couldn't be trusted not to screw it up, and Sgt. Welling was in court all day.

Andrea Hawkins wrote she'd seen her husband grab Officer Owens from behind by her hair. She was also a witness to his savage punch to her back. At this point, she moved inside and closed the door behind her. By the time she reached the second-floor apartment and looked down on the scene from a window, her husband had been handcuffed.

"Looks like you suddenly have nothing to worry about," Batista said as he got back in the vehicle. "She seems to have missed your horrendous display of police brutality."

"That's all on you, bitch, for not being there to have my back."

119

"Damn, sister. I was just having some fun and you make it all personal. You know I feel like shit about that," Batista said.

"Just messing with you. If it'd been the other way around, and I was in the car yakking on the phone, and you were having your ass handed to you by some wife-beating piece of shit, I would've taken my sweet time finishing up the call, too."

"Such an asshole. Just glad we're on the same team," Batista said. "We *are* on the same team, right?"

Owens raised her right fist. Batista bumped it with his, and they pulled out.

***

In an effort to take the initiative in the matter of someone, somewhere working furtively to hamper her career with the department, Owens was told by her immediate supervisor, Sgt. Welling, to go further up the chain of command with her concerns. From the vague picture she painted, Welling thought that whatever problem Owens was having, she'd need a hand from someone well above her sergeant's pay grade.

She managed to arrange an appointment with Inspector Washington Gates who had oversight of their small unit, among his many other responsibilities. Owens would have preferred to be in uniform for the meeting, but she had a tight schedule with class and another meeting with her academic advisor before seeing Gates. She had an appointment with Dr. Madeline O'Neill and a local congresswoman.

Owens told O'Neill about her meeting with Inspector Gates as they were getting coffee on the way to the congresswoman's office.

"Gates? Be careful with that one."

"Why?" Owens asked.

"You've never met him?"

"First time today."

"I've met him. He's as big as the doorway we just passed through. I'm probably not his type, but I've had complaints from two of my students working with him. 'Inappropriate as a motherfucker' as one of them described his actions."

O'Neill now had Owens's full attention.

"How so?" Owens asked.

"From what I got from them, he's just creepy as hell. They both felt physically intimidated by his complete disregard for personal space. One student said he was standing so close to her she could feel his dick touching her shoulder."

"Just what I fucking need right now," Owens said.

It was hardly necessary for a woman to have Owens's good looks to be the target of inappropriate behavior in the military and the Philadelphia Police Department; all women were targets. Owens had dealt with more than her fair share of abuse from her peers and superiors in both organizations, everything from gross staring to lewd comments, to even more toxic and threatening behavior from men in positions of power.

If ever a woman was capable of taking care of herself, that would be Elizabeth Owens, but the almost constant torrent of abuse men never had to deal with was simply infuriating for her. One of the most difficult situations for her to manage was when she was taken completely off-guard by blatant sexism when dealing with a superior.

121

During district roll call and other casual situations with other cops, Owens was always prepared to defend herself against her peers. When the same thing came from authority figures, it was usually unexpected, and her improvised response was not as determined or effective.

The heads-up from Dr. O'Neill was like being warned about an ambush. It could even work to her advantage in her predicament within the department.

The district headquarters was a former three-story brick firehouse built in 1916. It was an attractive structure built back when things were meant to last. Inside, it was pure government eyesore. The lights were too bright and everything else too dark, like the city got a deal on a million gallons of battleship grey paint.

Owens was running a bit late for her appointment with the inspector. She'd never been in the building before and asked the first person she met for directions. Finding a rugby scrum of overweight cops and workers waiting for the elevator, Owens took the stairs to the third floor.

As she entered the waiting area, the receptionist didn't even glance at her before grabbing her handbag and walking out of the office, closing the door behind her. Owens was alone in the waiting area and was about to have a seat when the office door opened.

What the hell was that? Owens thought before quickly connecting the dots: Gates had told his receptionist to clear out when his visitor arrived.

Damn, O'Neill wasn't kidding about the size of this guy: 6'5" and thick. Few would describe him as fat, but he could probably stand to lose seventy pounds, easy. Even so, Owens thought he carried his heft well.

He was wearing a dress uniform and Owens again regretted not wearing hers, not that her conservative business suit was in any way disrespectful. She was a detective, and they were required to be in plain clothes on workdays unless otherwise specified.

"Good afternoon, sir. I'm Detective Owens. I hope I'm not late," she said, looking at her watch.

She wasn't. Right on time.

"Detective Owens, yes. Come in, come in," Gates said as he motioned her into his office.

"Your secretary ran out of here as soon as I opened the door. Someone pull a silent fire alarm I can't hear?" Owens said, not moving to follow the inspector into his office.

Owens's volley caught the inspector by surprise, but he recovered with ease. He was a powerful man who rarely felt threatened or at any sort of disadvantage.

"Martha? No idea. Been with me for two years and has her own ways."

Gates walked into his office and Owens followed, trying not to show any sort of apprehension. Gates didn't walk behind his desk but sat on the edge of it while leaning toward Owens. There was a chair in front of the desk with Gates looming over it like a storm cloud. If she sat down, she'd have nothing in front of her but the huge man's lower torso—a crotch-level view. She remained standing a few feet away, about all the small office would permit.

Gates stared at Owens, slowly moving his gaze up and down before focusing on her chest.

"Damn, girl. You look good, real good. Totally my type, know what I'm saying?"

Owens was so glad she was prepared for this opening salvo of misogyny which would have come like a sucker punch. Her mentor's warning about Gates allowed her to keep her cool and focus.

"Pardon me?" she asked in a neutral tone, implying he needed to repeat what he said.

"I said you are one fine woman," he said, more clearly this time. "How come I never seen you before?"

Owens didn't answer, giving Gates some line.

"I'm a married man, but I could definitely make some exceptions with someone like you."

"You do know I'm here on official police business?" Owens asked calmly. "I made an appointment."

"Yeah, I got time. We can get to know each other a little. We should talk about this over a drink. Been a long day. What do you say?"

Owens lowered her head slightly, giving the inspector a bit more line. She was playing him like a fish already on the hook.

"If you want, I got a room down the street where we can have more privacy, just you and me and a little wine. Come on now, it's almost quitting time," Gates chuckled.

Owens took a step back and felt the door handle in her hand behind her. She was beginning to lose her cool.

"Don't be like that. I can be real good to you. Whatever you need, I can get it. Let's just play a little," Gates was getting into character.

He got off the desk and put his hands on her shoulders.

"Please take your hands off of me," Owens said, as calmly and as clearly as she possibly could.

"Come on, you know you want it," Gates purred.

Owens opened the door with her hand behind her back. She took a step backward out of the office into the waiting area.

"Inspector Washington Gates, how dare you treat me like this," Owens said, in a line scripted out of TV melodrama.

Gates didn't seem to take note of the histrionics and stepped toward her with a menacing look in his eye.

"I said I'll treat you real good."

"I've got nine years on the force, before that I was an Army MP. I got a fucking Bronze Star, something you'd know if you'd bothered to look at my record before taking this meeting. Now you're treating me like some ho you picked up in an alley on patrol?"

"Bitch, you have any fucking idea who you're talking to?"

Gates was starting to get steamed from the insubordination and rejection.

"Yeah, I have an idea. You're like the scum I see every day in Domestic Violence."

Gates took another step toward her. Owens maneuvered next to the corner of a coffee table reaching just below her knee.

125

"I got this all on my phone, by the way. You dumb motherfucking rapist pig."

Owens pointed to her phone hanging on the outside of her handbag and pointing directly at the inspector.

Gates was totally blindsided.

"Yeah, I've heard about you. I was warned, thank God," Owens said.

Gates had to make an awkward step around the coffee table as he lunged forward, trying to snag the bag on her shoulder, but Owens had anticipated his move and pushed her right foot against the inspector's left ankle as he lifted it to step toward her.

Against someone with more than twice your body mass, you don't have much of a chance in a physical confrontation. Once someone as big as Gates has his hands on you, it's already over. Owens had taken one aspect of judo and turned it into her first line of self-defense: the foot sweep. Before anyone can get their hands on you, they have to bridge the gap between the two of you, usually by taking a step or two.

*Ashi-Waza* is the Japanese term for this aspect of judo—the most subtle technique in the martial art. Owens would have never chosen to have a physical confrontation with a mountain of a human being like Gates, but she had trained for years and years for this sort of eventuality.

The key to a perfect foot sweep is to catch your opponent at the precise moment when they are shifting weight from their back foot to step forward. If you push on their foot too soon, while they have most of their weight on their back leg, you're relying solely on strength. With a man like Gates, that would be like trying to kick down a small tree. But if you apply a few pounds of pressure to the forward foot just as weight is leaving the back leg, you'll be using your opponent's weight against him, and the leg will move across his body while his weight is shifting in the other direction. For opponents who aren't suspecting this technique, the foot sweep is highly effective.

There is a definite truth to the adage the bigger they are, the harder they fall. Gates was an enormously strong man, but he was also morbidly obese at this stage in his life, and his extra weight made him extremely clumsy—imagine carrying seventy pounds while walking on uneven ground. He crashed to the floor, hard. He moaned in pain and let loose an avalanche of profanity aimed at Owens.

"Keep talking, I'm still recording," Owens said. "Wait. Did I say I was recording? I meant to say I was live-streaming. My faculty advisor at Temple recommended that. She's just outside watching the whole show."

Owens took her hand off her 9mm on her belt—her backup plan if things got out of hand with Gates. She'd also planned to scream at the top of her lungs. She looked over her shoulder just as the door to the office opened. Dr. O'Neill walked in with her cell phone in one hand. She left the door wide open.

"It's all on here," O'Neill said. "Nice work."

Dr. O'Neill sat down on one of the waiting room chairs, as did Owens, while Gates slowly picked himself off the floor, trying to determine if he was injured.

He looked at Dr. O'Neill.

"Who the fuck's this bitch?" he asked.

"You can just think of her as a witness for the time being," Owens said. "Please, have a seat, Inspector."

Gates sat down, more to alleviate the pain in his hip than to follow the instruction.

Owens played back the video she'd just made on her phone, holding it out for Gates to see.

Even on the palm-sized video screen, it was obvious Gates was ogling someone before he said, *"Damn, girl. You look good, real good. Totally my type, know what I'm saying?"*

"I wasn't really live-streaming this, but it's already out there to a few people I trust. How many other people see this is up to you."

"You think I'm afraid of some little video? Bitch, I'm going to have your head on…"

Owens shouted over him.

"Keep talking, lard ass, and I'll send this to the web so your momma and everyone else can watch it on the local news tonight."

Gates shut up.

"Just listen and you may salvage your miserable career."

Gates directed his attention to Dr. O'Neill.

"Who's this bitch?" he asked again.

"Do you know the city's already paid out over $350,000 to settle complaints lodged against this man?" Dr. O'Neill asked.

"The good news is I don't want money, Inspector. I just need you to do something for me," Owens said.

"You're blackmailing me? That's a felony if you didn't know," Gates said.

"Shut the fuck up," Owens said. "It's not blackmail. If you give me some information, I won't file a complaint against you that will burn down your damn house."

Gates had already been the subject of five investigations involving sexual misconduct, three of them serious enough to have been settled out of court with the Philadelphia Police Department paying the plaintiffs the sum O'Neill had mentioned. As he sat in a chair too small for his bulk, nursing his aching hip and shoulder injured in the fall, it was finally dawning on him he could be in serious trouble over this.

"What information?" he asked.

"Do you want to do this here, or should the three of us go out for that drink you mentioned?" Owens asked.

Philly dive bars all seemed to come from the same mold, and there were hundreds of them. The sort of places made for workers who rarely read anything but court summonses yet somehow featured the cleverest restroom graffiti. Owens and O'Neill sat across from Gates in a booth, with no one talking until their drinks arrived.

"I'm trying to figure out who doesn't like me in the department," Owens began. "I've got almost ten years in, with six more in the Army. Not bragging, but, as I said before, I have a fucking Bronze Star. My record at PPD is spotless—at least as far as records go. So why do I seem to get totally screwed at every step in my path here?"

"Do I look like some human resources hump? What the fuck you asking me for?" Gates asked, truly perplexed.

"Fair enough. I don't expect you to know about me, you don't even know my damn name, although you asked me to go to a hotel room with you. Jesus. What the fuck is wrong with you?"

Owens hesitated to collect herself.

"I just need the name of someone in or out of the department with the juice to screw me over without me even knowing about it. Someone with real power."

"You got enemies?"

"Obviously, I just don't know who the hell they are."

"Why do you think I can help you?" Gates asked.

"You gotta have names, people with money, people who pay to get things done in the department, make things go away—and I'm not talking about parking tickets. I'm talking about the power to make felonies go away…and screw over cops. You know anyone like that?"

"A few, maybe."

"So?"

"The mayor's office bailed out my fat ass when the shit got ugly. It wasn't exactly quiet, but they salvaged my career. Couple times."

"Mayor doesn't know me, not that I know of," Owens countered.

"I know a couple people. Rich folks. Philly's finest, as we call them."

Gates told a few stories about people moving backstage to make things go away. He rattled off a few names before Owens recognized one of them.

James McMillan.

"Tell me more about him," Owens said.

"I don't know much, but he's some sort of heavy hitter. I've never even met the man, but I've made some moves on his behalf."

"Like what?"

"Like damn near anything he wants. All I know is he's super-rich and a huge prick. Acts like we all work for him, like he's some sorta plantation overseer."

Gates stopped to take a big drink from his Hennessy.

"You got a history with the guy?" he asked.

Owens didn't answer. It wasn't anything Gates needed to know.

Owens gently tapped her cell phone on the table.

"You did good, Inspector. We're all square here."

"So let me see you delete that video," Gates said.

"Can't do it. I need insurance just in case you try to come back at me on this. I'm going to keep this nice and quiet, but you try to fuck me, or I even get a hint you're stabbing me in the back somehow…"

Owens gave Gates a second to let this sink in.

"You forget about this incident, and I will, too. You don't, I'll come back at you hard. You have my word," she said.

Owens looked over at her faculty advisor who was reviewing the video once again.

"She has you by the balls with this. My advice to you: listen to Detective Owens and get help with your attitude toward women. I'm available for counseling," O'Neill said, giving Gates her card.

O'Neill nodded to Owens.

"Almost forgot," Owens said. "I hear about another sexual accusation against you, I don't care if someone says you looked at them the wrong way, I'll make a formal complaint against you that will stick."

# CHAPTER 11 – SOCIAL MEDIA STALKER

James McMillan. Owens had almost forgotten the name, but as soon as Gates mentioned him, it all became clear to her that it was James McMillan. Batista heard the story about the guy but knew nothing about him, and neither of the two cops had any idea of the influence McMillan had in the city.

"Ungrateful prick should be sending me birthday cards after I dropped the charges against him," Owens said.

If anyone thought Owens and Batista spent too much time in bars, they didn't understand how police and ex-soldiers lived. Going to bars was as much ingrained in the psyches of cops and soldiers as profanity was embedded in their speech.

"He is one vindictive prick, that's for sure," Batista said.

"But could he really've been screwing me over in my career ever since that night? It just seems like something out of a Dickens novel."

"Who?"

"Even you ain't that damn ignorant," Owens laughed.

"Ha, you think you know me, but you don't," Batista said.

In fact, Owens knew Eduardo Batista better than anyone but his immediate family, or maybe a few of his brothers and sisters in the Army where he served for six years. He was a couple years younger than Owens, and both were made from the same mold of poverty, and a passion to rise from it.

His career had also been derailed a bit, but there was no mysterious villain working behind the curtain. He'd shot himself in the foot on a couple occasions, figuratively speaking. He hadn't shot anyone, which had been one of the strikes against him.

One night on patrol in the Frankford neighborhood, three cars were dispatched when shots were reported in an alley. Batista was on foot when a fourteen-year-old kid sprinted past him. Batista saw another officer on one knee aiming his pistol at the kid's back as he was running away. Instead of moving out of the line of fire, Batista ran after the kid, eventually tackling him a half block away. The kid was unarmed, and as far as Batista could see, hadn't thrown down a weapon.

The cop about to shoot the teenager in the back turned out to be a lieutenant on night patrol as part of a feature series the *Philadelphia Inquirer* was doing on high-ranking officers in the department. The lieutenant was on patrol for the first time in years to show how down-to-earth he was. He was furious the young officer had brought down the suspect he was about to shoot in the back.

Nothing too serious, but enough to ruffle a few feathers. Soon after, Batista found himself on what seemed to be a permanent rotation on mids, the dreaded 00:00 to 08:00 shift. After his fourth cycle in a row on the graveyard shift, Batista went to the office of the lieutenant and told him what he thought of his chicken-shit, passive-aggressive maneuvering behind his back.

This resulted in a very un-passive-aggressive write-up for insubordination. Again, not exactly career-shattering, but it set Batista back in the rankings for promotion. Months later while in another unit, when Batista should have put the whole episode behind him, he was playing against the lieutenant's team in an inter-district basketball game.

On four occasions, Batista allowed the lieutenant to drive on him on his way to a completely uncontested lay-up. On the fifth drive,

Batista posted and lowered himself just as the lieutenant was launching himself for what he expected to be another easy two points. Instead, he crashed to the boards and damaged his rotator cuff. It was a bit bigger payoff than Batista had anticipated.

"I'd've been satisfied just to see him fall on his ass," Batista said when he relayed the episode to Owens.

No foul was called on the play, but an avalanche of chicken-shit, passive-aggressive maneuvering behind Batista's back buried his career even further.

"I know you got shit for impulse control. That's why you're in this dogshit unit," Owens said.

Batista had rarely thought about it, and he most certainly had never told anyone what he felt would be the worst duty assignment he could ever imagine—his Fort Wainwright, Alaska—but the Domestic Violence Unit was definitely high on the list.

"So why do you want to give this Gates a pass?"

"I don't, but he played ball when I asked. Now I know who's out to sink me."

"How was Gates?"

"Total shitbag, should be in the Big Book. Makes Arthur Simmons seem like my soul mate in comparison," Owens said. "No tree-shredder big enough for his big, country ass."

"How many women has that guy ambushed in his years on the force?" Batista asked. "He's had five formal complaints, which means at least four or five times that, probably a lot more."

135

Batista was thinking this over, like having something stuck in your teeth you can't ignore.

"I just try to think what I'd do if that tub of guts pulled some shit like that with one of my sisters."

"I've thought a lot about Gates, too. He's definitely more of a shitbag than Arthur Simmons. He even has a nasty mustache like Arthur," Owens said. "Eew!"

Owens did an exaggerated shudder at the thought of disgusting mustaches and men like Gates and Simmons.

"But let's not digress. I need to deal with my James McMillan problem first."

"How do you deal with a billionaire who seems to be pulling the strings in our own department?" Batista asked. "You're the brains of this dynamic duo."

"Lord help us if that's true," Owens said. "I got his vitals: DOB, address in Gladwyne, plate number on three vehicles, and I still remember his little honey's address in Center City, if she's still with him."

"The fact he'd pay that much to blow up that bullshit Hawkins case against you sort of scares me. That shows a level of commitment beyond the criminals we're used to locking up," Batista said.

"Right? Like going to war against a force of nature."

"All because a guy breaks some cartilage in your nose, and you decide to give him fucking brain damage."

"Fuck you, and he's also a woman-beating shitbag, or didn't I tell you that part of the story?" Owens countered.

There was no longer any record of the night Owens and McMillan went toe-to-toe. It had simply vanished, along with the charges against him. Owens was going purely on memory of the years-old case. She thought she remembered the woman's age, but she wasn't sure.

Tanya Jenkins was in obvious pain when Owens took her statement after the ambulance crew hauled away her putative lover and abuser. She refused any medical care and said she'd fallen. She didn't press charges against McMillan. At the time, Owens wasn't too worried about that because he'd assaulted a police officer in front of another officer. She didn't need another witness to sink the guy.

The two cops thought the best way to begin looking into McMillan was through the girlfriend. It was a common name, but there was no trace of a Tanya Jenkins, no name on any lease in the Center City co-op where she lived. In fact, it seemed she'd never officially been a resident of the State of Pennsylvania, at least as far as Owens could ascertain. No driver's license, no state identification, and thus far, no employment history.

McMillan had surely moved on, said goodbye to Tanya Jenkins, kicked her out of the luxury condo, and probably installed another concubine. Owens needed to know who the new resident was in that fifteenth-floor apartment.

Even if the current resident had her name on the lease, which was doubtful, it would be difficult for the police to uncover this information without a warrant, and she absolutely had no basis for that. Owens also knew just setting foot inside the lobby of the exclusive high-rise was as difficult as breaking into a jewelry store. Her legal recourse in the matter was limited.

In a somewhat extra-legal maneuver, Batista was buzzed into the lobby, showed his police ID, gave the kid at the desk a tall tale and a fifty-dollar bill. He walked out with a name.

Rhonda Perry was born in Pottsville, twenty-six years old, two years of community college, and she was currently unemployed. This could mean she was with McMillan, who was paying her bills, or maybe she was a call girl with lousy money-laundering skills who didn't realize she needed some visible source of income. Batista's first thought was to break into her apartment and plant a camera, but the building was like Fort Knox and Owens couldn't afford the sort of bribe to actually enter someone's apartment.

Rhonda Perry was very active on social media. Owens and Batista had so many photos of her they could have mapped her daily aging process. What they didn't have was a photo of her and McMillan together. This wasn't strange since he was a happily married man, as far as the Philadelphia society columns were concerned. He'd never permit an indiscretion like a social media post with the two of them together. Another bit of information they didn't have on Rhonda Perry was her phone number.

All Owens had was the name of a beautiful young woman living at the same address as a former lover of James McMillan. Even if Owens had the time, which she didn't, she couldn't stake out the apartment waiting to see if McMillan visited Rhonda Perry. He could drive into the building's underground parking garage serving four buildings on the block, then take the elevator to the fifteenth floor, completely undetected. It would take an operation on the scale of the hunt for Bin Laden to snag McMillan in his presumed love nest.

Rhonda Perry had been a lackluster student in high school, and community college hadn't revealed her inner intellectual, but she tried to at least appear intelligent. Owens almost admired the woman for that. Rhonda Perry posted about going to gallery openings in

Philadelphia, although they looked to be little more than excuses for her to buy expensive clothes, drink wine, and to be seen with people she felt inferior to both socially and intellectually.

Rhonda Perry was so prolific on social media, detailing her daily schedule so meticulously, Owens knew her every move, but didn't know if she was McMillan's mistress.

With all of the photos of the beautiful young woman formerly of Pottsville, Pennsylvania, there were no pictures of her with any romantic interest. Owens knew call girls rarely had boyfriends—no time or inclination, usually. But Rhonda was a different kind of player, or so Owens guessed. She was a kept woman and had to keep her mouth shut about it.

After less than five days of stalking Rhonda Perry on social media, Owens saw she posted something about an art gallery opening on Saturday evening by an artist who went by one name: Armandiamo.

Arman-fucking-diamo, Owens thought, as she checked the guy out on his own social media platform. If Rhonda and James McMillan were going to be out together in Philadelphia that weekend, the gallery of this ridiculously named painter seemed like a likely spot.

She called the lawyer again to see if Noah Gottlieb thought she was on the right track checking into McMillan.

"While I can't say one way or another if James McMillan is the one working against you, he's certainly powerful enough to pull a lot of strings at PPD. He's also known as a vindictive prick," Gottlieb said.

"How so?" Owens asked.

"He went after a newspaper reporter after the kid wrote a mildly critical article about a few of McMillan's real estate deals. He used the police to harass him: parking tickets, moving violations for the smallest infractions, total bullshit. He ended up leaving Philadelphia, last I heard."

"How does he have the cops in his pocket?" Owens asked.

"It's pretty common knowledge. He gives out sweet property deals to the brass. Basically, they're bribes, but technically they aren't. He'll sell an assistant chief a house or apartment for what he paid for them years ago, after he had them as investment properties, renting them out at the top rates. On paper, the brass are paying what McMillan paid for the properties, so technically it's kosher, but McMillan is forgoing the opportunity cost of what he could have sold the properties for on the open market. Nothing illegal about it, but it's obvious he's getting something out of these deals. We're talking about discounts of hundreds of thousands of dollars on some of these arrangements."

Owens paused on her end of the phone.

"And now I have this guy up my ass…*and* he broke my damn nose."

"He's also very capable of the sort of financial transaction that hired me to go after you without it being traced back to him," Gottlieb said.

Owens told Gottlieb about her run-in with Inspector Gates.

"Detective Owens, do all of your encounters with powerful men end up with them getting pulverized?"

"I'm lucky that pig didn't rape me, because he definitely had that on his filthy little mind. If O'Neill hadn't given me the heads up on the asshole, I would've walked into some shit."

"I can't believe he still has a job. Someone needs to stop him before he ruins another woman's life, another cop's life," Gottlieb said.

"I've been thinking the same thing. Unfortunately, I have a James McMillan problem I need to take care of somehow," Owens said. "Mr. Gottlieb…"

"Please call me Noah, Detective Owens."

"Call me Beth," Owens said. "Noah, any advice you may have on how I should deal with McMillan, please feel free…you know, to pass it along."

"I'm way ahead of you. Thinking on it, I promise."

"Thanks, Noah."

"It's been a pleasure, Beth."

Then before he hung up.

"Beth, be careful with this guy. I know just enough about him to know he's completely ruthless."

It felt good to have one of the city's top defense attorneys on her side, but Owens wasn't sure how he could help her, and even less sure about her next play.

Her next move, her only move, was to scope out the gallery opening, but McMillan might recognize Owens, and Batista wasn't exactly the kind of guy who could navigate an art gallery crowd, although he graciously offered up his weekend evening to surveil the couple. Owens would keep her distance and see what she could learn about her secret malefactor.

It was easy for Owens to recognize Rhonda Perry when she arrived in a taxi. She was wearing the dress she'd posted on her social media page earlier in the day.

Owens sat in her unmarked car across the street from the gallery, which thankfully didn't have an underground parking garage, forcing guests to enter through the front door at street level. True to his unchivalric nature, James McMillan arrived over an hour later. Owens was exhilarated to see McMillan again. His imperious stature made him easy to recognize in the crowd, and even from across the street, she could see he was impeccably dressed.

Owens was now convinced the two were some sort of couple.

She wished she could have been inside, maybe get a photo of the two hanging on each other, but that wasn't going to happen. Owens called it a night.

"Nice work," Batista said later that evening.

"I guess, but I don't see what I can do with this except keep stalking the idiot on her social media platforms. I could die of boredom before I get anything I can use on McMillan," Owens said.

Before Owens succumbed to the mind-numbingly banal, multiple daily posts of the small-town girl in the big city, Rhonda Perry simply vanished.

# CHAPTER 12 – GHOST

The latest internet term for disappearing without a trace was "ghosting." In most circumstances, the term referred to a partner cutting off all contact with a former lover without explanation, often nothing more sinister than some passive-aggressive coward lacking the guts to confront an ex face-to-face. Rhonda Perry's version of ghosting was far darker.

The following morning, Owens discovered the young woman's social media platforms had all been deleted. Everything. It was like a wiretap going dead for no reason. Owens kicked herself for not being tech-savvy enough to have copied the young woman's internet postings, at least some of them. Why would she delete her entire internet presence without a warning just as her career as an influencer was on the rise?

Owens's first thought was McMillan had ordered his kept woman to take down her internet postings—the last thing the real estate developer wanted was his secret lover creating a fan base online. Of course, McMillan was behind it, but it went beyond deleting a few social media platforms. Even her email accounts were gone, leaving no online presence at all of the young woman. There was no missing person report on Rhonda Perry and no evidence a crime had been committed against her, meaning thus far, it wasn't a police matter. There could be a thousand reasons why Rhonda Perry had suddenly become incommunicado, but Owens sensed there was something more disturbing going on than a young woman deciding to drop out.

"Our girl seems to have gone underground," Owens said on the phone with Batista.

She explained Rhonda's abrupt and total withdrawal from the internet.

"I'll see if I can get into her building again," Batista said.

He was only a few blocks from the Center City high-rise apartment complex and was able to walk past the front desk while the concierge was busy signing for packages. He was just planning to knock on Rhonda's door but saw it was open with a cart of cleaning products blocking the entrance.

"Anyone home?" Batista called out, then again but louder.

He saw two women inside.

"¿Necesita algo, señor?" one of them asked.

He had no right to enter the apartment, but he showed the women his badge and pushed past the cleaning cart without any objection from them. He thought it better not to speak to them in Spanish which would make him easier to identify if anyone cared to investigate his illegal entry. Instead, he spoke to the women in English.

"I'm here for a follow-up interview with a potential witness by the name of Rhonda Perry. Does she happen to be home at this time?"

The two cleaning women didn't seem to know much English and weren't about to challenge a police officer, as Batista knew only too well of anyone with a questionable visa status or an illegal.

"If Rhonda Perry lived there, she's long gone. Not a trace of anything belonging to her," Batista said to Owens later in their PPD office.

"They let you inside?"

"I didn't ask. The door was open, sort of."

"So, nothing suggesting violence, I take it," Owens said. "Who knows, though, when you have two people cleaning up what could've been a crime scene."

"That's how the rich do it: fucking hire maids to clean up after their major felonies," Batista said.

"Maybe the kid will turn up."

"Her entire life seems to have been erased, and we saw her less than twelve hours ago," Batista said. "We don't even know for certain if she and McMillan were a thing."

"Other than his last girlfriend lived in the same place," Owens reminded him.

"Yeah, but nothing we can prove. Shit, we can't even prove he owns the place."

Owens contacted three of Rhonda's online "friends" via email. They all expressed concern about her disappearance, but none of them knew anything about Rhonda and had never met her in person. Something about this state of the online world reminded Owens of the question of whether a tree falling in the forest makes a sound if there's no one to hear it.

The detective tried to contact Rhonda's mother in Pottsville, this time in her full capacity as a police officer. According to Pottsville police, Rebecca Perry hadn't lived in the city for the last three years. No known address and the local police had zero interest in the woman or her daughter. They were a small department and had real problems to worry about that didn't involve ghosts who'd committed no crimes and weren't known to be victims.

145

Fair enough, Owens thought, but if Rhonda Perry was missing, it was also very possible there was a crime involved. She desperately wanted to be the cop tasked with interviewing James McMillan on the disappearance of the woman he was keeping in a million-dollar high-rise apartment in Center City, not that she could prove he owned the residence. All she could testify to in a court of law was she saw they'd gone to the same gallery opening. She couldn't even prove Rhonda had lived in the same apartment where Owens had first encountered James McMillan. In technical police and legal vernacular, she had fuck all.

Owens tried to find likely candidates who may have actually known Rhonda in the flesh and weren't simply people who connected with her on the web. From these, she selected three women in Rhonda's graduating high school class in Pottsville. She messaged all three with a semi-official police request for information on their former classmate.

One woman replied almost immediately saying she lived in Texas and hadn't seen Rhonda since high school. Another classmate didn't respond, and a third admitted she and Rhonda weren't close friends, but she'd be glad to help the police any way she could, leaving a phone number. Before calling, Owens tried to vet the woman the best she could with the information she had at her disposal. From her profile on three different social media sites, Amanda Torrance was probably voted most likely to segue from high school into spinsterhood. Most of her photos included at least one of her many cats.

Owens knew the type all too well from police work, the sort of person who never shuts up and rarely has anything worthwhile to add to an investigation. At this point in her discreet inquiry, she had nothing to lose.

Owens didn't mind at all when her instincts proved wrong.

Amanda Torrance had never left the small town of Pottsville, Pennsylvania, and she seemed to be the center of the universe for gossip on anyone and everyone who had ever lived there. For someone who claimed she wasn't friends with the missing woman, Amanda seemed to know everything about her.

According to Amanda, Rhonda was by far the best-looking girl in their graduating class, but she was of the white-trash, wrong-side-of-the-tracks variety of hot. She got into trouble, but nothing serious. No father and a strung-out mother, from what Amanda had heard, and she'd heard everything. She said Rhonda left Pottsville a few years ago to take a restaurant job in Philadelphia with the goal of becoming a model or a movie star.

Owens was surprised Amanda even could recall the name of the restaurant in the big city. However, as much detail as Amanda was able to give on her classmate, she didn't know the name of a single friend Rhonda may have had in Philadelphia.

"She seemed like sort of a loner, to be honest. She had men in her life, but no friends. Weird, huh?"

Not too weird, Owens thought. She knew a lot of women who fit that description, women who viewed other women as a threat and who saw men as cash machines. A woman without friends and family, a woman without a job or other responsibilities would be someone who wouldn't be missed. She could simply disappear.

In fact, Rhonda Perry had been so anonymous it was proving extremely difficult to prove she'd gone missing since it was impossible to prove she even existed in Philadelphia. Her social media followers vanished along with her internet history.

Owens had called Center City Tower, where Rhonda had been living in the fifteenth-floor condo, but the desk attendant said he wasn't at liberty to give out the names of residents. Rich people do love their gatekeepers, Owens thought. She also thought even for double Batista's tip, the desk guy wouldn't admit Rhonda lived there. He now talked as if he'd been coached. Something was definitely rotten. She imagined ownership of the condo was probably as anonymously layered as the fee paid out to Gottlieb in the Hawkins case.

She'd have loved to simply brace James McMillan on the matter, see how he handled himself in an interrogation room. Of course, that would never happen in a billion years, not for a billionaire. If she had a chance to talk to him at all, he'd be sitting on his lawyer's lap refusing to speak. Getting him on the phone was another thought, but she wouldn't know where to begin. People like McMillan probably had at least three people between them and anyone calling in an official capacity. The rich certainly knew the law. They should; they wrote most of them to cater to their needs.

How do you proceed with a case involving a woman who you can't prove is missing, and when absolutely no one seemed to care? Owens believed Rhonda was living in a luxury apartment provided by McMillan, but both her residence there and his ownership seemed, if not impossible, then extremely problematic to prove.

And fuck trying to establish motive, Owens thought.

But this wasn't some "gut" feeling on Owens's part. She had enough circumstantial evidence in her investigation to bear out her suspicions. She was also relying on her theory that a man who was capable of hitting a woman or a child was capable of murder. Had James McMillan not been hobbling her career at PPD, she thought she'd be a homicide detective by now. The irony he was now a suspect in her first murder investigation, although unofficial and off-the-books, wasn't lost on the young detective.

***

After another visit to the home of a battered woman, in another seedy district of Philadelphia, in the corner of yet another dive bar, Owens and Batista were having another beer together. Owens brought him up to speed on everything she had so far: diddly squat.

"So, this guy just disappears this girl and we can't even ask him about it?"

"That's about it," Owens answered.

"So, maybe we work backward?"

"How so?" asked Owens.

"We start with the other girlfriend, the one you met when McMillan broke your nose."

"I tried, but I got nothing on her but a name. Common as hell, no social security number, nothing. No DOB. No idea where she is now or where she's from."

"None of her info was on the arrest report back then?" Batista asked.

"That's the fucked-up thing about it. There was no arrest report, there was no arrest. Now, no report exists at all on the call. Expunged is the word rich folks use for it. I'm going on pure memory as far as her name. My partner left the department, kicked out for failing a piss test. Total stoner with the memory of a goldfish. Even if I could find him, he wouldn't remember anything."

149

She told Batista about her chat with the spinster from Pottsville.

"Maybe we ask in that restaurant where Rhonda worked," Batista offered. "We got nothing else."

They had nothing else. They had one card to play.

Owens showed up at the nation-wide franchise joint the next afternoon, not really knowing how she was going to proceed. All she thought she knew, according to what Amanda Torrance had told her, was this was the first job her classmate had in Philly.

She talked to a manager and told him she was working a missing person's investigation and was looking for employment records for Rhonda from approximately four years ago. On a whim, she asked if a Tanya Jenkins had ever worked there, giving the name of the girlfriend of James McMillan when he'd broken her nose.

Her whim, her gut feeling, paid off this time. Both women had worked at the restaurant, overlapping a few months. Owens now had a firm identification of two of McMillan's former mistresses. What brought them both to this restaurant? Did they know each other? Owens didn't believe in coincidences, so how could two of the billionaire's concubines have worked in the same place?

From the restaurant, Owens worked backward trying to locate Tanya Jenkins, much easier now that she had a social security number. As far as work and tax history, she found little on Tanya. Owens was able to uncover that she was four years older than Rhonda.

Tanya Jenkins was also missing, unofficially.

Women he was intimate with were disappearing.

Once again, proving Tanya Jenkins no longer existed seemed impossible.

Owens couldn't even prove she was the woman in the apartment the night she and her partner were called to the Center City Tower since the report on the matter had been removed from the record, a highly unusual move and something Owens had never come across before in her years with PPD. James McMillan had the power to make the incident disappear, except in the memory of the woman whose nose he'd broken. Owens wondered how many people had any memory of Tanya Jenkins.

She did a cursory search using Tanya's name and social security number. If this had been a true investigation instead of a detective working unofficially on a hunch, Owens would have had more resources to help in tracking down the girl. She was able to find a birthdate and a place of birth: Brazil, Indiana. After that, the trail went cold until Tanya surfaced twenty-five years later at the Philadelphia restaurant.

There were a lot of logical explanations for a lack of a documented work history. Tanya could have worked off-the-books in a number of capacities from babysitter to more sinister pursuits like drug dealing or prostitution. Owens could remember little about the woman from when she and her partner went to the high-rise in response to a noise complaint and a possible domestic violence case. Her partner interviewed Tanya after McMillan was hauled off in an ambulance and Owens talked with a supervisor while stanching the bleeding in her newly flattened nose, compliments of McMillan. All her partner had to say about Tanya was she was "hot as hell."

No one at the restaurant had worked there for more than two years, including the manager, so none of the current employees knew Tanya Jenkins or Rhonda Perry. While the manager was searching his computer archives for the records on both women, Owens took the opportunity to stand behind him and clandestinely take photos of the

151

screens showing lists of other employees during those years. Owens had mixed luck in tracking down any people from her highly illegal screenshot. Of the five she could contact who worked at the restaurant sometime around the years of Jenkins and Perry, no one could remember either of them.

"You've only contacted five people?" Batista asked.

"Boy, I have another job, in case you forgot. Going after McMillan is like a damn hobby at this point," Owens shot back. "Just matching the names of the former employees to existing phone numbers was a damn miracle of detective work."

"Right? Imagine back in the day when you could find names in a phone book. My grandparents got the same phone number since like 1960."

"Two of the guys I talked to were line cooks back then. Doubtful two hot women would have given them the time of day. I'll keep working the angle."

"I can't believe we can't just go to McMillan's house and question him like any other citizen," Batista said.

"He'd never talk to us. Hell, I'd never talk to us."

"Hell, no," Batista agreed.

You have the right to remain silent as stated in the Fifth Amendment to the United States Constitution, something lawyers, judges, and cops teach their children along with the ABCs.

"No person shall be compelled in any criminal case to be a witness against himself," Owens recited from memory. "Words to live by."

"The good news for cops is most folks are too stupid to get this and they spill their guts in the interrogation room. It's not even like the old days when cops would beat confessions out of people, stupid fucks just give it up."

Instead of the rubber hoses and blackjacks the police once employed to coax admissions of guilt from suspects, they used the threat of taking cases to trial and handing out the maximum in sentencing guidelines. Most suspects took the carrot, admitted their crimes, and accepted a plea arrangement. Sometimes they admitted to crimes they didn't commit to avoid long stretches in prison.

"No way McMillan would ever talk to the police on this. Not a word, not even 'I don't know what you're talking about.' The more I think about this, the more convinced I am he murdered both of these women. We can't even prove he knew either one of them, not yet at least," Owens said.

"We need to get the old band back together and Arthur Simmons this motherfucker," Batista said, making a questionable verb coinage Owens didn't address.

"Except making this prick disappear would cause the shitstorm of all shitstorms."

"We'd be lucky to get into the same area code as James McMillan. Still, how cool would it be to make him go away?"

"It's not like I haven't thought about it...a lot," Owens said.

After Arthur Simmons had been "Arthur Simmonsed," Owens rode her bike past his last known address. Less than two weeks after his exit from this world, she saw a pile of trash in the street in front of his apartment building. Arthur's landlord didn't waste any time making

153

his apartment available. Owens took a peek at the remains of his life, at least the stuff that wasn't sold or carried off by the neighborhood scavengers.

Among boxes of old clothes and knickknacks, there was a cardboard box with framed watercolors. The paintings were puerile and clumsy attempts at landscapes. In the corner of one mountain scene, Owens saw the signature of Arthur Simmons. Even in this shitty area of Philadelphia, no one thought the paintings were worth hauling away, even for free. It was a fitting tribute to the legacy of a wicked man.

Washington Gates had a wife and two children. Owens could only imagine his wife probably knew her husband was a world-class shitbag. Her main concern would be his steady government paychecks supporting the family. Maybe he was a decent father, but it was hard for Owens to see how such a total creep like Gates could be the sort of decent human being that makes an effective parent.

James McMillan had two kids, a son who was now twenty-two, and a daughter three years younger. From what Owens found in the press, both kids were typical rich kid fuck-ups, into drugs and flunking out of private schools and public universities right and left. Their father had probably been too busy with work and having affairs with waitresses half his age to steer his kids down the right path, not that he'd know where that was.

Would it surprise his children to know he was a murderer? Perhaps a serial killer?

Owens knew she was being somewhat hypocritical, but she never considered herself to be a murderer. She was a killer. She thought about it quite often, and not once did she feel she'd murdered those seven insurgents on the highway in Baghdad. They gave her a medal for it. She deserved another medal for preventing Arthur Simmons from harming another woman or child.

James McMillan was a whole other level of malevolent. As more about the man was uncovered in her digging, Owens had little doubt she could walk up to him in public and shoot him in the face. Not much of a plan, but at this point nothing else occurred to her. There was still no justification for a police investigation into the young woman from Pottsville, Pennsylvania, and even less for an inquiry into the whereabouts of Tanya Jenkins. Owens was chasing ghosts.

# CHAPTER 13 – WAR

"Mr. Carmichael, my name is Elizabeth Owens. I'm a detective with the Philadelphia Police Department. I'd like to talk to you about James McMillan if you have a moment."

Thanks to Noah Gottlieb, Owens got the name of the reporter formerly with the *Philadelphia Inquirer* whose career was allegedly derailed by the billionaire after Joseph Carmichael had written articles critical of McMillan. He was now working in Seattle as a tech writer.

"McMillan? Why, is he still trying to destroy me? I thought he already won that battle?" Carmichael said.

"In fact, I have reason to believe he's out to destroy me these days," Owens said.

She explained her history with McMillan to the former reporter, as well as her current suspicions about the real estate mogul, careful to warn Carmichael these were nothing more than her own entirely unsubstantiated observations. Carmichael made it clear he despised the man and there was no need for the detective to tiptoe around her suspicions.

"No need for you to mince your words with me," he said.

The reporter knew nothing of McMillan's extracurricular sexual activity but didn't seem at all surprised two of his secret mistresses may have vanished, especially after hearing about how McMillan had punched Owens in the face. He agreed with Owens's statement that a man who could punch a woman could also commit murder.

"That's very true, Detective," he said. "It's a sign of a true sociopath."

He had other reasons not to be surprised about the missing women.

While digging into his past in the course of his investigation into McMillan's real estate dealings, he interviewed people who knew the man from his days at one of Philadelphia's most exclusive high schools. From three separate classmates at the academy, Carmichael heard a rumor of a young immigrant woman disappearing while working in the McMillan household in their rambling Gladwyne estate.

When he was sixteen, McMillan had bragged to his classmates he was having a sexual relationship with a young housekeeper. The three classmates had been to the estate and seen the woman who lived in the servants' quarters along with two other full-time domestics. All three said when in his presence, the young girl seemed terrified of the young McMillan.

And then she disappeared, or quit, or moved away. When they asked their classmate about the beautiful young housekeeper, James said she was fired for stealing.

"What do you expect of a Romanian gypsy?" McMillan reportedly said to one of them.

Three years later, during a drunken and drug-fueled reunion, James confessed to one of the classmates he "killed the bitch." The other two couldn't corroborate this part of the story, but they said it wouldn't have surprised them about McMillan. Carmichael could find nothing about a Romanian housekeeper working at the estate. His investigation simply died in its tracks, almost as dead as Owens's current probe into the two women.

He promised Owens he'd enlist the aid of friends still working at the Philadelphia newspaper to look into the story of the two women presumed to be missing.

"Ever since I started reporting about the man, I always thought he was nothing less than a son of a bitch," Carmichael said before they ended the call. "From what you've told me, he's obviously much worse."

If no one else was going to concern themselves with the disappearance of Rhonda Perry, Owens would take on the task. She made flyers with a recent photo of Rhonda with the message:

*Missing. Have you seen Rhonda Perry? She hasn't been seen since April 20. All information is welcome and confidential.*

Owens left the phone number of a burner phone she found during an arrest years ago and had kept active, along with an email address. She posted the flyers near the Center City Tower and near the restaurant where Rhonda and Tanya had worked, thinking someone must remember the beautiful woman from her days as a waitress.

She paid a young boy to post one hundred of the flyers around an office building in the downtown housing the offices of one of McMillan's major real estate enterprises. She thought seeing these flyers should at the very least let McMillan know Rhonda Perry had someone looking for her. Two days later, when Owens rode her bike around the McMillan office building, she couldn't find a single one of her flyers.

"The prick paid someone to go around and take down our damn flyers," Owens said.

"Then we put up a hundred more, and this time we make it harder to take them down," Batista said.

This time, they paid a kid to paste up every flyer, instead of just using masking tape. If McMillan wanted them taken down, it was going to cost someone a lot of work. Owens managed to clandestinely post several of the flyers inside the McMillan building.

"I pasted flyers in two of the elevators. McMillan may not even go in that building, for all we know. But you have to think someone who works there had seen McMillan and Rhonda together at some point," Owens said to Dr. O'Neill. "I worded these a bit differently."

She gave one of the flyers to her professor.

*Missing. Have you seen Rhonda Perry? Girlfriend of James McMillan. She hasn't been seen since April 20. All information is welcome and confidential.*

"Even a photo of McMillan. I love how you're turning up the heat," Dr. O'Neill said. "But you aren't you afraid of legal ramifications from McMillan?"

"Me? I didn't write these. I have nothing to do with this. Nope, not afraid of legal ramifications in the least. I doubt McMillan would even go there."

Her professor and faculty advisor had become somewhat obsessed with the intrigues of her policewoman student.

"I could almost talk myself into thinking McMillan had just paid these girls to go away, but after hearing the story of his childhood housekeeper—as unsubstantiated as it is—I can't help but lean toward a more sinister version of their disappearance," O'Neill said.

Owens didn't comment.

"How's the job?"

O'Neill knew changing the subject to Owens's police work was no way to lighten the mood of their coffee break conversation.

"The job is killing me. I need out of the unit. We had another woman beaten almost to death by yet another name from the Big Book of Shitbags."

"Wanda Evans. I read about it yesterday," O'Neill said as she pulled out a sheet of paper from her leather portfolio. "According to your latest records, she'd made twenty-four calls for assistance."

"I want to work homicide. At least there you don't have the names of the perps until you catch them."

"No arrest yet in the Evans case?"

"No. That's even more insulting to me as a cop. First, we have the guy's name written down in a book saying he's likely to do something awful. Then, when he does, we can't find him. I could have found him easily enough two days ago before he almost murdered his ex-wife."

"Maybe you should have?" O'Neill said.

"Maybe I should have what?"

Of course, Owens knew what O'Neill was getting at, but she played dumb, wanting her professor to come out and say it.

O'Neill hesitated, as if preparing to give a long statement.

"Maybe you, or someone, should take the worst of these predators off the streets before they destroy the lives of the people around them."

Owens laughed at this.

"Is that something a social scientist can recommend?"

"Fuck social science, and fuck the law," O'Neill blurted out. "After your run-in with that Gates monster…I don't know. I'd never witnessed anything so terrifying in all of my years in social work. I've read case after case, literally thousands, but to actually witness it firsthand? I still tremble with fury just thinking about it."

"That? With Gates? I've experienced a lot fucking worse, so don't feel bad for me."

"I was so terrified for your safety. Then when I came into the office and saw him splayed out on the floor with you in total control…damn, you're my hero, Beth."

O'Neill was crying just a bit.

Owens wondered if her academic mentor's opinion of her would be improved or destroyed if she knew about the Arthur Simmons affair. Then Owens thought perhaps "affair" wasn't the precise word for it. Like the military juntas in Latin America who invented the term, she had "disappeared" him. Instead of flying out over the Atlantic Ocean in a helicopter and throwing out trade unionists and leftist organizers as they'd done in Argentina, in a perfect world it should be the Washington Gates, James McMillans, and Arthur Simmons of the world being launched into a dark sea in the middle of the night.

Owens wanted to talk to O'Neill to find out everything she could about her adversary. Not that a humble university professor moved in the same world as a billionaire real estate mogul, but Dr. O'Neill was a well-respected member of the Philadelphia community, a city where she'd lived her entire life.

"He fancies himself a philanthropist," O'Neill said. "The thing is, for people of his economic status, philanthropy is pretty far from charity. For James McMillan, it's business. I'm not a tax attorney, but

161

I'd wager the man has made money on every one of his putative donations to the Philadelphia Art Museum. It's mostly about ego with people of his ilk. As much as he'd like to think otherwise, all he's ever done in his life is make money, or make more money, because he was born rich. Having his name on a foundation, or a wing of a museum is a way for him to wash away his sins."

"From what I think I know about him, he definitely has a heavy bill of penance to cover," Owens said. "He should be doubling down on the charitable donations."

"He's probably never given a cent without getting two back in return," O'Neill said.

This brought to mind something her new lawyer friend had relayed to Owens.

"Gottlieb told me even his bribes to police officials are money-makers for him, something about declaring losses on the properties he sells to them way under market value for tax purposes."

"That's the way the rich do it. They have the money to buy off the police and the judicial system, and if that isn't enough, they just pay politicians to change the laws in their favor. We make a big show about putting cartel leaders in jail, but they allow opioid pharmaceuticals to bury us in pill versions of heroin."

"The thing about McMillan that bothers me almost as much as the fact that he may have murdered three women, is no one even knows about it. I'm a cop and I can't even find a name of the young girl who worked at his house when he was in high school. It's like I'm swatting at an armored vehicle with a broomstick," Owens said, always more comfortable putting metaphors and analogies into military parlance.

"It's because it makes you feel utterly powerless. Join the club, Beth. One of the things I most admire about you is you've shaped yourself into a person who has to take less shit than any woman I know. I've watched the video of you putting Gates on his fat ass about a million times, and I smile every time. I wish I could show it to every woman on the planet."

"If I hear he's molested another woman, the whole planet will see that damn video. I wasn't kidding about that; I just hope he knows it."

"I think you got your point across. That's what I love about the video: you changed him from hunter into your little bitch just like that," and O'Neill snapped her fingers.

Owens got a good laugh at this.

"Now Madeline, I'm paying you to turn me into an educated East Coast elite, but it seems like I'm turning you into a girl from the hood."

"I wish. Knowing what you knew before you went in to see Gates…I never would've had the nerve to do that."

"You had my back. I was OK."

"Had your back, my ass. The only thing I had was a fear of shitting myself."

Owens laughed again.

"But if I'm such a superhero, why can't I even question McMillan about three possible homicides?"

"It just proves how much extreme wealth poisons democracy. If McMillan were simply a millionaire, he couldn't keep himself so

163

insulated. As you told me about him, it's not just that he can buy a luxury downtown high-rise for his fuck buddies, it's you can't even prove he owns it. That's a level of wealth that shouldn't even exist."

"The damn police can't even talk to this guy, yet he can rattle my cage without me knowing about it. Or I should say he has his flunkies at PPD do it for him. That guy probably hasn't ever pumped his own gas in his life," Owens said.

"Pump his own gas? He's probably never bothered to flush a fucking toilet in his over-privileged life."

"Ha, girl, you sound more like cops and Army every time we get together. I must be a bad influence."

Maybe Dr. O'Neill was starting to think more like a cop. She had an idea of how to get around the walls surrounding James McMillan.

"You need to talk to his wife, or at least one of them."

"He's been married more than once?" Owens asked.

"Twice, but in his usual fashion, he basically made the first marriage disappear, or at least he paid her off to go away. He was only married for a couple of years. The typical story of rebellious youth marrying someone beneath him, in this case a girl he met in Italy while he was flunking out of his first university."

"I've never heard this story. Definitely not on his website," Owens said.

James McMillan actually had a website outlining his many accomplishments but mentioning only his current wife and two children.

"No kids with the Italian girl. She moved back to Rome after their divorce, more of an annulment really."

"You think I should try to talk to her?"

"I doubt she has much to say, at least nothing interesting. I'm talking about his current wife."

"You think she'd talk to a cop? She comes from money, too, from what I've read. Rich folks hire cops, they don't talk to us."

"I just imagine she hates the man. How could she not hate him? I think under the right circumstances, she could be a good source of information, maybe give you a new angle on him," O'Neill said.

This had occurred to Owens, too, but she soon discovered the wife had built a formidable wall around her life. She traveled constantly, spending most of the year at the couple's estate in Palm Beach, Florida. Just tracking down the woman's phone number ranked up there with the hunt for a top ten most-wanted fugitive, except some of those investigations had a happy ending, like an arrest. Owens also knew McMillan's wife wouldn't dream of acting against him unless she knew there was a one hundred percent chance of putting him away.

Owens thought a one hundred percent chance of locking up James McMillan would be somewhere around zero. What little Owens knew about the rich was they weren't often arrested, rarely went to court, and never lost in open court. They paid people like Noah Gottlieb to ensure favorable outcomes in the worst-case scenario they ever went to trial for sins committed, or allegedly committed.

Generally, they were never arrested, never booked, never printed, and never locked up for their crimes. "White privilege" had recently come into the vernacular to describe the societal benefits white people had over non-Whites, but rich privilege had been around since one man had two of something while the other guy had one. James McMillan had known nothing else in his life. Empathy for the less fortunate wasn't part of his inculcation into society. He learned others were lesser beings who didn't deserve the advantages he had in life, not that he ever thought of them as advantages. They were his birthright, his inheritance.

On the complete opposite end of this spectrum was Elizabeth Owens, born in a different hospital than McMillan, but only twenty minutes away. Was it possible for empathy to work uphill? Could Elizabeth Owens imagine the problems of the young James? Was his father abusive? Did his parents ask him about his day when he returned from his elite private schools? Perhaps the real estate scion had been as abandoned in his childhood as she was growing up on the streets of South Philly.

From what she'd learned about her nemesis, he couldn't be bothered to stop and think for even a split-second about how his actions impacted the lives of people around him. McMillan thought so little of them he may have killed three people, three women he had intimate relations with. For Owens, this made his heinous crimes even worse. Killing a stranger or a rival was unthinkable but murdering someone you had sex with, a lover, was positively diabolical. Someone needed to stop him.

That "someone" wasn't going to be the PPD which appeared to be just one more of the man's possessions. McMillan was like an animal who had no natural predators. Owens hardly felt she was any match for a man with his money, connections, and the power that came with them. At this point, she only had one thing going for her. James McMillan wasn't aware Elizabeth Owens had been investigating him.

She'd been cruising behind him in his blind spot waiting for him to reveal a weakness in his defenses, a vulnerability.

The "Missing Woman" notices she'd posted weren't a total failure. She received calls from a half dozen people, none of them knew Rhonda Perry beyond commercial transactions. Owens interviewed a girl who worked at a coffee shop near the Center City Tower. She said Rhonda came in at least three mornings a week. She said Rhonda was a big tipper but not the talkative sort, at least not with her. The barista said that on two separate occasions, a couple of months apart, she noticed Rhonda had bruises on her face she couldn't quite cover up completely with heavy make-up. She said she never saw her with anyone.

A bartender who worked at a chic restaurant about equidistant from the Center City apartment and McMillan's real estate headquarters said he'd seen her at the bar quite a few times. He said she was always with someone, an older gentleman, perhaps different men but it could have been the same guy each time. He was able to identify James McMillan from a group of photos, but he wasn't willing to swear to it.

The other people Owens spoke to were even less helpful, in spite of the fact they all seemed very concerned about the woman. None of them even knew her name. No one had filed a missing person's report, and it was unlikely anyone would at this point, several weeks now since Owens noticed Rhonda wasn't engaging on social media. There was not a trace of Rhonda Perry on the internet.

It would have been easy enough for James McMillan to place a program on Rhonda's computer to trace her every last keystroke, fish out her various accounts and social media sites, then find the passwords necessary to delete everything. Owens was competent

167

when it came to computers, but she needed help to delve into Rhonda's internet history.

She decided to go outside of the department and asked her old U.S. Army friend for help in the matter. Chuck had been an Army medic she met in Iraq and now worked in Philadelphia at a burgeoning engineering firm he helped to create. His nickname was "Google" back in Iraq because during the frequent interruptions in internet connections in the Green Zone Army ghetto, people would ask Chuck stuff they'd normally look for on the internet search engine. A brilliant, polymathic workaholic was the only way Owens could describe him.

Less than twenty-four hours after Owens explained her dilemma to Chuck, and giving him every shred of information she had on Rhonda Perry, her phone rang at one in the morning.

"Owens?"

"Who the fuck you think it would be? It's my number," Owens said, instantly recognizing the voice and not surprised in the least at the strange hour, but curious. "It's 01:35."

"Sorry, I'm in L.A. on a job site. Sending you everything I have so far on your girl."

"Talk to me about it, but like you're talking to someone who isn't an engineer."

"When she went off the grid, she really went off the grid. From what you told me about her, she doesn't seem to have the skill set to do this good of an erase."

"Meaning what?" Owens asked.

"She probably had help, someone who's good at this. There will still be traces of her out there, but only the people she messaged privately will have access to it. She didn't seem to have many real friends, just the creepy internet type of non-friend."

What Chuck had was a photo of Rhonda with James McMillan at what looked to be an art gallery gala. The photo showed them standing next to each other in front of a large, blank canvas. Chuck noted he found the photo attached to a message Rhonda had sent to a blog about the Philadelphia art scene. When he went back to the site an hour later, the photo and comment had been erased.

Whoever was ghosting Rhonda was still working ardently to finish the job, taking the trouble to contact other users, and asking them to remove her comments.

"This McMillan really wants every trace of that woman deleted," Chuck said. "Just the little I've found on the guy, he's a dangerous man to have as an enemy, but since you're already on his shit-list, offense is the best play."

"What I'm thinking," Owens said.

"It's like a chess game and you had to begin without a queen and a bishop," Chuck said. "That's how rich people play the game."

"If he's going to play that way, maybe I need to change the rules."

"Exactly."

Owens already had a few thoughts on how she'd stack the game in her favor.

"Thanks, Chuck. I owe you…again."

"We're cool, Owens. Anything else you need from me, call any time. I sleep, but it's not something I hold very dearly."

Owens laughed at this because back in their days as soldiers, Chuck used to rant about how useless sleep was in human evolution, and how we needed to find a way around it. Owens wasn't a big fan of sleep, and these days she felt like she needed to keep one eye open when she did.

Once again, there wasn't a bit of proof of it, but since her violent first meeting with James McMillan, he was working assiduously to bushwhack her career. This had proved not entirely successful and only hobbled Owens when it came to being assigned to elite units. Even the highly-connected real estate scion didn't have the suction to negate her departmental test scores and excellent performance reports. She had also entered the department as a highly-decorated military veteran with years of active-duty experience in the military police.

McMillan was acting completely out of spite and a desire for vengeance. If he were to learn Owens was gunning for him, she thought it highly probable her nemesis would up the ante in his attacks, possibly escalating to violence.

# PART 2

*«Le secret des grandes fortunes sans cause apparente est un crime oublié, parce qu'il a été proprement fait.»*

*"The secret of great fortunes without apparent cause is a forgotten crime, because it was properly done."*

*Le Père Goriot, serialized in "Revue de Paris" in 1834 by Honoré de Balzac.*

Commonly translated as, "every great fortune was born from a crime."

# CHAPTER 14 – THE MCMILLANS

James Hawthorne McMillan was born in Philadelphia in 1958, the only child of Harold McMillan and Dorothy Landen McMillan. He was the third generation of his family born in the United States. The city of Philadelphia dated back to well before the American Revolution, and among some elite families in the city, third generation American was synonymous with "fresh off the boat," or carpetbagger, or some other pejorative.

One rule of society is that no matter how high you rise, there will be someone who wants to look down on you, making the snobbery of the local gentry class one of the primary motivations in the business career of James McMillan. He decided that if he couldn't be from one of the oldest families in the city, his would be the richest.

There is a point where money trumps pedigree, even in the stuffiest parlors of Boston, New York, and including London.

His great-grandfather was the first McMillan to step on the shores of America, at least to take up a permanent residence. John McMillan was eighteen years old, broke, and entirely alone when he arrived at Ellis Island in 1898. The first decade in his newly-adopted country was a record that seems to have been expunged. He never talked about these years with the family he formed beginning with his marriage to a young Irish immigrant. There are no records of his early years, no witnesses came forward, he was never arrested, or at least never charged. Even the rumors of his time in the streets of the city seemed to evaporate with every step up the ladder in his fabled success story, but there were a few who remembered John's violent past.

The immigrant McMillan had learned a few important things in life—the first being the importance of owning property which could always earn money. Being from a poor Scottish family, he'd seen the power landlords had over the property-less peasants. He was drawn to America by the promise of its endless expanses where any man could own land. He'd originally planned to move to the western states, but never made it past the banks of the Delaware River.

His plan was to work in Philadelphia long enough to stake his dream of journeying westward and becoming a landowner. Even with the new century breaking on the horizon, the streets of Philadelphia were still rife with the wild stories of men who'd made their fortunes in the vast territories in the Far West. California was the end of the continent and the dream of every penniless immigrant on the streets of the cities on the east coast. John's movement westward was cut short by the skill he showed in his first violent act in America.

He was sweeping out several shops along a busy street near the docks, the only job he could find, and he was glad to have it. One of the men who gave him a few pennies to clean up around his barber shop a couple hours a day also ran an illegal lottery operation. He tried to entice the young Scot immigrant to take numbers instead of his pay, but John was observant enough to see the only person coming out ahead in the numbers racket was the corpulent barber. He chose the few coins he was offered and passed on the chance for greater riches in this stacked game of chance.

The shop catered to the sailors and stevedores from the docks who happened to be about the roughest men in the city. Many were degenerate drunks and gamblers and couldn't resist a game of chance any more than they could another round at the bar. They were ungracious when they happened to win, and unbelievably contentious as losers. They lost more often than they won, as is the inherent nature of gambling.

Well before noon one morning, a tremendously drunk and spectacularly huge stevedore barged into the shop holding a fistful of paper slips representing his losing numbers in the lottery from the day previous. As the barber was occupied shaving a client, the stevedore

173

reached for the first person he could find, which was John busy sweeping the floor.

"Someone's going to pay me for this useless script," he bellowed, grabbing John by the collar of his shirt.

The man was at least a head taller than the boy and heavier, yet John didn't so much as blink an eye before punching the drunk as hard as he could under his chin, knocking him out cold and dropping him onto the pile of sweepings. John simply rolled the unconscious man over and swept the hair and dirt into the mouth of a coal shovel.

He didn't even know it himself before the incident, but John McMillan had a talent, not so much for fisticuffs and brawling, but for having nothing in the way of fear if he needed to step into a violent situation, and zero compunction of doing serious physical harm to his opponent. The barber instantly realized he needed a man like this as he'd been forced to excuse a lot of losses to men he didn't have the stomach to confront. For a percentage of the money owed for the bad bets, John would step up to the deadbeats and convince them to make good.

After a few deadbeats challenged him and desperately wished they hadn't, his reputation spread through the neighborhood, the stories of his brutality gaining with each embellished telling. Most of his collections involved little more than tracking down debtors and asking them politely for the money. Most men would much rather pay up than find out if what they'd heard about John McMillan was truth or fiction.

He hired out to other people running numbers games. He became known simply as "The Collector" in the neighborhood. He took to wearing suits and walking with a stout walnut cane which he rarely used in any acts of aggression, but soon he was the source of dozens of stories and rumors across the city all emphasizing his vicious nature and his pitiless attacks with the cane against anyone who refused to take him seriously.

With the modest amount of capital he'd saved from this time among the criminal elements of the city, he bought his first property in the form of a duplex apartment. When this initial investment began to pay off, John McMillan saw that this success was easily duplicated. He soon learned about bank mortgages for buying investment property. Most of the other aspects of managing rental properties he'd already mastered during his years as "The Collector."

His tenants learned very quickly being late with the rent was a foolish move. Rent was due on or before the first of every month. On the second day of the month, John McMillan would walk into the apartments where payments were overdue. Hardworking, industrious, indefatigable, clever, motivated, and many other adjectives could be used to describe the young man from Scotland. "Patient" was not on the list of his virtues. "Forgiveness" was also a word lacking in his vocabulary.

"I don't care how you get me my money. You can borrow it, steal it, sell your children, sell your wife's body, makes no difference to me. Just get it. I'll be back tomorrow. Pay me or move out."

Not paying rent was almost unheard of in his units because on the third day of the month, the delinquent renters wouldn't see John McMillan at their door, but a team of movers who loaded up any possessions of value on a horse-drawn wagon while leaving everything else on the curb. John McMillan would keep the one-month deposit tenants had paid, charging them for the entire month even though they were evicted on the third. He claimed the money from their confiscated possessions as his right so he could pay the "movers" along with a cleaning fee.

Word got around quickly if you rented from McMillan, you'd better pay and pay on time. By the time he celebrated his tenth year in the new country, he had twenty-two rental apartments and was well on his way to becoming—for lack of a better description—a slum lord. Even when he started to buy higher-priced properties and rent to respectable businessmen, his collection strategy was just as brutal.

When his first and only son was born in 1912, John McMillan was well on his way in creating a dynasty and becoming a wealthy man.

Barely literate, he made sure his son, Robert McMillan, would have the best education possible. Contrasting with the sod hut in the Scottish Highlands where he'd been raised along with seven siblings, his son grew up in a three-story townhouse in one of Philadelphia's best neighborhoods. Robert would be tutored in math and French. John McMillan thought a fine house without a piano wasn't much of a house at all. Then there was the matter of having someone who could play it. John McMillan harbored the feeling a true gentleman, among many qualities, should be competent on a musical instrument. His son would also receive instruction on the piano from a woman who was considered the best teacher in the city.

John McMillan had grown up being ashamed of the life he'd been dealt. He was ashamed of his family's poverty, of his filthy siblings, he even became ashamed of his almost unintelligible and uneducated Scottish brogue. He was ashamed of his shame, the shame he felt about his own mother, a broken woman who looked thirty years older than she was. He was ashamed that by the time he'd earned enough to send money back home, he received news his mother had died of tuberculosis. He wanted more than anything else for his child to be proud of everything around him in his life, but especially that the boy be proud of his father's accomplishments.

It had never occurred to John McMillan that with his growing fortune, he could have learned to play the piano and furthered his own formal education which had stopped when he was ten years old, although adult education was a concept still years away. The father had only one path to proving himself as a human being: the accumulation of wealth. To John McMillan's credit, he managed this exceptionally well, although he left a considerable amount of pain and misfortune for others in his wake.

Robert, an only child, had a life of privilege and comfort. His father's fortune would explode in the early 1920's providing the young heir with even more of the training his father thought was essential in shaping the sort of man he felt he could never be. John adored his son and spoiled him shamelessly. Robert, in turn, loved his father and wanted nothing more than to please him, like most sons of powerful men. Robert had no inkling of his father's ruthless reputation in business.

John had learned to pay off the local police, sometimes even hiring them to carry out his violent evictions. The former criminal was astounded to learn how supposedly legitimate businessmen acted with complete impunity in dealings considered high felonies among his former colleagues in the street gangs of early twentieth century Philadelphia. The rich didn't break the rules, they made the rules.

The boy excelled on the piano, applying the work ethic he'd learned from his immigrant father to his tortuous, self-imposed practice regimen. His father worried the boy worked too hard at his musical studies. He would have been satisfied with a child who was able to tap out a few popular tunes of the day at family gatherings, but young Robert was working his way through the complete book of Bach's forty-eight preludes and fugues before he was sixteen.

The following year, the American economy collapsed, something John McMillan had foreseen, as did most wealthy men at the time who weren't heavily invested in the stock market. For the McMillans, the

177

Great Depression simply represented a few years when the family fortune stagnated, although John was able to buy up a staggering number of properties. While these holdings were a poor investment in the short term, for anyone in a position to weather the crippling deflation of the early 1930s, they would prove to be like so many gold mines once the American economy awoke from the nightmare.

Thanks to his father's vast fortune, Robert was completely insulated from the ravages of the worst economic downturn since the beginning of the industrial age. He left at age eighteen to study music in Paris where his father's generous allowance enabled Robert to live like a prince. He bought a baronial residence on the top floor of an historic building near the Jardin du Luxembourg on the Left Bank. With his social graces, talent on the piano, and most importantly, his money, his parties were the envy of the elite in Paris.

Because of his father's insistence he learn French as a boy, after a year in Paris, Robert was a native speaker of his adopted language, only adding to his ability to charm the bourgeoisie, even though still a teenager. As comfortable as his life had become, he could see he wasn't destined for a career in music. He continued to work himself half-to-death on the piano, but he knew he lacked a few subtle degrees of talent to be someone who would stand out in the world of music. He also knew he had little interest in his father's growing real estate empire.

At the age of twenty-two, Robert married a woman of the minor French aristocracy, ten years his senior. Their first and only child was born five months later and was named Harold McMillan after a brother of the child's grandfather who had died in Scotland the year John arrived at Ellis Island in 1898. John McMillan felt his grandson was the greatest gift he'd ever received. He was assured his legacy would carry on well beyond his own lifetime.

Although John had just turned fifty and looked ten years younger, he was becoming obsessed with his own mortality. His guiding ethos at this time in his life was to secure his place in history. He wanted to be remembered as a great man, like the earlier America industrialists. He'd go to any lengths, pay anything he could, if only his name could be attached to a building, or a city park, or even a dusty lane on the outskirts of the city he felt could one day become a place his heirs could look to with pride.

Even in his philanthropic endeavors, John McMillan was mocked by the Philadelphia elite who considered themselves to be the city's Brahmin class, especially compared to a quasi-literate immigrant. They joked McMillan would pay to have his name put on a sewer grate.

McMillan's focus was on the world of art, at least once he understood how the old money people put such importance on paintings, even though none of them knew much more than the Scotsman about the subject. John figured out quickly money was the key into this world, and he had as much money as almost any of the snobs.

He offered the city a fortune to erect a museum in his name. Although he'd become one of the richest men in Philadelphia, the city's fathers felt an art museum bearing the McMillan name would reflect badly on the city. Not only was John McMillan not the sort of man to take "no" for an answer, he also wouldn't ask twice.

Instead, he bought a beautiful public-school building in the city center, built in 1866, but scheduled to be demolished. He had the structure painstakingly restored to its former glory. Once again, the city aristocrats mocked the idea of putting an art museum in a former schoolhouse, but this was more a reflection on their complete lack of vision than in John McMillan's pedestrian artistic sense.

179

In the coming decades, everyone would agree the John McMillan Art Museum, nicknamed "The Schoolhouse," was a gem and the decision to spare the building from destruction was a move of historic preservation years ahead of its time.

By 1937, the writing was on the wall in Europe, and even the head-in-the-clouds heir to a fortune and accomplished pianist knew it was time to return to America. In his seven years in the French capital, his mother had visited him twice, but his father could never steal himself from his work. Robert had returned to America to visit his family on three separate occasions, most recently a year after his son was born, but he was going to make Philadelphia his home again.

His ever-indulgent father put no pressure on his son to go to work, but Robert, although an artist and dreamer at heart, had also inherited his father's passion for hard work. As much as the piano meant to him, Robert had known for years it wasn't a career, not for him. He went to work with his father and was determined to learn the business from the ground floor. His father had never been happier with his son than when they went together to collect rents and talk with tenants. To have someone of Robert's education and refinement talk to renters about problems with the plumbing in their buildings was an overkill on the scale of having the Pope hear your confession, but the young man was loaded with empathy and charm. He was genuinely good at the job.

Robert would never compare to his father in the business world, but he was a competent middle executive who could handle a lot of the day-to-day affairs his father found tedious. John McMillan was also the sort of man who would work until the day he died. John may have had a criminal attitude in his financial dealings, but he had no vices other than work. He was destined to live a long, healthy life.

If John could have been accused of pampering his son, he was even more indulgent with his grandson, Harold. All of this was fortunate for the grandchild, because his own father was an indifferent parent and his mother, the minor French aristocrat, was slipping slowly into alcoholism and mental illness. If Robert had taken even the most cursory glance into the family of his bride, he would've seen a history of both afflictions.

Harold would prove to have the spirit and grit of his immigrant grandfather. By the time the boy was ten years old, in the final year of the Second World War, his mother was a mere shell of a woman, while his father spent his days shut up in his study playing the piano. Harold was being raised by his nanny until his grandfather stepped in and all but adopted the boy as his own. Robert didn't put up a fight when John took young Harold to live at his new country estate in Gladwyne, northwest of the city. The boy was torn by the fact he was losing his parents, but delighted in the indulgence of his grandparents at their sprawling country estate.

John McMillan's wife had been raised in rural Cork Country in Ireland and never felt comfortable living in the city. She raised chickens and a few sheep at their Gladwyne mansion, which was yet another impediment to the McMillans being accepted into the Philadelphia high society. Harold worshipped his grandparents and as soon as he was old enough to sense the resentment against them by families well below the McMillans in economic terms, he grew to despise them.

Harold also began to resent his parents: his mother because of her alcoholism and increasing insanity, and his father because he sat back and did nothing, retreating into his music room, no longer even bothering to work in any of the family's growing concerns. Harold begged his grandfather to let him come to work for him at his elegant office tower in the city, this when he was just fifteen.

Robert and the boy's grandfather had both wanted the boy to study piano, as well as take on other pursuits of someone of his stature, but

181

Harold refused to play the piano and confessed to his grandfather he thought it a pastime for women. He told his father he wasn't interested in ever visiting France and thought learning the language was a waste of time. His grandfather had to bribe him to pursue a university degree when he was eighteen. It was a combination of threat and bribe: finish a four-year degree and he could begin work as a junior vice president, skip university—as the boy begged—and he'd begin at the very bottom.

Harold was expelled from two universities, once for cheating, and another time for an assault charge that was covered up. By the skin of his teeth, a lot of cheating, and a few bribes, he finally received a degree from a lesser state university, fulfilling his part of the bargain with his grandfather. Harold was a good head taller than his grandfather and had the body of a professional athlete. A bully by nature, and completely incapable of empathy of any sort, he was well adapted for the world of finance and real estate.

While his grandfather tended to over-compensate employees let go for any reason, and his father too meek to fire anyone at the company for any reason whatsoever, Harold relished the job of the firm's hatchet man. In his Saville Row suits, his nickname was "the well-dressed grim reaper," at least behind his back as no one would've dared call him anything but "Mr. McMillan" to his face. He'd heard the rumors and welcomed the fear he inspired among the staff. Harold wasn't trying to gain respect or become a popular leader. He was just a step away from the top the day he started working. He was a son of a bitch and didn't care who knew it.

People like Harold were commonly just referred to as "total assholes" until sociologists diagnosed this condition and decided to call them sociopaths. Sociopaths often make for good businessmen, perhaps the best businessmen, although no one refers to the captains of finance and industry as sociopaths, unless their empire is completely in the criminal world.

Harold McMillan definitely would've never thought there was anything wrong with him as a human being, and he felt his actions in commerce were a model to anyone interested in amassing wealth, or as in his case, growing an existing fortune. Ruthless was the most common adjective associated with his practices in real estate. The same could be said of his actions in his private life.

He would marry and divorce three times in his life, although he only fathered one child with his first wife: his son James McMillan. If there was one thing high society didn't tend to judge, it was a man's marital life, but in the case of Harold McMillan, he was such a complete monster with women, it was even easier for the Philadelphia elite to shun the family of the real estate mogul—not that Harold cared at all about the hoary gentry class of the city.

Harold wasn't much of a parent, even less than his own father had been. He had no time for family life between his work and his endless string of women. As a boy, James grew up spending less time with his own father than he did with his tennis instructor, a man who was later accused of child abuse. A psychologist had interviewed James when he was twelve, a year after the tennis teacher was convicted for molesting two other children. James steadfastly denied he'd been a victim. Many people who knew the McMillans thought Harold had ordered his son to say nothing of his history with the pedophile because he didn't want the shame of the affair to affect the family name.

The tennis instructor was found beaten to death only two months after arriving at the Eastern State Penitentiary. Harold could think of no better therapy for his son than knowing his former abuser had his skull crushed against an iron stair railing by convicts doing the

183

bidding of the McMillan family of Philadelphia, although this wasn't even hinted at by the police. Harold presented the news of the death of the tennis teacher to the young boy as if delivering a birthday gift.

While Harold had his grandfather to steer him in the direction of proper conduct in society, James was completely off the leash for his entire upbringing. Although possessing above average intelligence, according to his testing, he was a poor student and a constant discipline problem for the half-dozen schools he attended. James was expelled from three different private academies, an almost impossible feat considering how much his family contributed to their operating budgets, but they all had limits.

James was constantly testing limits, the limits of society, the limits of humanity. He wanted to see how far he could push before he felt any consequences. He didn't consider expulsions from the schools he hated as anything resembling punishment. James was completely flabbergasted at how much he could get away with. In his early teens he passed through a shoplifting phase in which he stole thousands of dollars of insignificant items he didn't want before he was finally caught by a store detective at a jewelry store. He was released less than an hour later and never heard a word from either of his parents about the felony, and, of course, nothing more from authorities.

This happened just when the household had hired the beautiful Romanian girl as a live-in servant. James lived with his mother, the first wife of Harold, and since he was the heir, his father was exceptionally generous to his mother. The estate had three live-in servants, or employees as James's mother insisted on calling them. There was the chef, a butler, and a cleaning woman who all lived in a guest house on the estate. The butler and chef were permanent fixtures at the guesthouse, but the housekeeper position wasn't as well paid, and the turnover was much higher.

A nineteen-year-old girl without working documents in 1974 was about as invisible as a person could be. When she disappeared after only three months working at the McMillan estate, everyone assumed she'd simply moved on to another off-the-books job. Her position was filled two days later. Life at the McMillan mansion didn't miss a beat.

James didn't miss a wink of sleep.

By the time James's family had bought him into a decent university, he began to understand to get what he really wanted in life, he'd need to apply himself, at least a bit. He had his own system for success at the University of Pennsylvania where he was definitely fighting over his weight class academically when he was admitted, thanks to several enormous grants from the McMillan Foundation.

James didn't study much at Penn. When he did actually crack a book, he had a highly-qualified upperclassman tutor spoon-feeding him exactly what he needed for the next exam. Well before the era of the disgraced American cyclist, James was the Lance Armstrong of cheating at Penn, except he was never caught. He paid for stolen exam questions, had other students take tests in his name, and did everything and anything to make it to graduation at the Ivy League school of his hometown.

If his behavior at university was under-handed and criminal, his tactics in business from the start were diabolical and pitiless. In the world of commerce, these were two admirable virtues. James McMillan could have toured the world giving inspiring talks on his contempt for anyone he faced in a negotiation. He was the ultimate "tough guy" in Philadelphia real estate ventures. His toughness didn't stem from his own inner strength, but from the financial dominance he had over his rivals.

Taking after his father, James was tall and athletic, but he'd never been in a physical confrontation with another man in his entire life. He'd abused women in his life, but he'd never stood up to another man. It had never been necessary. He always knew he could pay someone else to stand in his place, like the rulers from ancient times who would have a champion do battle in their stead, like the men who hired his great-grandfather to do their dirty work.

# CHAPTER 15 – BORN ON THIRD BASE

The McMillans were finally able to shed their outsider status among the city's elite after James managed to leverage the family's real estate holdings by liquidating certain key assets during a boom period in the early years of the twenty-first century. The real estate sell-off provided the McMillan clan with truly stratospheric wealth. One of the properties sold off in the frenzy was meant as a final and very cynical finger in the eye of the Philadelphia elite.

James had been hounding the city council of Philadelphia to help cover the expenses of his great-grandfather's eponymous art museum in the refurbished schoolhouse. The city refused to allow city funds for the museum under its current charter with the McMillan family in complete control. Without a representative from the city council on the board of the museum, no public funds could be allocated to help with the upkeep of the art gallery.

After quarrelling for a decade with the city council, James announced he was selling the museum. The city arts council tried to stop the sale, but they hit a legal brick wall immediately. The museum and everything in it were the sole property of the McMillan family under a trust now controlled entirely by James. The museum had served the family well as a tax deduction, but James had been working on the sale for over five years and planned to make upward of half a billion dollars.

The contents of the gallery had been accumulating and appreciating in value over the course of almost seventy years. There were many "priceless" treasures among the collection, but of course, everything has a price. James McMillan wanted very much to find out the exact worth of everything within the walls of the former public school. There was one painting in particular motivating James to carry out the entire piratical venture.

From 1892-93, Paul Cézanne created one of his most renowned series, *The Card Players*. John McMillan purchased a painting from the series of five oils in 1913. The other four were housed in other superlative museums around the world, including the *Musée D'Orsay* in Paris and the Courtauld Institute of Art in London. Since James was old enough to understand the worth of the painting, he'd dreamed of selling it. In a complicated and quasi-legal arrangement, he made nearly two hundred million euros in Europe on the deal and didn't pay a penny in taxes in the United States or anywhere else.

John McMillan had meant the museum to be a monument to his success and standing in the community, but James had the legal authority to do anything he wished with the collection and the building. When the last painting, the last sketch, and anything else of value in the museum were sold off, including the furniture, he oversaw a repurposing of the building into a condominium of twenty luxury apartments. Unlike his great-grandfather, James cared nothing about creating a legacy for himself in the city of his birth.

He suddenly had a huge reservoir of stagnant cash he sat on patiently. The financial meltdown of 2008 came two years later, as if James had orchestrated the world crisis for his own gain, but, of course, he wasn't nearly that clever. He wasn't very clever at all, according to anyone who knew him. He'd simply been born into wealth, which makes it incredibly easy to increase wealth. He could only be accused of being at the right place at the right time.

With the precipitous fall in property values after the crash, James was able to buy enormous swaths of downtown real estate at as much as a forty percent discount. He'd had an insider's view of the real estate market during his entire working life, so he knew which property owners were already highly-leveraged before the financial collapse and was able to take advantage of their vulnerable positions.

His initial move to liquidate the museum and its collection had been criticized in the financial world as a short-sighted and irresponsible move dishonoring his great-grandfather's wishes. There was nothing in the way of criticism when James leveraged the cash from the museum fire sale to buy up a staggering array of properties from people desperate to get out from beneath their toxic positions.

One common bromide tossed around in the real estate world is that the three most important aspects of a property are location, location, and location. This is similar to the saying about the importance of being at the right place at the right time, which is more or less the cousin to the old joke about the rich kid who thought he hit a triple because he was born on third base.

Whether it was by luck, inheritance, or his ruthless business acumen, in 2012, James McMillan was officially among the elite class of people who could call themselves billionaires. It was a completely meaningless distinction as far as his material well-being was concerned. What could a billionaire hope to buy unavailable to someone worth a bit less than ten figures? There were scientific studies showing you couldn't buy happiness. After a very modest income guaranteeing stability and security, more money didn't contribute to a person's positive mental state. The monetary figure studies pointed to was in the neighborhood of $75,000 a year. This wasn't to say people making less than this weren't capable of happiness, but there was no correlation of people being happier because they had more money than this modest figure.

To people of James McMillan's financial status, their net worth was an almost meaningless concept, except for their own egos. Members of this exclusive club had egos that could fill an entire stadium, or a skyscraper, or a 4,000-acre ranch where they went a few times a year to play cowboy, or an island in the Caribbean where they

189

could pretend to be a tribal king, or whatever motivated the man who literally had everything.

James McMillan was as materialistic and egotistical as any other man in the billionaire fraternity, and it was mostly a fraternity. There were some women in the ranks, but just like in the realm of serial killers, most were men. While serial killers were most certainly psychopaths, scientific evidence was showing that many of the top men in the business world fell into this category. Detective Elizabeth Owens believed James McMillan was both a billionaire and a serial killer.

She knew he was involved in the disappearance and deaths of three women, two in the past three years. Did he kill these women himself, or did he hire someone, the same way he paid people to clean his mansions or mop up after the murder in the Center City apartment? She knew firsthand he was violent toward women, as he'd beat up Tanya Jenkins on the night Owens responded to the call at the Center City Tower. Of course, then he'd attacked Owens. He assaulted her while she was in uniform and on duty as a city police officer. He came at her in a blind rage, first hammering her in the face with his fist, and then lunging at her to do more damage. How far would he have gone had she not been able to defend herself?

The biggest question Owens had at the moment was what was James McMillan doing now? Who was his latest mistress and where did she live? Men of his stature were almost impossible to locate, maintaining a half a dozen homes around the world, flying on private aircraft, and rarely showing themselves in the world of mere mortals. He may have never set foot inside a supermarket in his entire life or performed any of the other mundane tasks that made up the quotidian life of most human beings on the planet. They lived on top of the modern equivalent of Mount Olympus, but with fewer responsibilities than the Greek gods.

They were referred to as the hyper-rich. They occupied the top one percent on the economic ladder, or higher still. A couple thousand people in this exclusive club controlled more wealth than the bottom half of humanity, or almost seven billion people. These new masters of the human race were much, much more powerful than the Greek gods. Even though the ancient deities were merely legends, they were still bound by certain codes of conduct. The aristocrats in medieval Europe were also held to some constraints since they had to govern their subjects. The new billionaires outsourced the messy work of condemning workers to little more than indentured servitude.

They delegated.

Owens was certain James McMillan had committed his share of economic crimes in his career, but those weren't her domain. She'd been briefed by Noah Gottlieb about the shady and criminal underbelly of the McMillan fortune. As Gottlieb told her, it wasn't that his crimes would be difficult to prove in a court of law, but no one had the will to go after him. The McMillans had a reputation of being vindictive in their victories and preferred to completely vanquish rivals so they wouldn't have the resources required to fight back. The McMillans ruined their opponents.

What Owens wanted to prove was James McMillan had murdered women, or he had them murdered. She knew the young Romanian woman from his teen years was impossible to investigate, and she had little hope in her investigation of the two former residents of the luxury apartment in Center City. After so much time feeling she could do nothing to strike out at McMillan, she was running her own clandestine task force to bring down the billionaire.

The task force was entirely unofficial and included her partner, Ed Batista, Noah Gottlieb, and her academic advisor, Dr. Madeleine O'Neill. They met irregularly and at different pubs in the city, mostly

191

in the Center City neighborhood because they all lived near there except O'Neill. The first order of business was to discuss news of his whereabouts.

Gottlieb and O'Neill had some intersection with Philadelphia's elite, and they had often heard of McMillan having dinner at one of the city's better restaurants, or him attending some sort of exclusive cultural event—he rarely condescended to go to a normal performance of the philharmonic or the opera. He'd become a pariah in the cultural world of the city after he sacked the schoolhouse museum. Of course, McMillan despised the self-proclaimed leaders of the city's arts community and sold off the museum precisely because he knew it would infuriate the blue bloods.

He was still a patron of local artists, primarily for the investment opportunities of buying cheap and selling dear, and he liked the attention he received at gallery openings because of his reputation as a buyer. Dr. O'Neill was married to a prominent cardiologist and she and her husband were also avid buyers of local art. They weren't in the league of people like McMillan, but they were consistent customers, and they encouraged friends and colleagues to support the local art community. Among her crowd of mid-level patrons, Madeleine always asked discreetly about James McMillan.

Noah Gottlieb was one of the most successful trial attorneys in the city and was now becoming the face of local activism. If there was anything happening in a Philadelphia courthouse, he was a phone call away from hearing a full report. His bread-and-butter fare was almost exclusively in criminal law, but he had his ear to the ground for James McMillan in civil cases involving property disputes. There were absolutely no circumstances under which the billionaire himself had to step into a Philadelphia courtroom, but Gottlieb knew if the case were sufficiently important, McMillan was in town to keep a close eye on the proceedings.

Batista had little to say at most of these reunions. He played the role of muscle for Owens when she needed it. Ed Batista was the kind of man many monumentally foolish people underestimated. He was a really good cop, but he would've made a phenomenal mafia enforcer or a medieval knight. He was patient and insightful, and his opinion was often solicited.

During his combat tour in Afghanistan, the Army did a series of psychological tests on soldiers in the field to see how they dealt with stress under fire. Batista was at a very forward outpost in the Kandahar valley with a company of soldiers who were under almost perpetual fire. During brief lulls in the fighting, so brief the enemy may have just been taking a cigarette break in one of the rocky crags surrounding the outpost, an interviewer would present cognitive tasks the individual soldiers had to solve. The tasks ranged from math problems to chess moves to disassembling and reassembling a rifle or sidearm.

Eduardo Batista scored higher on these stress tests than any soldier who was then in country. He'd performed much better under stress on many of the problems than he did in a relaxed, controlled situation. Batista's marksmanship scores were also significantly higher when he was in jeopardy than when he wasn't. That was simply how he dealt with stress.

What the Army psychologists never asked Batista was whether he felt stress when he was in combat. The truth was he felt no more stress in combat than most people felt just performing the simple tasks asked of them in their daily lives. Although he never had a chance to carry out the experiment, Batista wondered if his chess game would improve if he challenged someone in his company to a match during a Taliban attack. Batista knew other soldiers with similar coping mechanisms, and he knew being cool under fire didn't mean you wouldn't suffer from Post-Traumatic Stress Disorder once you were

193

taken off the line and sent back to civilian life. Luckily, he had sidestepped that scourge of many people who'd served in a forward area.

Owens dealt with street criminals in her career in the force: thugs, drug dealers, thieves, drunks, and punks, and most recently, wife-beating pieces of shit. In her military days, she dispatched Iraqi insurgents, Syrian and Saudi jihadists, as well as the run-of-the-mill Army law breakers. Philly street cops didn't deal with villains who had private jets and provided luxury apartments for women they were screwing. With McMillan, she felt unarmed and out of her league.

Owens had news to share at this meeting, another stop on their Center City pub crawl as the four had grown to enjoy each other's company. She'd convinced someone working in missing persons to send an inquiry to James McMillan about the disappearance of Rhonda Perry. The inquiry was in the form of a phone call to his office and then a follow-up letter. It asked for any information he might have regarding Rhonda Perry. Owens didn't expect McMillan to answer the inquiry, as he had absolutely no legal obligation to do so.

The officer in missing persons received a letter from McMillan's office stating he had no knowledge of the woman, and he wasn't in Philadelphia on the dates surrounding Rhonda's disappearance. The letter was typed and unsigned.

"So, my question is this, if he didn't know Rhonda Perry, why would he provide an alibi?" Owens asked her three colleagues.

"I can't believe he responded at all. He certainly wasn't following legal counsel in the matter. I would've never allowed a client to respond to such a vague query. There's nothing to gain and the letter can be used in court," the lawyer Noah Gottlieb said.

"He thought it was a way to get us off his back. Beth's been bombing the area around his office tower with notices about Rhonda," Batista said. "There's no way for him to avoid all of them."

"Someone who works for McMillan must have seen the two of them together and also seen those posters," Dr. O'Neill said. "Sooner or later, they'll come forward."

"I wouldn't be so sure. From everything I know about the man, he doesn't tolerate anything less than blind loyalty from the people working for him," Noah said. "There's also the possibility no one who worked for him ever saw the girl."

"That's what I'm thinking," Owens said. "Every aspect of his life was set up to shield him from scrutiny. The night he attacked me, what pissed him off the most was just having someone at his door who wasn't welcome. The doorman said he'd never seen McMillan before. I believe him. He drove into the garage and took the elevator up to the fifteenth floor. The damn elevator even has a program so it doesn't stop on other floors."

"What I don't get is if the guy's such a kook about privacy and security, why does he allow his little girlfriend to run rampant over social media?" O'Neill asked.

No one answered.

"Maybe he didn't know," she said, answering her own question.

"Significant, if not very useful from a prosecutor's perspective," Gottlieb said.

"How so?" Batista asked.

195

"It means even if the girl was blabbing about their relationship, there's still no evidence of their alleged affair," Noah said.

Gottlieb pondered this for a few seconds.

"It's a complete dead end, legally. He won't say anything. He's not obliged to say anything. I'm flabbergasted he sent that mealy-mouthed denial."

"Flabbergasted. Ha, ha, I love it," Owens said with a laugh. "I've never heard anyone use that word in conversation. Only fucking Noah."

"That's why I make the big bucks, as they say. It's all about vocabulary."

Everyone at the table knew Noah Gottlieb amounted to much more than a good vocabulary. He made the big bucks, as he said, because he was as fine an actor as he was an attorney, and in jury trials, being something of a master thespian was at least as important as knowledge of the law. Gottlieb had made a small fortune giving lectures and video courses on how psychology and playing to the jurors won more verdicts than an encyclopedic recollection of legal precedents.

After his second failed marriage, he'd lost any love he once had for the law. He parlayed his good name and spotless reputation into a fortune defending some of the most notorious criminals to set foot in courtrooms in Pennsylvania and New York. The money was staggering, but more than anything, he loved the limelight these cases brought him, even if it meant more infamy than fame. He'd always been handsome and fit, making him a favorite on television news reports covering these show trials like the best kind of reality TV.

When his third marriage turned into yet another smoking hole in the ground, Noah began to think his downward spiral had to be reversed. Immediately. He and his good friend, now the crusading District Attorney of the city, a man who was the new hero among liberals and villainized by conservatives, had a frank discussion one night at a bar favored by courthouse lawyers.

"You need to use your powers for good, not evil," Larry said.

Noah could have objected and given his often-repeated speech on how everyone has the right to the best defense, how this was the cornerstone of American jurisprudence, but if he did, he never would've stopped vomiting on his own bullshit. His friend was right, as he always was. It was time for Noah Gottlieb to become a very different kind of lawyer.

# CHAPTER 16 – LOGAN

Batista drove as he and Owens were on their way to take a statement from another abuse victim. This time, the woman had only called for police assistance on twenty-one previous occasions. Her husband of three months had blackened both of her eyes on the previous call, but had done no permanent physical damage, at least not yet. The wife refused to press charges. Owens was in no mood for the piece-of-shit husband or the wife unless she was willing to cooperate with them.

"Someone was in my apartment," Owens said to her partner.

"When?"

"Not sure, I didn't notice until this morning. I came home late last night and went right to bed. Yesterday or the day before"

"How do you know? Forced entry?" Batista asked.

"Nothing like that. Big time stealth. I can't even be sure, just gut, like I can tell when someone rides my bike. Can't say how or why. I just think someone was in my place."

"Nothing taken?"

"This wasn't a break-in. This was some asshole spying on me. Like the shitbags in the Big Book who snoop around in their ex's panty drawers."

"They were in your…"

"Shut the fuck up," Owens cut him off. "This was a whole other level of professional. I mean, I think. All the windows were locked. If someone was inside, they were good. Like creepy good."

"Had to be someone sent by McMillan, right?"

"That was my first thought," Owens said. "Like I need another reason to hate that motherfucker."

"Let's check your place out right after this call."

Owens had placed a marker on the door to detect if anyone had entered since the last time she'd left. She hadn't been paranoid enough to do this before. The marker was still there. She and Batista entered and began a thorough search. Of course, there wouldn't be prints, so they didn't bother looking or worrying about tainting a potential crime scene.

"You should throw out everything you'd either eat or drink."

"Good call. Fucked up and it freaks me out, but good call," Owens said.

She reached for an empty garbage bag and started throwing things out of her fridge.

"Good news is I have next-to-nothing to eat in this place. Don't even have any booze."

"If they aren't out to kill you, what else could they get here?"

Owens had to consider this as she spent so little time at home.

"I just sleep here. I rarely even shower at home," she said. "Right now, I can hardly see straight because all I can think about is how much I want to fuck this guy up for being in my home."

"Maybe they're looking for personal stuff, family and friends they can use to get to you."

"Look around, *compadre*. I don't have a single photo."

199

"You're right. Your place has all the charm of a hotel room," Batista said. "A listening device?"

"To listen to me snore?"

"Maybe they're just messing with you?"

"Bingo!" Owens almost screamed. "It's working because I feel violated. I hate feeling like a damn victim."

"I'd like to victimize that shitbag. I've never even seen McMillan before and I want to stomp a mud puddle in his chest," Batista said. "Maybe you should stay somewhere else."

"Whoever did this won't be back. Too risky, and if they were just messing with me, their job's done. Still, I'd like to put his foot in a bear trap if he comes back."

Batista picked up a laptop computer from the desk.

"Password protected?"

Owens frowned.

"Do I look like James Bond? Besides, there's nothing on there; I barely use the thing. I'm pretty good about not putting anything in emails I wouldn't want someone else to read."

"Someone should check this out for you. They could've installed something."

Batista handed the computer to Owens who pulled a case out of one of the desk drawers and placed the laptop inside.

"I got a guy," Owens said.

"We need to tell Madeleine and Noah about this, too. If this has anything to do with McMillan, he must know we're hanging out—probably knows we're talking about him"

Owens was way ahead of him and in the middle of texting both of them.

"Done," she said after sending it.

"Let's take care of this right away," Owens said, holding up the computer.

As Batista drove following the directions Owens had on her phone, he'd been mulling something over before he finally articulated his thoughts.

"I think Noah is the one who really needs to be worried."

"I was thinking the same thing," Owens said.

"He's a civilian and untrained in any of the messy shit done by whoever the hell broke into your apartment. Plus, if McMillan secretly paid him to bring you down in that civil case, he'd be pissed to find out the two of you are pals."

Chuck had a work area in a retail zone south of Owens's apartment. It was the original office of his engineering firm before it took off financially and moved out to the suburbs. He kept the old space and used it as a tech-geek clubhouse.

Of course, there was no parking. Batista stopped in a loading zone. The door to the shop was locked and it looked closed, hell, it looked abandoned. Owens rang the bell and was buzzed in thirty seconds later.

"The fuck is this place?" Batista asked.

They walked through a room full of computer husks, piles of cables, and dozens of monitors stacked on one wall. They passed through another door into the rear of the shop. This area was brightly lit and looked like it might have been an office at CIA headquarters. Organized, tidy, with a minimal amount of top-of-the-line computer equipment.

"Batista, this is Chuck. Chuck, Batista."

The two shook hands, and that was it for pleasantries. Owens handed Chuck the laptop. He placed it on a large counter, and took a seat on a stool. Batista and Owens remained standing—there was no place to sit. After less than five minutes, Chuck turned toward them.

"There might be more, but there's a program that allows someone to remotely see everything you're doing on this, as long as the machine is connected to the internet. As I said, there might be other things, but this is all they really need."

"Can you remove it?" Batista asked.

Chuck gave him the "of course" shoulder shrug.

"Maybe I don't want him to," Owens said. "Why would someone do this?"

"Lots of reasons I can think of, but I don't know your situation. This is shit parents, jealous ex-boyfriends, and husbands install to spy on people. You can even see through the camera at them, but I see you have tape over your camera lens," Chuck said.

"No freeloaders allowed when I'm walking around naked," Owens said. "If I remember, you told me to do that way back."

Chuck laughed.

"Back to your point, do you want to remove this? It could be a good way to steer this person where you want them to go…as long as they don't know you know the computer was hacked."

"That's what I was thinking. Just show me how to remove it when I'm ready."

It was a fairly simple process and took Chuck less than five minutes to explain.

Now Owens just needed to find a way to make this spyware work for her.

McMillan's man was called Logan. From what he'd seen of her apartment, and from what he already knew about her, she was the workaholic type. Little food in the fridge, no sign of hobbies other than exercise, no family, no regular boyfriend. She worked, worked out, and studied for her master's degree which was work-related. Not the sort of cop you'd care to have looking into your life. The most important thing he found out about his target was she was someone you'd never want to underestimate.

McMillan was incredibly vague with Logan about what he wanted from him. He wanted the cop "checked out thoroughly." That could mean a lot of different things to a lot of different clients, running the gamut from getting bank account numbers to copying home-made sex tapes off their computers to getting the names and addresses of everyone they cared about. In this particular case, Logan guessed McMillan didn't know what he wanted other than avoiding getting blindsided down the line.

A smart move, something Logan had taught his billionaire sponsor years ago when they first started their relationship. The truth was Logan didn't have a very high opinion of the wealthy heir and doubted McMillan ever had a good idea of his own. From what he'd seen of the man, he was astounded he hadn't lost every penny of his family's money. He had the impulse control of a Molotov cocktail and the critical thinking skills of a panicked moth. McMillan wasn't sitting in a prison cell thanks to actions Logan carried out on his behalf. Logan wondered how McMillan managed before he started cleaning up after him.

But McMillan couldn't want him to kill this cop. A woman, a good cop—from what Logan had found out so far—with a decade on the force, an Army veteran with combat service in Iraq, and to top it all off, a Bronze Star recipient. It would stir up about as much muck as a political assassination. In the spoiled real estate tycoon's defense, the cop had fucked him up, but good. Still, he had it coming from what Logan heard through the grapevine.

Logan thought McMillan should quit while he was ahead, but if every rich asshole did that, Logan would have to go back to being a security consultant, which meant giving up his pride and joy: a Beneteau fifty-four-foot sloop moored in Key Biscayne. He'd have to give up other things, too, but the sailing is what he'd miss the most about his financial current position.

The richer men became, the more screwed up they were, at least this was Logan's experience. The good news for them was they had the money to cover their tracks, which came in the form of favors, hand-outs, bribes, pay-offs to witnesses, and hiring people like Logan. The wealthy really needed help with cleaning up the truly epic mistakes, like beating a girlfriend to death because she told you she was going to have a baby.

He'd met McMillan before, but their relationship solidified when he called Logan after killing a young girl at one of his hundreds of apartments in the city. Logistically speaking, it was an easy problem to make go away, but Logan knew this wouldn't be a one-time job for McMillan. This woman-killer would be his ticket to retirement in five, or at the most, ten years. McMillan hadn't been clear about what he wanted with this cop, but he didn't balk when Logan told him anything to do with police was going to be expensive.

Money had never been a problem for James McMillan, Logan thought. He'd read up on the family before he ever met the guy. McMillan wasn't the easiest guy to vet, as the billionaire had done a thorough job of keeping his private matters very close to his chest. He wasn't a publicity hound, not in his youth and definitely not at this point in his life as was common among other children of the rich who were often starved for attention. Logan assumed his client always had a lot to hide. If he did, he was doing a great job at keeping it buried.

Whatever secrets McMillan kept hidden, Logan had a pretty good picture of the man to know he was full of anger. He'd cleaned up after three murders, all young women, all beaten to death. Logan's service was to disappear the "subjects" as he euphemistically referred to the victims, not only their physical presences, but also as much of their internet history as possible without attracting undue attention. He was no wizard when it came to technology, but if you had the subjects' passwords for their various accounts, it was a simple affair.

From early on in his career as a fixer, Logan had worked among people who had the skills he needed while he had talents he could lend out to them. One of his contacts was a techie whose field of expertise was manipulating certain social media sites. All Logan had to do was pass along a name, and that username would be completely eliminated from the entire platform.

After the women McMillan had discarded were erased from social media and their other internet history scrubbed thoroughly, it was like they'd never existed. This was partly due to the fact Logan had begun vetting the women before they were introduced to James McMillan. He knew what the man was looking for, and he went out and found them. Three of them worked at a restaurant where Logan paid the manager for access to their employment records.

It was getting easier and easier to learn everything about these girls just from their internet history. He always looked for women who were new to the big city, preferably from as far away as possible. Logan looked for women from broken homes which often meant weaker family ties than those from two-parent households.

The women needed to be poor, of course. The poorer they were before they came to Philadelphia, the better. These factors suggested they usually had nowhere else to go. They were vulnerable.

Logan always justified what he did as intelligence gathering, at least that's what he told himself. He didn't consider himself a pimp or a trafficker in human flesh; someone else was responsible for bringing the women to McMillan. His job was to match the physical profiles McMillan craved with personal backgrounds mostly lacking in anyone who'd come looking for them. It never occurred to Logan he was setting these women up to be murdered, at least not until two of them were dead and he was summoned like a janitor to clean up the mess, both literally and figuratively.

This cop Logan was vetting looked good on paper, but he wrote off many of her accomplishments as tokenism. His was a typical opinion of mediocre White males who believed their lackluster careers were hindered by affirmative action policies. Like so many others who discounted the ability of Beth Owens, Logan was allowing his narrow, misogynist, and possibly racist views to underestimate the Philadelphia detective.

He knew that targeting a cop would draw a lot of heat, if that's what McMillan wanted, but he didn't think it would prove much of a problem. It could be his big payday, liberating him once and for all from monetary concerns.

His vision was hindered by greed.

# CHAPTER 17 – AFTERNOON INTERLUDE

The next time Owens, Batista, Gottlieb, and O'Neill met, they followed some simple security protocols to foil anyone attempting to eavesdrop on their conversation.

"It's not being paranoid when you know someone's spying on you," Owens said in her message to the others.

They still met in a Center City pub, but they took slightly circuitous routes. They were also aware of other customers in the place. When you have four people at a table glancing around the room at random intervals, it's a simple yet highly effective way to foil intruders and eavesdroppers.

"Still no luck trying to convince anyone in homicide to take a look into these disappearances?" Gottlieb asked when they'd all settled in with their pints.

"There were 365 murders last year in Philadelphia, many of them unsolved and without suspects. The last thing homicide wants is to try to make a case when there's not even a body," Owens said. "We knew this from the beginning."

Owens told Gottlieb and O'Neill about the break-in at her apartment and warned them to be more aware of their own security, both at home and in every other aspect of their lives, something she and Batista knew instinctively.

"It just seems if McMillan had someone break into your home, he's upped the ante in his aggression toward you," Madeleine O'Neill said.

"Definitely. I just want to know how we can turn the heat up on that bastard," Batista said. "It's like we're just sitting around waiting for something bad to happen while we can't even ask him a few questions."

"He's tipped his hand for us twice now. He provided an alibi for Rhonda's disappearance, which tells us he has something to hide, and he's got someone creeping around in Beth's life," Gottlieb added. "Unfortunately, we can't do anything with this, not from a legal standpoint."

"I'm tired of worrying about the legal channels in this. I'd just like to meet the guy face-to-face," Batista said. "Ten minutes with him and I'd wrap up both disappearances."

Owens didn't react to Batista's macho outburst.

"I'm worried someone will come after you two," Owens said, indicating the two civilians at the table.

"I doubt anyone would break into my home. It just wouldn't make sense. I don't really have a part in this. Besides, our apartment is like a fortress," O'Neill said. "And we have two big dogs."

"I agree with Madeleine. I don't think they have anything to gain coming to my house or office. It's Ed I'm worried about."

"Shhhhiiiit," Batista sighed. "They may get *in* my place, but they aren't getting out in one piece."

Everyone stared at him waiting for an explanation.

Owens didn't even want to know what Batista had rigged up in his place. She thought the worst-case scenario for an intruder would be to break into Batista's house while he was home. She'd put all her money on Batista against anyone McMillan hired.

"Since Beth told me she'd been creeped, I've been more vigilant than usual. I'd know if anyone entered my place," he said, toning down his braggadocio.

209

Batista knew anyone who came into Owens's house while she was home, even if she were asleep, was at a distinct disadvantage, even if there were more than one of them. He knew her.

Gottlieb laid a printed sheet of paper on the table.

"Here we have a list of the philanthropic events McMillan could possibly attend in the next six months,"

"Where'd you get this?" Owens asked.

"McMillan has a lot of people working for him who hate his guts. I run into them at the courthouse. They'd love nothing more than to see him in handcuffs."

Owens thought she'd like to see him in a shallow grave.

She picked up the paper and scanned the list of five upcoming events: three openings at the studio of artists and two galas at the Philadelphia art museum.

"What are we supposed to do? Walk up and arrest him?" Batista asked.

Gottlieb just shrugged his shoulders in reply.

"How likely is it he'll actually be at any of these?" Owens asked. "He hasn't been spotted in the city in months."

Gottlieb put his finger on one of the dates.

"He's been a patron of this painter for a few years. She happens to be young and beautiful. If I had to bet, I'd say he'll be at this one."

"So let me get this straight," Madeleine said. "This guy is a suspect in two homicides, and the police can't even question him? You're reduced to ambushing him at a charity event? There's something severely wrong with the system."

"You're beginning to understand police work," Owens said. "Just like our Big Book of Shitbags, we mostly watch crimes happen and try to clean up later."

"Speaking of which, I'd imagine McMillan has a new girlfriend who really needs someone to tell her what she's gotten herself into," Dr. O'Neill said.

"I'd walk right up to her and tell her as much with McMillan standing next to her. At this point, I don't know if I can even trust myself to be around him in public without opening his skull with a hammer," Owens said.

"I hear that," Batista concurred.

"Not that I'd ever see him in public," Owens said.

The lawyer in Gottlieb cautioned them both not to do anything they'd definitely regret later, as McMillan would bring down the full force of his power and influence in the city, and especially the PPD, if he were assaulted.

"We're cops, Noah, but we're not completely stupid," Owens said. "Still, I'd definitely push him down a flight of stairs if I thought no one was looking."

At this point, running into James McMillan was becoming a very remote possibility. He was keeping a very low profile and may have been away from Philadelphia for months. The art opening Gottlieb mentioned was their first lead on his possible future whereabouts since Rhonda Perry disappeared.

Owens had put in for a transfer to homicide with assurances from Inspector Washington Gates it would be approved, but these internal moves often took months to happen.

Work in the Domestic Violence Unit plodded on in what for Detective Elizabeth Owens was an inexorable slide into despair. She couldn't imagine any type of police work less rewarding for a cop, as completely necessary as it was. She never felt like she was protecting the women. She thought the system was shielding the abusers.

Owens's tech guru had programmed her unit's files to count the number of complaints from the women in the database. When the number of calls reached twenty-seven, Owens would receive an alert. There was nothing much the unit could do when this benchmark was reached, but either Batista or Owens, or both, would check up on the women filing the complaints.

The following afternoon, Owens was responding to in Nicetown in North Philly when Batista called.

"What?"

"Your gal just made call twenty-seven. A patrol unit left there fifteen minutes ago," Batista said.

"Damn, I just talked to her like two days ago."

"Her ex wasn't at the scene, just stayed around long enough to beat her up pretty good. Neighbors witnessed the whole thing, some of it on video."

"Got an address on him?" Owens asked.

"We have him at 44845 North Delhi."

"A unit heading there?"

"Fuck if I know. They may not have the address."

"I'm ten blocks out; I'll stop in and talk to him," Owens said as she took a hard left turn. "Wendell Prude, right?"

"That's our shitbag."

"Later."

Owens sped down the one-way street with cars parked on one side. When she got to Wendell's house, she parked the car on the sidewalk and put her flasher on the roof. The car blocked the entire sidewalk and part of the narrow street lined with two-story townhouses. As soon as she got out of the car, people started walking out of their doors and stared at her from their stoops or small front porches.

She wanted desperately to be in uniform to put more of an official air to what she was about to do. Instead, she tucked the right side of her jacket into her waistband to show her service weapon. She had her detective shield hanging from a lanyard around her neck before she bounded up the four stairs, taking out her expandable baton as she approached the door.

She rang the buzzer. Then again, still without an answer.

She knocked violently with her fist, then with her metal baton, finally screaming out his name.

"Wendell Prude! Police. Open the fucking door and come out, or we're coming in!"

Safety in numbers was always a good plan, even if it wasn't a reality. Batista would make sure at least one patrol car was on the way, but as they said in the PPD, they'd get here right on time and ten minutes late, which made no sense at all to anyone but a Philly cop.

213

The neighbors were already starting to congregate, not only on their front steps, but a half dozen of the curious were standing beside the police vehicle parked in front of the run-down townhome. Reality TV had nothing on daily life in this North Philly neighborhood.

Owens hadn't let up, alternating on the door buzzer, an old school model which literally had a hammer pounding on a bell, and using her steel baton as a knocker.

"Wendell Prude, I saw you through the window, so I know you're home. Just open the damn door so we can talk."

Owens stopped the ringing and banging and turned around to look at the neighbors.

"Nothing to see here folks. Just some parking tickets to clear up."

No one was buying it.

The front door opened slowly, but there was still the metal security gate separating the cop and the occupant.

"What you want?" the enormous man said.

Owens already knew enough about Wendell Prude so there were no surprises. 6'2," forty-four years old, served four years at Chester for assault. And then there were the many, many calls from his ex-wife.

There was also the latest assault, but this one was different.

There were witnesses this time, witnesses who were willing to cooperate, witnesses with video. Wendell Prude was definitely going to jail this time around.

"Open the damn door and come out here and talk to me, Wendell."

Wendell stood behind the steel bars. For once, the bars were keeping the law out and weren't keeping him in a cage.

"What? You can use your wife as a damn punching bag, but you're scared shitless of little old me?" Owens taunted.

"I ain't a scared a you, bitch."

"Bitch? I see a little bitch hiding behind his door," Owens countered in her best street dueling lingo.

The peanut gallery in the street and on the stoops was becoming increasingly animated by the spectacle, although there wasn't much to it just yet. The Phillies must not be playing today, was all Owens could think, or they'd have something better to do.

Where in the hell is my backup? She looked down the narrow one-way street and saw a growing line of at least eight cars, some to watch the show, others stuck behind them. She gave up on the idea of help.

People at the back of the line of stalled traffic started leaning on their horns, adding to the chaotic atmosphere.

"You're under arrest, Wendell. You fucked up this time, you beat your old lady in front of witnesses willing to testify. Hell, they're dying to testify."

"None a they damn bidness."

"Hell yes it is, when you do it right out on the stoop of her house."

Wendell didn't budge.

"People don't like men who beat on women and kids, Wendell. The law doesn't like it either, that's why you're under arrest, or you will be as soon as you come out here."

"Why would I do that?"

"Because if you don't, Wendell, we have to come in and get you. If we do that, we aren't going to be nice about it."

"Who the hell is *we*? All I see is you out there."

"Don't think I couldn't do this myself, but patrol's gonna be here soon enough. You make any fuss, and you'll have resisting arrest tacked on to the assault charge."

Wendell was thinking, something he didn't seem to do often enough upon any examination of his life choices so far.

"Look at you, Wendell. You want to go to district in those filthy shorts and no shirt and shoes? You want your neighbors to see you dragged out of here like a fucking animal?"

Owens knew he didn't.

"Listen, I'm going to sit down on these steps and wait. I'll give you twenty minutes to shower, shave, brush your teeth, put on some clothes, maybe make a phone call or two. Then I take you in with no cuffs, sit up front with me, like we're friends going for a ride."

Wendell's head sank down.

"That sound good to you? You and the court aren't my concern; that shit ain't my job. I'm a cop. My job is to bring you in. Who knows, maybe you can work something out, you know how it goes with the law. Fucking OJ walked."

Wendell looked her in the eyes and bowed his head.

"You're definitely making the right decision," Owens said, knowing she had him.

With that, Owens turned around and sat down on the stoop. The peanut gallery broke apart immediately and the traffic started moving again.

*** 

"So now you're doing things all civilized. No cracked head this time, or just no visible marks left on the arrestee?" Batista said back at the station.

"Fuck you. Once again, would it kill you to have my back? I thought your mostly-worthless ass called for patrol?"

"I did."

"Like hell, you did. Police didn't make it by in the forty-five minutes I was there. It was like I was General Custer all alone at the All-Black-Folks Little Bighorn."

There was only a bit more of this back and forth between the two cops before they ended up back at Batista's place.

Again.

They always went to Batista's place, although they'd only hooked up about ten times, each encounter separated by a week or two. Owens always initiated the move. Batista was more than satisfied with the arrangement as he was as averse to relationships as Owens. They were just partners and really good friends...and two people who had sex once in a while. Owens would've preferred to have it more often, but that would complicate things.

Batista had other women in his life, although none of them would've understood his relationship with Owens, so he never mentioned it. Owens never asked him about the other women, and he never volunteered any information. Batista felt men would have a much easier time getting laid if they could just learn to shut their damn mouths about it afterward. Owens agreed with him on this point. He was good at keeping secrets.

Owens didn't meet a lot of men whom she found attractive. Most cops were just plain stupid and pigs when it came to women, like Washington Gates. Civilian men were too soft, even the muscle-heads who lifted weights five days a week. She actually considered going home one night with Noah Gottlieb. He was a good-looking older man, educated and cultured, rich, and he seemed like he was good to women, although three divorces didn't argue in his favor in that department.

After one of their group meetings at a pub, she and Noah left at the same time. She was about ready to make her move as they walked down South Eighteenth Street near Rittenhouse Square. A car backfired just behind the couple and Noah jumped out of his own skin. That was all it took for Owens to lose all interest in the man, at least as a potential lover. It happened that fast.

Batista may not have been the most sophisticated guy she knew, but she dug his toughness. He was the sort who wouldn't take shit from anyone, yet at the same time he was as nice as they came, still visited his grandparents every Sunday. From what she'd seen, he was good to women. He just didn't want to get married and have kids, at least not yet, for a lot of women a total deal-breaker—not for Owens. His mother was always hoping he'd fall for one of the young women from her church, a parish exclusively made up of immigrant Latin American families.

They always went to Batista's place. Owens didn't tell him this, but she never wanted anyone to spend the night at her apartment. At Batista's she could make the decision when she wanted the date to be over. She always went home before morning and woke up in her own bed—after a shower. She was also turning inexorably into a clean freak and the idea of some guy peeing all over her bathroom didn't sit well with her.

They made it back to Batista's apartment in the early afternoon after she'd booked Wendell Prude. They usually worked until 20:00 on Thursdays but had skipped out three hours early thinking they'd go back to the unit later.

Owens was lying in Batista's bed half-asleep with a hint of the afternoon light making its way through his bamboo window shades. She noticed Batista wasn't in the bed as she struggled to pull herself out of her short nap.

Batista had put on a pair of boxer shorts and was making coffee in a small stove-top mocha pot when he heard a scratching at his front door. He walked over to the door in his bare feet and pulled a child-sized aluminum baseball bat out of the umbrella stand. He hadn't bothered to lock the deadbolt on the door when he and Owens came in, so it was quick work for the person on the other side to pop the door open.

Things were about to get very difficult for the person entering illegally.

The door opened slowly with the light from the outside hallway illuminating the small entranceway in the apartment. Batista raised the bat as if he were preparing to hit a home run. A tall man stepped into the apartment and was struck in the stomach with the bat. Luckily, Batista had choked up on the swing and instead of a home run, he only went for a single. The man went down in a heap, making a sound that could only be described as a death rattle as the pain Logan felt made him wish he were dead.

Owens heard the commotion from the bedroom and immediately reached for her service weapon. She slid across the bed and popped out of the bedroom with the pistol drawn. Batista looked over and laughed.

"I think 'Mostly-Useless' just fucked up McMillan's champion," he said.

Owens saw the man writhing on the floor, but her first thought was how she was delighted Batista had used a word from a book on Greek history she'd pushed on him, thinking he'd never read it in a million years.

It was obvious Logan was an experienced B&E guy. He was wearing expensive slacks and a finely-tailored sport coat, a ruse to dissuade anyone from suspecting wrongdoing. If he were caught in the act by a neighbor, he could claim to be a realtor and few people would challenge him further.

Batista rolled him over on his stomach and pulled a small semi-automatic pistol from his belt, then took another small-caliber pistol from an ankle holster. Next, he pulled a large lock-blade knife from the right pocket of his slacks.

Still completely naked, Owens walked up and handed Batista a pair of handcuffs. She stepped lightly on the back of Logan's neck while Batista cuffed him.

Owens looked over to see the mocha pot steaming on the stove.

"God damn," she said. "You made coffee, too?"

# CHAPTER 18 – QUEEN TAKES KNIGHT

Before Logan had fully regained his senses after being slammed by Batista, the two cops had dressed and were having their post-coital *cortado*. Logan was still on his stomach and looked up to see the cops with their small cups sitting at the kitchen bar counter.

"Sorry, I only made enough coffee for two. Gotta call before stopping by."

Batista had bound Logan's feet with two flexi-cuffs so he'd be able to shuffle, but that would be about the limit of his mobility. He was treating his prisoner as some elite operative and wasn't taking any chances, especially while he was having a coffee with his beautiful partner.

Owens looked at her watch.

"We need to take our sweet time getting him booked so he'll spend the night at the district. We get him in too soon and he may be out in a couple hours," Owens said.

"I got nowhere to be. We could go back in there," Batista said, motioning with his head toward the bedroom.

Owens laughed.

"With this hump on the floor? Maybe just another coffee."

When they'd finished, they both hoisted the prisoner to his feet.

"Here's the deal. You may be some sort of ninja assassin or ex-spook, or whatever, considering the job you do, but if you fuck around here, even a little bit, your next stop will be the emergency room," Owens said. "Got it?"

Logan nodded.

The two cops had to hoist him under his arms to the street as the ankle restraints wouldn't allow him to manage stairs on his own. They put him in the back of the unmarked police cruiser.

Batista read Logan his rights on the way to the station and he was booked at their district. He had no identification and refused to give a name. The cop doing the booking was a cheery Black woman who looked more like a game show presenter than a Philly cop.

"That whole 'you have the right to remain silent' really doesn't cover giving us your name. We'll get it sooner or later, and if it's later because you're just being an asshole, well, that won't be good for you," she told him.

Logan remained silent.

"See, honey, what we do is lock you up with the worst of them here. No phone calls for people with no names. You sit tight until we find your name. Can take days, sugar."

Her charm seemed to work because he caved in and gave her his name.

Charles Logan.

Logan didn't hand out résumés. For the past seven years, his clients had sought out his services through intermediaries. When a client inquired about his background, he'd shroud his responses in vague generalities sounding like false modesty and subterfuge to those listening. He'd hint at "special ops" and elite services, but the truth was he'd been an enlisted soldier in the Army who'd never seen combat. He knew the jargon of the military through his service, but he also knew better than to spell out any specifics of his military service.

Any non-veteran who claimed military service would struggle to survive three questions from anyone who had. This much Logan knew as well as any veteran. His service had been honorable, but he wasn't the elite warrior he hinted at for the sake of his clients.

The morning after his arrest, Batista and Owens had an adequate profile on their prisoner and were ready for their first interrogation, but if he wasn't willing to cooperate, they'd do all the taking.

Logan sat in the small interrogation room handcuffed to the table. He was trying to appear unconcerned and hadn't contacted a lawyer. He was thinking of his fine Beneteau sailboat drifting further away from him with every hour he was behind bars. He had a pretty good idea he was screwed.

"You know you're screwed, right?" Owens asked in her first salvo upon entering the room, before she and Batista had even sat down.

"Dude, you are so fucked," Batista said. "Breaking and entering, illegal possession of firearms—plural—unregistered firearms. Shit, just the knife charge could put you away for two years. We don't play around in Philly."

"I know you were in my place, too. Can't prove it, don't need to. Why? Because we got you dead here, brother. You are screwed. Completely," Owens said.

Logan was maintaining his right to remain silent.

"There is no scenario where you walk away from this without at least two years in prison with no chance of early release. You could easily get four."

Logan stared at the wall feigning boredom.

"There's no 'good cop, bad cop' here today, just two cops spelling out your very unfortunate future," Owens said. "You have one card to play, and one only, and we both know what that is."

Logan was trying desperately to appear stoic and tough, but he could see his lovely 54-foot sloop sinking with every minute, with every word these cops used to describe his predicament.

"Give us James McMillan and things'll go much better for you," Batista said.

Logan sank even deeper into silent remorse.

"Charles," Owens said, calling him by his first name, a name he hated. "No one's coming to save you. There's no happy ending to your story. The prosecutor will have two decorated officers testifying against you for some very serious charges. There's no lawyer dumb enough to take this case to trial, not even the worst of the public defenders. You try to run with this case in front of a jury and some grumpy-ass judge may give you five years."

The silence in the small interrogation room was total. Both Owens and Batista knew this was the moment to let the words sink in. They controlled their breathing to increase the silence.

"A White defendant on a gun charge? There isn't a judge in this entire fucked-up town who wouldn't put you away for that. Makes it easier for them to deflect criticism about all the racist shit aimed at the Philly judicial system."

"I want my lawyer," Logan finally said.

Owens stood up and moved back from the table where she faced the prisoner.

"That's your right, that's the law. But. The second you lawyer up; any chance of a deal is off the table. We'll come down on you hard, like with everything we have. Why wouldn't we?" Owens asked.

She leaned back against the wall.

"Why wouldn't we come down on you like a ton of bricks? You broke into a police officer's private domicile, armed like a killer. What were your motives? An assassination?"

Owens stepped back to the table and picked up a printed sheet of paper.

"Says here you own a yacht. I don't even know what the fuck that means except people who own yachts don't break into a cop's apartment to steal a TV. I'll admit we won't be able to prove your motive was to murder a cop, but we can definitely hint at it."

Logan sat up straight.

"I wasn't out to kill anyone."

"He speaks," Batista shouted. "I was beginning to wonder."

"Keep talking, Charles. You may just talk your way out of a prison cell," Owens said.

Logan recovered from his one-line outburst and went back to the silent act.

Batista and Owens just stared holes into their prisoner.

"I need to talk to a lawyer before I say anything."

Owens and Batista had nothing more to say to their prisoner before Logan was returned to a holding cell. They both knew their threat of taking any deals off the table if Logan talked to a lawyer was a bluff.

He'd be a lot stupider than they thought if he *didn't* confer with a lawyer. It was all just bullshit cops threw out in an interrogation room. Of course, they'd work a deal with Logan if he testified against McMillan. It was strange he hadn't already secured legal representation. They figured he must've been waiting for McMillan and his cavalry to come through and get him released.

"Should we be worried about this guy's safety in lockup?" Batista asked.

"I was thinking the same thing and the answer that keeps coming up is 'hell yes.' They already told me they're totally jammed up in holding, like thirteen violent felonies pending."

"You think McMillan will make a move on him in lock up?" Batista asked.

"Why wouldn't he?"

Batista was scanning the sheet they had on Logan as the two walked back to their office.

"We can't go too soft on him considering he's a definite flight risk. We got his home address as Fort Lauderdale. He could be down there on the next flight and then out to sea in that big boat. He's got no visible means of support for the last three years."

"Then again, knowing what he knows about McMillan, he may be safer in the holding pen than running around out there. But I guess even this résumé-padding asshole can take care of himself, inside or out," Owens said.

"Then we do everything to keep him locked up if he doesn't play ball and soon. We'll lay it on the judge at the bail hearing."

"Any Philly judge would love to have an excuse to refuse bail for a White defendant, just to make his record a little less than totally lopsided."

Philadelphia's court system had a bad reputation for keeping poorer arrestees in jail awaiting trial while those with more resources—White defendants—could easily manage to pay their bail and go home pending trial.

"I almost feel bad for this Logan dipshit," Owens said. "Or I would if he didn't break into my house. He's either looking at a few years in prison or dealing with the wrath of James McMillan if he cooperates. Even if he gets bail, he has to worry about McMillan hiring some other goon to put him down."

"McMillan needs to vet these guys better. Logan was just some Army REMF admin guy. How'd he parlay that into being some sort of super-sleuth?" Batista asked.

Batista knew he didn't need to tell Owens that REMF was army slang for "rear echelon mother fucker."

"Everyone lies on their résumés," Owens said.

"We also have to consider there's the distinct possibility he doesn't know anything and can't give up McMillan."

"He must have something on him unless he just started. If he's been with him for a while, he'll have something to bargain with. He may literally know where the bodies are buried."

Batista considered this.

"Either way, dead would be better than alive for McMillan. I mean, if he had his way. He murdered at least three women that we suspect, so he's not a big fan of the whole 'value of human life' thing."

"The arraignment's set for the day after tomorrow, eleven o'clock. Logan shows up without representation means he doesn't want McMillan to know he got pinched," Owens said.

"We lay it on thick with the D.A., let her know everything we suspect this guy's done, not that she'll be able to use it, but it'll put the prosecutor on our side. We have enough on him as a flight risk to deny bail."

Logan pleaded not guilty at his arraignment two days later. He wasn't represented by a lawyer and was denied bail by the judge on the grounds he was a flight risk. He'd be off to county lockup in his new orange jumpsuit. After the arraignment, Owens stepped over to the accused and warned him to watch himself in the holding facility.

"If McMillan wants to get at you, county's no place to hide. He has friends all over the department. Some guard will leave you locked in a corridor with three gangbangers and McMillan's worries are over."

Logan stood at the table as a bailiff started walking over to take him away. Owens held up a hand asking for a minute with the defendant.

"He even know you're in here? If so, why didn't he have one of his lawyers for this? Even without a guy like McMillan out to do you harm, county ain't no joke, especially for a middle-aged White guy."

Logan wasn't talking.

"I can't help you if you don't help me. Got it?"

Logan just nodded. The bailiff led him out of the cramped courtroom, making room for the next sorry soul in the Philadelphia criminal justice system meat grinder.

"See you later, Logan. Maybe."

James McMillan was told what happened with Logan five days after his arrest, but it took another week before he learned he was in lockup awaiting trial for breaking into the apartment of the cop who worked with Owens. From what his sources were able to uncover, Logan had yet to talk to a lawyer, either state-appointed or otherwise. He wasn't cooperating with prosecutors.

From what McMillan's attorneys could glean from his accounts about his relationship with the accused, Logan could make things difficult for McMillan. But what Logan had to say against him would come down to one man's word against the other, and one of them was in jail. However, even if what Logan could testify to wasn't enough to file charges against the real estate mogul, it could prove to be an exceptionally ugly affair in terms of his public image, an ugly affair McMillan would rather avoid at almost any cost. He had already decided Logan deserved to go down merely for his utter lack of competence.

McMillan had a few buffers between him and his police contacts. He usually met the highest-ranking members of the force at society functions. He'd shake hands and have a drink, but he never discussed business with anyone directly, even with his top contacts. He always worked through a filter, one of his subordinates who'd pass on his messages, return their messages, and make pay-offs.

He sent his subordinate out with a valise stuffed with bundled, well-worn bills, directing him toward an official who worked directly under the commandant of the county jail. The request was received, the money was accepted with assurances of success, but the message back to McMillan was that another payment was necessary for such a brazen act. It wouldn't have been any problem at all except the D.A. was working desperately to get the defendant to cooperate. He was in protective custody. Just what the prosecutor expected from Logan wasn't clear to the commandant's underling.

What they were asking was a ridiculous sum to take out some half-assed B&E artist, but McMillan was so furious with the man's ineptitude he would've paid twice that amount. He'd paid millions over the years to keep the Philadelphia Police Department more or less on retainer, much like his law firm, and their seeming unwillingness to help him now made him wish he could take them all down.

For now, he'd settle for eliminating the cocky fixer who'd promised him the two cops and the lawyer he wanted taken down would be easy work with no blowback. Logan had done quite a lot of work for him during the past few years and up until now, it had all gone off without even a minor problem. Had the man's luck simply run out? Not that McMillan believed in luck.

James McMillan never considered that Logan had simply been outmatched by the two Philly cops.

McMillan would take care of Owens soon enough, and the Puerto Rican kid, or whatever he was, would have to wait his turn. He had another priority that could directly concern his well-being, something that could make his life extremely difficult and even lead to his arrest. As much as he tried to limit his exposure with the fixer, Logan knew too much about the affairs of James McMillan.

# CHAPTER 19 – PHILADELPHIA LOCKUP

Curran-Fromhold Correctional Facility (CFCF) on the Delaware River north of Philadelphia's downtown, housed up to 2,000 male inmates of all custody levels. The facility was part of the Philadelphia Department of Prisons (PDP) and was the largest in the system. It had four buildings, each with eight housing units and was further broken down to contain thirty-two cells. The units were divided into two separate tiers. Inmates housed on each unit had access to indoor and outdoor recreation, a medical facility, and a library.

And the facility was a total hellhole. The murder rate for Philadelphia prisons was four times higher than the national average. There was a constant deluge of complaints about inadequate staffing and deteriorating building conditions. One of the complaints was that in some of the cells prisoners were able to breach the locking mechanisms and basically come and go as they pleased. Curran-Fromhold Correctional Facility had been built only twenty-six years earlier and was quickly falling into rubble.

The assistant district attorney assigned to the case managed to have Logan placed in protective custody at the facility, even though the prisoner hadn't agreed to cooperate in any way with prosecutors. The promise of release from confinement was already on the table. All Logan had to do was give prosecutors a case against James McMillan.

He maintained his right to silence.

Charles Logan, now L-34-7245, was definitely out of his element in prison. The population was eighty-two percent Black, fourteen percent Hispanic, leaving Whites at four percent. They all wore the same uniform of a denim shirt with navy-blue trousers, but there was no way for Logan to blend in. He could've been spotted in the prison yard from a satellite photo. One of the basic rules of prison life is not to stand out from the crowd.

The commandant at CFCF was the truly greedy link in the chain if someone were looking to kill a prisoner in protective custody. One of McMillan's contacts at PPD offered him almost half of the cash McMillan had originally put up for the job. The commandant had worked extensively with elements at the facility who'd be willing to kill a prisoner for a few hundred dollars in their commissary account, but he saw this as an opportunity to make a sizeable contribution to his own retirement plan. His corruption over the years had been considerable but not sufficient to liberate him from monetary concerns, if that were ever possible. Losing his job and his pension would be a disaster, so he was always on the lookout for an insurance policy, a golden parachute.

He also knew he'd only get one chance at taking out the prisoner. He was going to give the gang leader he worked with in the prison a huge sum, but he'd insist on hearing about the plan from the gangster, and then a backup plan. An over-used phrase had been a big part of business culture for years and was repeated in boardrooms and in locker rooms: Failure is not an option. The commandant knew too well failure was most certainly an option. It was always an option, only a complete idiot would think otherwise. Anyone with any common sense and even a shred of life experience knew this. The way to avoid failure was redundancy.

The commandant didn't repeat this trite aphorism to the prison gang leader. Instead, he told him if the first attempt failed, there had to be an immediate second attempt. Then another if that failed. He let the gangster know he didn't care how clumsy the killing was, or how brutal, or how inhumane. Charles Logan needed to be dead. The commandant would worry about the negative fall-out later.

McMillan's proxy and his conduit to the Philadelphia police let the cops know Logan wouldn't be missed, not much. He wasn't local. His

233

crime was breaking and entering, hardly the type of crime to garner time on the local news stations. The prosecutors couldn't even suggest a link to James McMillan as the prisoner hadn't offered to cooperate, at least not yet.

Logan was a nobody. He wouldn't be missed. He would be quickly forgotten.

The commandant had given the gangster, who went by Malcolm Z at the facility, a hefty advance for the hit with the remainder to be paid immediately upon completion of the task. He couldn't give an inmate cash as there wasn't much prisoners at the facility could do with it. He delivered it personally one evening to an address in an area of the city where even a high-ranking law enforcement official didn't feel completely safe.

Four days later, the commandant pulled up to the same address in his obscenely-expensive SUV and parked. This time he had a small gym bag with the second payment. He strode up to the door as confidently as he could and rang the buzzer of the townhouse with the deceptively shabby façade like the rest of the entire neighborhood.

A sliding peephole in the door opened showing the face inside, a young Black man with a bandana on his head.

"Wha," the kid stammered.

"I'm here to talk to Sebastian," the commandant said. "He's expecting me."

The door opened and the commandant walked into a room that looked like the waiting room of an expensive plastic surgeon. The seven people sitting around were the usual drug lord entourage of beautiful women, and three soldiers.

The commandant followed the kid through the gallery to a back room of the house looking into the interior courtyard of the block. Behind a state-of-the-art laptop computer sat a thirty-something Black man wearing a white shirt and blue blazer. He looked like he stepped out of an ad for English country living.

"How do you do?" he said, extending his hand. "I'm Sebastian."

The commandant left him hanging.

"OK, no handshake, like I give a fuck. Just trying to be polite."

"We don't need polite here, this business," the commandant grunted.

"Fine by me. What do you have for me?"

The commandant set the gym bag down on the desk. The GQ man picked it up and started counting.

"It's over," the commandant grunted again.

"Excuse me?" Sebastian asked.

"The count is over. There's extra in there," the commandant said. "For a job well done, and all that bullshit."

The GQ guy stood up shaking his head.

"Well, while your tip doesn't move the needle very far in this organization's income, it's the thought that counts, right?"

The commandant relaxed a bit.

"Just…" the commandant stuttered, "…that whole suicide aspect was fucking true brilliance. Hanging. We didn't even discuss that. I didn't even think of it."

Sebastian's idea, but he didn't give this away to the cop.

The Commandant was turning to leave when Sebastian spoke again.

"My boy Malcolm Z doing Ok at your place? Anything I can do to make his life easier?"

The commandant turned back around.

"Z has it as good as it can get for him. Good as it gets in prison," the commandant said. "He keep doing good by me, he keep living like a king in my castle."

*** 

News of Logan's "suicide" made its way to Owens and Batista the next day.

"I almost want to congratulate McMillan for this one because I don't know if it was a suicide or just meant to look like one," Owens said. "The man *was* desperate."

Batista was equally impressed and confused by the news.

"I was thinking the same thing. Either way, we have zero on McMillan at this point. If we're playing chess, he's winning," Batista said.

"I hate chess. Fucking stupid game, passive-aggressive bullshit; some kind of gauge of a person's level of intelligence. Maybe it does come down to a person's IQ, but who the hell would spend time studying a damn board game?"

James McMillan would have agreed with Owens on this point. He didn't have time for games. He received the news regarding Logan almost immediately. If only Logan had carried out his orders with the same precision and ingenuity as the thugs contracted at Curran-Fromhold Correctional Facility. His police contact sent word to him that although the suicide would be investigated, it was unlikely to be challenged.

McMillan also didn't have time to consider he was literally getting away with murder yet again. Murder wasn't something that gave him pleasure, not particularly. He enjoyed the power of killing someone without consequences, but the murders in his life were simply solutions to problems, beginning with the young Romanian housekeeper at his parents' estate. He was sixteen years old when she began working as a cleaner. She was one of the live-in domestics who shared a small residence behind the main house. At first, the young heir had spied on her through the windows of her bedroom. His voyeurism soon escalated to harassing the young girl every chance he ran into her.

At first, his perversions were passive. He'd make sure he was naked when she came in to clean his room. If his parents weren't at home, he'd masturbate in front of the terrified girl. She was nothing more to him than another family possession and he knew he could do with her what he pleased. If she didn't like it, she could quit. One afternoon, when she resisted too much, he killed her to keep her from screaming for help. He threw her body in the trunk of his car and buried her in the woods surrounding an abandoned quarry north of where he lived, a place he and his friends often went to swim, drink beer, and smoke weed.

237

Her body was never found. In fact, she was never reported missing. At the McMillan household, her absence was simply seen as just another example of an immigrant unwilling to work. In a week, she was forgotten

He was a young, rich, and handsome boy, and at sixteen he was popular with the girls his age, many of whom were more than willing to have sex with him, but the Romanian maid was a bigger thrill to him for reasons he couldn't understand at that time. He felt she belonged to him, or so he thought. It was a feeling he couldn't duplicate with the women he dated, or with the women he married.

This feeling of ownership only returned when he started keeping young women in one of his many luxury apartments around Philadelphia. He actually called these women his pets. He rarely tried to mask his low opinion of women, his vast, intimidating fortune shielding him from any sort of backlash against this behavior. Some women paid a heavy price for his hatred of their gender.

It was Logan who discovered Rhonda Perry was chronicling her entire life on her internet pages, like she was someone famous. McMillan was furious as he'd warned the girl from the beginning that she wasn't to talk to anyone about their relationship. She was living like royalty at his expense, with an almost unlimited credit card account. All she had to do was be beautiful and keep her mouth shut.

After Rhonda, he had another girlfriend living in an even more spectacular apartment, an eighteenth-story penthouse in the center. She was even younger than his last pet and seemed even more subservient, more submissive, at least at times. She participated enthusiastically in any and all of his lurid fantasies. She enjoyed it when he invited a creepy older woman into their bedroom to film their acts. The truth was McMillan's "perversions" were mostly pathetic and mundane. He certainly had no future in porn.

He soon tired of this young girl, booted her out, and found another beauty who was installed in the same apartment. New was always good for McMillan.

He'd dodged what could have been an extremely complicated situation with Logan, but now he wanted the woman cop dead. He didn't care who he had to hire, or what he had to pay to make it happen. He wondered if the prison thugs were as capable of the same operational talent in the streets of the city as they'd demonstrated in lockup. He knew better than to go through his police channels to contact whoever these people were. His police connections were the most corrupt public officials he'd ever worked with anywhere, but they'd balk at killing one of their own.

McMillan's proxy with the police let a top official know the real estate tycoon wanted to open a direct line of communication with whoever had carried out the hit at the correctional facility. The proxy was given a name and a number.

McMillan's go-between was a twenty-four-year-old just a few years out of The Wharton School, a sharp kid who found himself way over his head in the world McMillan had sent him to navigate. He was the type of native, affluent Philadelphian who'd panic at the sight of a Black man walking toward him on an empty street.

Normally, if you were White, Ivy League, and a financial hot shot, you had the world by the balls, but not when you were in a gritty Philadelphia police district working out the intricacies of a bribe with a hulking Black giant of a police inspector.

When the Ivy Leaguer communicated McMillan's request to meet directly with the gangbangers from the prison, the police inspector laughed in the young man's face.

"Boy, you from Philly, right?"

"Born and raised," the kid said proudly.

"Travis, you ever been near Kensington and Allegheny?"

Travis had never been near that corner.

The highly-privileged, young financier knew the area, as did anyone from the city, infamous from the countless news reports of murders and shootings. It was ground zero for drug and gang activity in Philadelphia, and one of the most dangerous corners in the entire world.

I'm certainly not fucking going there, the whiz kid thought. He was just a middleman, paid to do McMillan's bidding, but this was above and beyond, like several neighborhoods beyond any he'd entered.

"I hope you people know what you're doing, boy," the inspector said as he handed the kid a piece of paper.

It finally dawned on the boy he was expected to actually visit this blighted area of his city. It was like asking him to enter a burning building.

There were no further instructions from the police inspector who simply pointed to the door. Travis tried to act confident as he strode out of the noisy district precinct house. He didn't look at the slip of paper until he was on the sidewalk.

Sebastian #543-34-2291.

He texted the number when he got to his car. "This is Travis," was all he was told to write.

He was in no hurry to run this little errand, but he received an answer almost immediately.

"22557 Jasper Street. 18:30. Come alone."

Travis had about forty-five minutes. He pulled away from the district and headed toward the war zone he'd heard so much about on the local news broadcasts. About the only landmark in the area that didn't look completely threatening was the train station at Kensington and Allegheny. The rest of the bombed-out area was littered with check cashing services, dollar stores, small convenience markets, and bars he'd never enter in this lifetime.

He turned right on Jasper Street and found the address of yet another two-story townhouse, the sort making up so much of the Philadelphia urban landscape, both the good areas and the very bad. He was five minutes early and sat in his higher-end BMW four-door sedan, wondering if it would still be there when he came out from his meeting.

There wasn't a single pedestrian on the street as far as his could see in any direction. He didn't know if he found this comforting or terrifying.

Before he reached the stoop, the door opened from the inside. Travis skipped up the steps and entered. As he did, a young kid wearing a Phillies ball cap brushed by him and stood on the top step. Another man stood in the doorway.

"I'm Sebastian," he said, extending his hand.

Sebastian was once again dressed in what looked like English gentry casual: a custom-made white shirt, blue blazer, dark wool slacks, and black leather shoes with a single buckle. Travis suddenly felt underdressed in his khakis and button-down blue shirt and tie.

"Jacob here will keep an eye on your wheels, so nothing to worry about. This is actually a better neighborhood than everyone thinks."

Yeah, Travis thought, who would mess with anything belonging to this ruthless crew? He followed Sebastian through the house to the modern kitchen. It didn't appear anyone lived in this house, Travis thought. There was no indication in the kitchen food had ever been prepared there since it was remodeled. They sat at the table for six.

Sebastian told Travis to get immediately to the point.

Travis took out his tablet and set it in front of Sebastian.

"Enter the day and year of your birth in the space, then hit enter. An encrypted message will appear and then remain on the screen for two minutes. It will delete itself."

Sebastian did as he was instructed. Travis had no idea what the message was and was grateful for this ignorance. He attempted a poker face and studied the man whose services he was trying to enlist.

Sebastian wasn't playing poker and made no attempt to mask what he thought of the offer.

"We don't do that, Mr. Travis."

"It's just Travis, that's my first name."

"Excuse me, but as I said, we don't do that."

"If it's a matter of money…"

"It's not about money. We don't kill cops. Period."

The boy's poker face suddenly changed to one of pure panic. Kill a cop? He had no idea his little errand today was to broker a contract killing…of a police officer. Travis was no lawyer, but he knew this amounted to a first-degree murder charge.

"Meaning we take care of them; they stay the fuck away from us," Sebastian finished.

Travis realized not only was he implicated in a murder-for-hire scheme, he also had to report back he'd failed in his mission.

"Anything else you need today?" Sebastian asked after what he thought was the conclusion to their meeting.

Travis was too stunned to speak and drove out of the war zone, barely conscious.

# CHAPTER 20 – CONSPIRACIES

Sebastian looked even better in workout apparel than in street clothes, but then he had a body that seemed more built in a laboratory than sculpted by exercise. He casually strode up to Owens as she was working out on an assisted pull-ups machine. That area of the gym must have been out of fashion because they were the only two people in the room.

"Detective Elizabeth Owens, my name is Sebastian Martin."

Owens stopped in the middle of her set to turn around to see who'd addressed her in this, her sanctuary. She saw the exceptionally handsome man and couldn't place him from anywhere in her memory. Definitely not a cop, too articulate to be a criminal, must be a lawyer, her least favorite of those three choices.

"Do I know you? You know me?"

"I'm Sebastian," he repeated, "but no, I don't know you. I'm here to relay some information."

Owens stepped down off the machine and took a drink from a bottle of water on one of the stairs.

She thought about asking him a few preliminary questions but decided to get directly to the point, whatever that was.

"Go ahead," she said, staring him straight in the eyes.

"Someone's looking to kill you."

Owens took another drink from her bottle.

"Can you be more specific?" she asked calmly.

Sebastian laughed at this bit of sangfroid he wasn't expecting.

"James McMillan, to be precise."

This got her full attention.

"Where'd you get this?"

"From the horse's mouth, or from the horse's flunky. He came to us directly."

"Who's we?"

"That's something falling under the auspices of the Fifth Amendment, but let's just say I have an acquaintance known as Malcolm Z."

She knew Malcolm Z was currently serving time at Curran-Fromhold Correctional Facility. Owens had to take a beat or two before her next question.

"You're telling me McMillan had someone contact your people to take me out," Owens said before asking, "So, why would you tell me?"

Sebastian looked her in the eye.

"Because it seemed like the right thing to do."

"My fucking ass," Owens almost choked saying this.

"Seriously. I told his flunky we don't kill cops."

"You kill a fucking lot of people, so excuse me if I'm not overwhelmed with admiration for you and your people."

For the first time, Sebastian seemed to falter in his discourse.

"I promise you we're working on it, the killing, but that's a discussion for another day."

Sebastian was trying to distance his organization from the senseless killings defining the drug trade in Philadelphia. He had a long, long way to go.

"Once again, why are you telling me this?"

"The truth? Because I admire you," Sebastian said. "I told him no and then looked you up on the internet. War hero, Bronze Star, cop, Philly girl makes good. Temple graduate. Now a graduate student there."

Sebastian took a step backward as if to refocus his eyes.

"And you're totally gorgeous, but I didn't know until just now."

Owens ignored the compliment. She had to admit this guy could get away with that kind of remark to a woman he'd just met. In the military, the saying was "rank has its privilege,' but so do extraordinarily good looks. An ugly guy compliments you and it could be creepy; a guy this gorgeous says the same damn thing and few women would complain.

"Your people know you're talking to me?" she asked.

"They aren't the understanding type if you really want to know. This is strictly between the two of us."

"The thing is, I'm not afraid of my people like you are. They aren't out to kill me," Owens said.

"I wouldn't be too sure," Sebastian said. "Once again, just between the two of us, McMillan contacted my people through your people."

"What the fuck does that mean, exactly?"

Owens was beginning to lose her cool, just a bit.

For the first time, Sebastian wasn't being extremely polite.

"It means your department is up to its eyebrows in fucking filth. Maybe they didn't know what McMillan was looking for when they put us together. Maybe they did."

Owens took a few moments to register this along with a few sips of water. She softened her tone.

"Thanks. I have no idea what I can do with this information, but thanks. I think."

Owens hesitated a few seconds.

"Why did you ambush me here," she said, looking around her gym.

"I just figured you wouldn't be carrying a gun. I hate the things, personally."

"You're in the wrong fucking job if that's true, no matter what the hell you do for whoever you work for."

Sebastian didn't blink at this.

"Nice gym, for a cop," he said, changing the subject.

Owens heard the insinuation in this remark, like she couldn't afford these surroundings on her salary.

"My one indulgence, but I figure you either pay now for your health, or it comes back a hundred times more expensive when you reach fifty. This," she said as she motioned around the elegant health facility, "this is an investment."

Owens started to walk away, thinking the exchange had played itself out.

"Can I call you sometime?" Sebastian asked, with a hint of shyness a man of his looks and economic stature seldom felt.

Owens stopped dead in her tracks as she was walking away and turned.

"You're asking me on a date? I hate to break this to you, but you got a much better chance of me arresting your ass than you do seeing what's under these sweaty, stinky clothes."

Sebastian laughed at this and seemed to take it as a challenge. He took a business card out of the back pocket of his shorts and held it up in front of him.

"If I can't call you, you call me. You need anything, you let me know. The mess you're in, you may need some allies."

Owens didn't take the offered card.

Sebastian took this as a challenge.

"You want to know why I told you this? Because I hate people like McMillan, White, over-privileged aristocrats who make the laws and always keep themselves above them, no matter what. Meanwhile, my best friend has spent most of his life in jail. Not saying he's innocent, but people like McMillan have done worse, I'm sure."

"The shit that man has done," Owens said as she took Sebastian's card. "Brother, you have no idea."

***

The protocol for McMillan's employees was for all of his commands to go through the man he called his executive officer, a forty-two-year-old lawyer named Drew Rice. As a lawyer he'd pushed the envelope on the line between legal and illegal, coming so close he was almost disbarred in Pennsylvania. His loose interpretation of the law and willingness to cross the line, and then some, made him a perfect candidate to manage the many quasi-legal and illegal operations in McMillan's enterprises. He was the only link between James McMillan and whatever criminal acts were carried out to further his business deals or solve problems in his personal life.

It had been Drew Rice who sent Travis on his little errand to Kensington and Allegheny, and now the young man was back to report. Rice had an office in the corporate headquarters, but for security reasons he issued his orders and listened to the reports from his many lieutenants outside the building. He met Travis at a downtown bar that was all mahogany, potted plants, waiters who'd worked there for at least a quarter century, and a collection of over two hundred different bottles of fine scotch whiskey.

When Travis entered, it took a full minute for his eyes to adjust to the dim lights as he stumbled to a back table that seemed to be Rice's private domain within the establishment. Rice was drinking a Manhattan and tapping on a device. Without looking up, he pointed for Travis to have a seat.

Travis could have really used a drink after his ordeal in the roughest area of the city he'd ever seen first-hand, but the waiters knew not to approach the table of Mr. Rice unless they were summoned. They weren't summoned. Travis's next hope after a stiff drink was that this wouldn't take long.

The kid sat down and immediately began on a highly detailed account of his meeting.

Rice stopped him with a raised hand.

"The important part of this story was his answer was no. Correct?"

Travis started to explain again what Sebastian told him of the gang's prohibition against killing police officers.

"It wasn't a question of money?"

"No, he made that quite clear," Travis muttered.

Rice knew this punk financial wizard should've never been sent to do a man's job. That would have been a task for Logan, a position for which Rice was desperately seeking a replacement. He'd do a better job this time of vetting the candidates. He took some comfort in how easy it was to solve his Logan problem. A bit expensive, but mostly due to the unmitigated greed of the Philadelphia police elite.

Rice dismissed the young financier and texted McMillan immediately. This was news that couldn't wait.

McMillan responded immediately. He'd be there in fifteen minutes.

Rice knew this could mean up to an hour or as little as five minutes. People of McMillan's stature had little concept of time unless it concerned them. He ordered another Manhattan and considered what he should tell his boss.

Rice was well aware his only real talent as a lawyer was his willingness to break the law if he felt the risk was acceptable. He'd also been talented at calculating risk. He hadn't said anything about it to McMillan, but he thought this whole campaign against the woman officer was going down a very dangerous path. He would've sided with this gang leader, Sebastian, if they both were arguing the point to McMillan.

The real estate magnate entered the bar exactly thirty-eight minutes after sending the text message saying he'd be there in fifteen. As he found his way to Rice's table, he signaled for a waiter who met him precisely when he sat down with his underling.

It may have been Rice's table, and his bar, but it was McMillan's city and the workers seemed to intuit this.

"A gin martini, with olives. Something special concerning the gin, and I don't mind the vermouth part."

McMillan wasn't a big drinker, but he enjoyed it when he did.

Rice had worked in this capacity for McMillan long enough to understand the man never solicited opinions about the orders he issued, either. Even Rice's position as "executive officer" hinted at military hierarchy where strategy, as well as orders, always flowed downhill. As lofty and as highly-paid as he considered his position in the company, he and everyone else were downhill from their boss, and McMillan was never shy about reminding them.

Rice recounted what he'd just heard from Travis, but he began with the part about "no" as the final answer, so as not to waste any time.

"Do you think he did enough, this, what's his name?" McMillan asked.

"Travis."

"He didn't seem to represent himself very well. From my perspective, it looks like he simply walked away completely defeated in a negotiation."

McMillan hadn't finished his thought and took a sip of his drink before continuing.

"Maybe he didn't offer enough. I made it very clear money wasn't of any concern."

"I wouldn't put this on Travis. These people are nothing if not capitalists. Money isn't a problem for them. What they're after is power and insulation from their crimes," Rice said. "As their representative told Travis, they work with PPD."

Of course, they do, McMillan thought. He was familiar enough with the police department to know they'd work with or for anyone if there was money in it.

After Rice gave him all the details he had on the meeting, McMillan sat back and took a long pull from his drink. He didn't like that some gangbanger had basically told him to fuck off, not to his face, but by proxy. He'd destroyed men for a lot less. He'd like to send a message to these people that they needed to treat him with a lot more respect, even when he sent his subordinates. He expressed this to Rice.

"There's no up-side, James," Rice said, ignoring his usual policy of not giving his opinions on the orders he was given.

"I'm not afraid of these pimps and drug dealers," McMillan shot back, his veiled racism not too veiled this time.

"That's not the point. All I'm saying is what could you possibly gain by striking out at those people?" Rice asked. "Besides, the kid Travis dealt with today will probably be dead in a week anyway. If those people make it to thirty it's a minor miracle, or they all end up in prison eventually."

Rice could sense his boss wasn't listening and already regretted voicing any sort of counter-argument. This very conversation highlighted the danger in going against McMillan's interests as he was about to lash out at a hyper-violent drug cartel because they turned down his outlandish request to assassinate a city cop.

McMillan wasn't thinking of getting into a shootout with the drug cartel. His usual methods of castigating anyone who defied him were through financial channels or crushing them in real estate deals.

"Tell Watkins to give me everything they have on this kid Travis met today."

He left his drink and walked away without another word to Rice.

The Watkins his boss had mentioned was another high-ranking police inspector they had on retainer. Rice was certain a first name and an address in the war zone area of the city were sufficient to pass on to the inspector to identify the subject of McMillan's current interest. He was positive going after this person was foolish, probably dangerous, but he wouldn't offer further opinions. He'd do his job like before, but at this point he'd also keep an eye on the emergency exit, of walking away. He didn't want to end up like Logan, now laid out on a slab in a prison infirmary.

The police inspector knew the name and told him over the phone that afternoon. Sebastian Franklin, thirty-three years old, born and raised in North Philly. Father unknown, mother, Sandra Lee Franklin, living in the same North Philly neighborhood where she, too, was born fifty-two years ago. Two other children. Andre, thirty-seven years old and serving twenty years at United States Penitentiary Canaan, in

Waymart, Pennsylvania, on a drug charge. Another son was shot to death on a street in Philadelphia four years ago. There were no suspects in the slaying and no arrests were made.

The police didn't have a current address for Sebastian. He'd never been arrested, not for anything. He'd never been issued so much as a parking ticket. The inspector told Rice he assumed Sebastian Franklin had never owned a car in his own name and avoided driving at any cost. Driving was about the surest way to have a run-in with the police, whether you were a drug cartel executive or a real estate magnate.

If you drove, you ran the risk of being pulled over, especially if you were a young, Black man. Sebastian had never bothered to get a driver's license after seeing the dangers of driving while Black. He knew lots of White people whose lives had been disrupted considerably because of driving, showing there were limits to White privilege. If you were in an accident while under the influence of alcohol, you were screwed no matter who you were. But Blacks had a significantly greater chance of being pulled over with nothing in the way of probable cause.

The inspector had no explanation as to how a young Black kid growing up in North Philly could side-step the police his entire life, especially since it was common knowledge Sebastian had worked his way up through the ranks in the Black Mafia street gang, or whatever they called themselves now. The original Black Mafia had splintered in the mid-1990s. They were some sort of Muslim sect as many members had converted while in prison, although much of the rank and file, including Sebastian, were non-believers.

The current leader, who now went by the name of Malcolm Z, was awaiting trial on a drug charge at Curran-Fromhold Correctional Facility where he ran the gang operations from his cell. The police inspector had little idea what role Sebastian played in the Black Muslim Mafia hierarchy, but from what the PPD knew of him, it was significant. The major gap in police intelligence regarding the group was what the gang did these days to make money.

The knee-jerk answer was drugs, making up a considerable part of their income, but their influence was reaching out into the community like the tentacles of a rapacious octopus. Sebastian Franklin appeared to be one of the few gang members who'd ever held a legitimate job. Oddly enough, he'd worked as a real estate broker for three years. Without any proof, police suspected the gang was working with a North Philadelphia real estate firm to help low-income families purchase their own homes. This was coming at a time when property values in the most blighted areas of the city were plummeting while rents continued to rise with unrelenting regularity.

It was impossible for anyone, even the most astute forensic accountants, to tell whether the gang was actually committed to this policy of aiding the poorest families in the city, or it was a money-laundering scheme with a level of sophistication never seen in a street-level criminal organization. A third alternative was the housing initiative was little more than a cynical public relations campaign to win favor in the poor areas and insulate the gang further from police scrutiny. Whether they were ushering poor families into home ownership or not, their record of violence was a horror witnessed every day and chronicled in the Philadelphia press.

The city had one of the worst homicide rates in the country, and very often was ranked at the very top of this shameful list. Rice didn't know if his boss even read the local press to know the sort of people he was now planning to attack, or undermine, or challenge openly. Rice couldn't imagine what McMillan hoped to gain in his campaign of spite, grudges, and in this case, petty revenge.

Rice hadn't worked for the man long enough to understand this was what got McMillan out of bed in the morning. Even when he won, he was vindictive. He wouldn't tolerate the smallest act of insubordination among his employees. He was thrown into vengeful furies at the slightest gesture he felt showed a lack of respect. Criticizing James McMillan was something he considered an act of war, and he overreacted accordingly. He preferred to inspire fear and terror in people, believing respect and admiration had little value in business.

McMillan never had to worry about the sometimes very expensive nature of his vendettas and never had to suffer any consequences. His wealth had insulated him from his bad judgment and fiery temper throughout his entire life.

# CHAPTER 21 – BEHIND THE FINANCIAL CURTAIN

McMillan had interfered in the career of Beth Owens for years, although she had no evidence. Now he was conspiring to kill her, according to the handsome representative from the Black Mafia, while all she could do was sit back and wait for him to make his next move. While Sebastian told her his organization had rejected his offer, there were dozens of street gangs in Philadelphia who'd do anything for a few thousand dollars. Most of the kids in these gangs were nihilistic half-wits who murdered people over ten-dollar drug deals that went wrong. Killing a local cop wouldn't exactly violate their moral code.

Owens did as much as she could to hide the source when she reported Sebastian's message to her immediate supervisor, as per department protocol. Sgt. Welling sent the message up the chain of command, yet after two weeks, Owens hadn't heard anything from the department. Nothing. No one-on-one with an inspector or anyone else. Owens felt there was little else she could do. If the department wasn't taking the threat seriously, she thought at least they'd want to talk to her about it, just to cover their asses if something did happen.

Then again, she thought, there was little the department could do, not without any proof or someone willing to come forward to report the threat. Sebastian certainly wouldn't go on the record. Owens knew it wouldn't make a bit of difference, as there was still nothing to implicate McMillan—his errand boy had never mentioned his name. Owens had referred to Sebastian as a "confidential informant" in her report. What she did know for sure was if McMillan had sent a representative to talk with a local cartel leader, she needed to take the threat very seriously.

After several weeks of varying her routine and keeping as vigilant as she could, Owens was approached again by Sebastian, this time in the pub near her apartment where she was somewhat of a regular.

She was sitting at a back table with a book, but she noticed him the moment he entered. Imposingly tall and impeccably dressed, he was hard to miss. After his eyes had adjusted to the dim lights, he spotted her and walked to her table.

"Mind if I join you for a minute, detective?"

"You can call me Beth, I'm off the clock."

"Can I get you another beer, Beth?"

She nodded.

Sebastian returned from the bar with two pints and sat down at the heavy wooden table.

"See, that's what I don't like about electronic books: you can't see what people are reading to make conversation."

"Sorry technology is screwing with your pick-up routine," Owens said.

Sebastian laughed.

"Did you come here to talk about books?" she asked.

"We can, but I have other matters to discuss."

Owens took a sip of her beer.

"Wait a second," Owens said. "Since you told me McMillan is looking to kill me, I've been trying to be more security conscious, yet you've had no trouble tracking me down twice now. What am I doing wrong?"

"I've had two kids checking on you."

"Checking on me? Spying?" Owens asked. "I don't know whether to feel thankful or pistol-whip you."

Sebastian was almost certain she was joking.

"Just keeping an eye on your apartment a few hours a day," Sebastian said. "I told them to be unobtrusive."

"They must know what that word means because I haven't spotted them, and I've been looking. Hard, really hard. Maybe give them a raise?"

"Anyway, kid called me saying you were here."

"And here we are. What can I do for you?"

Sebastian sat back and put his hands on the table.

"I'm not sure there's anything you can do for me, but we now have an enemy in common. Someone's been harassing my mother lately and I suspect it's McMillan."

Owens waited for more.

"Her water was shut off for no reason. Then the electricity, so no air conditioning during these dog days. I cleared it up, but there was no reason for it, not anything she did. Now her next-door neighbor is being evicted—a family that's been renting the house forever. The building has a new owner, and they want the tenants out. These people are like family to my mother, so it's been traumatic."

"And you think McMillan is pulling the strings?" Owens asked.

"No proof, but who else has that kind of power? I assume I'm on his shit list because I rejected his offer to kill you. Now he's rat-fucking my mother."

Owens was proud of herself for understanding that word after recently having it explained to her by O'Neill, who was around during the Nixon administration.

"Rich assholes don't like it when you tell them no," Owens said. "Believe me, he's done worse things for a lot less."

"Like what?"

"Like firing a secretary because she didn't change the cartridge in the office printer fast enough, this after she'd worked for him for four years. He fired a driver because he wouldn't drive down a one-way street," Owens said. "How about murdering one of his girlfriends because he didn't like that she was on social media?"

"Why don't you arrest him?" Sebastian asked.

"Ha, arrest him? We haven't even questioned him on anything. It's like we don't have the elevator key to get to his floor. It's called being above the law. Shit, he was born above the damn law."

"Let me talk to him," Sebastian said.

Owens gave a mocking laugh at this.

"This guy isn't like you and me. It's like he travels around in secret passages or something. From his car to a protected garage, to a private elevator, to a secured floor at his headquarters. Flies on a private jet. Helicopters to rooftops. He has security like the president, and his schedule is a lot more private. We can't get near him, and even if we could, his lawyers would tie us up like calves at a rodeo."

"I'd like to tie a noose around his neck," Sebastian said.

"Take a number."

They both took a pull from their beers. Sebastian took an appreciative look around the pub.

"Nice place. This your spot?"

"I come here enough. Sometimes not enough. It's quiet, except when it isn't—they have Premier League football matches sometimes. I like it both ways, depending."

It was quiet now.

"I just want you to know I'm in this with you now. You can see it as one of those 'the enemy of my enemy is my friend' situations."

"You're not my enemy, Sebastian. As a cop, I don't have enemies," Owens said, not entirely believing what she said.

"This guy wants to kill you…"

Owens cut him off.

"Oh, that motherfucker? He's definitely my enemy. It's not even about me being a cop or dealing with the law. He's crossed so many lines at this point he's more of an enemy to the people of this city than anyone in Iraq I was ordered to kill. Shit, I even respected many of them. We were in their damn country. This guy thinks this country belongs to him."

She told him the story of how she cracked McMillan's skull when she was on patrol responding to the abuse call.

"I did as I was told, dropped the charges against him, and he still comes after me, to this day. I want to tell him to move on with his life, but mostly I just want to be alone with him for about thirty minutes, make him talk, make him fess up to everything he's ever done, everyone he's ever killed or had killed."

"You know as well as I people like McMillan almost never go to jail, right? Meanwhile, my best friend is serving time for punching a cop who threw his girlfriend down some stairs at a club."

Malcolm Z, a.k.a. Malcolm Arnette. Owens had checked up on Malcolm, but there was nothing in the police report about the cop throwing Malcolm's girlfriend down a flight of stairs. She didn't doubt Sebastian's account, and nothing involving the corruption of the Philadelphia Police Department could surprise her at this point in her career.

"As I told you before, Malcolm's a criminal, but they could never pin anything on him. Like McMillan. So why can't they throw McMillan down some stairs to provoke him like they did to my friend?"

It was a good question and one that wasn't going to be answered over microbrew ales in a Philadelphia Center City pub.

"My academic advisor at Temple calls it the financial curtain, the wall people like McMillan hide behind while they do whatever the fuck they want. Their money is every bit as effective as the castle walls protecting their ancestors from the wrath of their enemies. They still have plenty of physical walls to protect them, but it's mostly about their wealth which buys power...and stops the police dead in their tracks."

"Money worked for OJ," Sebastian said, before reconsidering. "At least it did until it stopped working for him."

"I work in the Domestic Violence Unit, so excuse me if I don't get excited about raising that wife-murdering bastard up as a standard to bear, but I get your point."

Sebastian paused a moment to reset the conversation.

"I just came here to tell you if there's anything I can do to help you in anything regarding James Hawthorne McMillan…"

"His middle name is Hawthorne?" Owens asked, shaking her head in disbelief.

"I guess that's to sound more English to make up for his Scottish surname."

"White people have some weird issues," Owens said.

"Yeah, they do," Sebastian said. "I just wanted you to know not to hesitate if there's anything I can do."

Owens would have been less impressed with this offer before she was told a couple of gangbanger kids working for Sebastian had been surveilling her and she hadn't picked up on it. Of course, she couldn't help thinking if Sebastian's people hadn't assassinated Logan while he was in lockup, she might've had a real case against McMillan. It reminded her of the complicated military alliances the U.S. Army had forged in Iraq. She only hoped this one with Sebastian would end more favorably than the U.S. Army in the war she fought.

"I'm sorry, but I wish there was something the police could do to help your mother. What kind of man would do something like that?"

Owens had a pretty good idea of what kind of man McMillan was and decided he wasn't much of a man at all. At least the Mujahideen and jihadists she fought in Iraq believed in something, even if she thought it was hateful and completely misguided. McMillan only stood for himself.

Sebastian had his own motives in his anger toward McMillan, but his offer of assistance was more than her own police department gave after she reported the threat. At this point, she didn't know if the PPD was afraid to act on her allegations for fear of bringing down the legal wrath of one of the country's wealthiest men, or if McMillan's influence in the department was deep enough to completely extinguish the complaint.

There was also a strong probability McMillan had abandoned the idea of having a cop killed. While Owens found this to be very likely, she knew it would be foolish to accept the idea. She knew what it was like to live with a constant threat of death. Her entire time in Iraq was one of vigilance bordering on paranoia.

The difference was in Iraq, she was absolutely certain of the constant danger. Not a day went by without some sort of incident which was part of the daily briefing to the MP brigade, as if any of them needed a reminder of the perilous nature of their deployment. Most of the casualties were the result of IEDs or sniper fire, with very few soldiers killed or injured in direct combat, at least during her time in country.

Owens kept changing her routine daily, walking and biking in different directions to get to work and to her gym. Her Achilles' heel was her apartment in a not-very-secure building. A key was needed to get in the front door but that was really no obstacle, even for the people passing out pizza flyers and restaurant coupons who just kept ringing doorbells at the entrance until someone buzzed them into the lobby. There were too many units in the building for a stranger to stand out, and she rarely ran into any of her neighbors to have much of a relationship with most of them.

She bought a motion-detector alarm she put in the big area of the apartment which included the kitchen, dining room, and living room. The more she considered the problem she discussed with Batista, Gottlieb, and Dr. O'Neill, the more she felt she was safe in her apartment. It would be a risky move to attack her at home with a high probability of failure, as Logan had discovered the hard way at Batista's apartment.

When it finally happened a few weeks later, it was just how Owens had been describing the plan for the perfect crime for anyone who was willing to listen.

"If you want to kill someone and get away with it, just run the motherfucker over in your car. Those people never go to jail. Ever. Unless they're drunk or high, they walk."

Philly's homicide rate had been a total disgrace for years. The vast majority of these murders were young Black men killing each other, most related in some way to the drug trade. The city had twenty-four pedestrian deaths the same year, and the number of cyclist deaths had more than doubled over the previous year. If you weren't a young Black man involved in the drug trade, the city was considerably safer. For Whites, Philadelphia's murder rate was about the same as Portland, Oregon. However, deaths involving pedestrians and cyclists crossed all racial and economic barriers.

Owens had a couple of bikes in her stable. Her pride and joy was a cyclo-cross bike she loved for its stability. It was slower than a racing bike, but infinitely sturdier on the rough pavements and cobblestone streets of Philadelphia, and could also handle the gravel roads and dirt paths she encountered in her excursions on the Wissahickon Bike Path, and trails farther outside the city.

For her day-to-day riding and commuting to work, she had a single-speed bike she had custom built from parts she provided, including an indestructible aluminum frame, disc brakes, and a rack for her custom-made leather saddle bags. The bike was sound but purposely looked like hell to limit its appeal to thieves. It was her workhorse.

This was what she had beneath her as she was cruising to work on Fifteenth Street when she heard a car accelerating behind her. She instinctively moved as far to the right as she could along the line of parked cars. The driver had plenty of room to maneuver around her as traffic was lighter at this off-peak hour, and she was in the bike lane, although it was just a line of paint and wasn't protected by a barrier. Owens noticed someone in a parked car ahead of her who looked about to open his door, then she saw him check his side mirror. Not everyone in Philadelphia was out to kill cyclists, she thought.

She threw a quick glance over her left shoulder and saw the car behind her coming up quickly, too quickly and too close. She pedaled harder and passed the guy about to open his door. He was parked two cars from the intersection. Just as she rolled past his car, she heard an explosion behind as her pursuer ripped the door off the car just as the driver opened it.

Owens braked hard and turned even harder to her right just in front of the car parked at the intersection. The car behind her side-swiped it, moving it forward just enough to bump Owens off her bike. She'd come to a complete stop a split-second before, and her fall was just a matter of tipping over.

She picked herself up immediately, but by this time the car was speeding away down Fifteenth Street.

Even the stunned pedestrians at the intersection could see this was an attempted homicide. Owens identified herself as a police officer and asked if anyone could contribute to what she recalled about the incident, which amounted to almost nothing beyond the fact it was a dark blue sedan. She checked on the driver who lost his door. He was speechless but unharmed. No one knew anything more about the car or the driver, not even a single digit of the plate or the gender or race of the driver.

Owens was on the scene for forty-five minutes talking with other cops responding to the call. She took her own photos of the two damaged vehicles before finally riding the rest of the way to the district. There wasn't much to be gained on the investigation into the hit-and-run. Whoever did it had probably already left the car—obviously stolen—in a pay lot where it wouldn't be noticed for a week, perhaps longer. She knew any effort in that investigation was a total waste of resources.

There was no question this was a direct attempt on her life, something she immediately sent up the chain of command. It would be impossible for the department to ignore her claim, but there was still nothing linking McMillan except the word of a criminal who wouldn't give an official statement.

"So, after coming about one bike length from getting mowed down today, I'm still at square one with McMillan," Owens said to Batista.

They were in the unit office along with Noah Gottlieb who'd come by after she phoned him earlier. She showed the two her photos from the crash. Batista was nonplussed, but Gottlieb was horrified.

"How are you still alive?" Gottlieb asked.

"I got lucky, this time."

"At least we know Sebastian was telling the truth," Gottlieb said.

"I was sure before," Owens said. "He had no reason to lie about it."

Done with showing the photos, Owens put her phone away.

"I'd give anything just to have him in an interrogation room, just to talk," Batista said.

"McMillan'll never talk to the police," Gottlieb said.

"Talk to him? I've never even fucking *seen* the guy before, and he had a thug break into my house, not to mention he just attempted to kill my partner," Batista said. "It's like we're up against the invisible man."

"If he were anyone else, we could just go to his damn house and knock on the door. He wouldn't have to talk, or even answer the door, but he'd at least see us, and his neighbors would see us. I don't even know where he lives, not with any degree of certainty, but wherever it is, I'm sure it has a wall around it, or a secure entrance with a guard or two in the lobby, and then a private elevator," Owens said.

Owens had run headfirst, once again, into the financial curtain.

# CHAPTER 22 – POLICING

The following morning, Owens had a meeting with the Deputy Commissioner of Investigations during which she was told exactly what she was expecting but didn't want to hear. That the department was doing everything in its power to find the individual or individuals responsible for the egregious hit-and-run incident where, thankfully, there were no injuries. She was told she had the full support of the department, that she'd have a patrol car passing regularly by her apartment, and if she needed absolutely anything, she shouldn't hesitate to call.

She asked the officer wearing a full dress blue uniform if they were pursuing James McMillan as a suspect.

"Did you see him behind the wheel?" the Deputy Commissioner of Investigations asked with a straight face.

"Motherfucking Deputy Commissioner actually asked me," she relayed to Batista after the meeting when they met to drive to the home of a recent domestic abuse victim. "Told me there was absolutely no proof to implicate McMillan in the crime, how he's a pillar of the community…"

"Did he really say, 'pillar of the community'?" Batista asked.

"No, but something equally insipid. I couldn't tell if he was being prudent, or if he's stupid, or he's on McMillan's payroll."

"Could be all three," Batista said.

Batista pulled the unmarked car up on the sidewalk in front of a shabby duplex.

"Another day, another shithole," he said as they walked up the two stairs of the stoop and knocked.

There was definitely a *déjà vu* element to their police work, especially in the Domestic Violence Unit, and especially in the poorer neighborhoods of the city that looked strikingly similar. Most of the city was made up of two and sometimes three-story row houses. Owens had grown up in places just like this. She remembered six different apartments in her childhood and every place was as ugly and hopeless as this block. Her question wasn't why would anyone choose to live here, but why would anyone build a city like this? She had trouble believing these areas of the city were ever decent places to live.

Upon returning to the city after her military service, as soon as she could afford it, she moved to Center City where she could walk or ride her bike everywhere. Most of these towering urban neighborhoods were pedestrian-unfriendly, to put it mildly. The poor woman Owens and Batista were seeing now probably had to drive a mile to go to a supermarket. Owens had two within three blocks of her place.

She looked along the street and saw lines of automobiles on both sides of the street, cars none of these people could afford, two lines of dormant heaps of metal serving absolutely no purpose during most of the day except to make the city even uglier.

A car cruised down the street, and she could hear the beats from the sound system a good half a block behind her. She instinctively turned and put her hand at her side where her weapon was holstered on her hip. Relax, she thought, if they're coming for you, you won't hear them from half a football field away. Batista was on the same page of paranoia at this point in the game. He'd jumped down off the two-step stoop and had his hand on his service weapon.

"Chill, dude," Owens said, exasperated.

The car drove past.

"Better safe, and all that," Batista said.

Just then, the door opened and another tall, fat, shirtless man stood facing Owens.

"What the fuck you want, bitch?"

It was all Owens could do to keep herself from grabbing the slob by the waist of his filthy cargo shorts and pulling him down the stairs, but she was on her best behavior, a direct order from the Commissioner. He told her she needed to be squeaky clean—his exact words—if the department had any chance of pursuing James McMillan in an investigation. The smallest policy infraction on her part would give his lawyers more than they needed to dismiss any accusations.

She had to play nice.

Batista didn't.

He was still on the sidewalk and to the right, out of view from the doorway. He jumped up the stairs and walked into the house, standing with his face so close the fat slob could feel his breath.

"That 'bitch' is a Philadelphia Police Department detective here to take a statement about some wife-beating piece of shit. You the wife-beating cocksucker?"

The fat slob was too stunned to answer.

"I said, you the wife-beating shitbag bringing us here on this fine evening?"

271

Owens backed up a step. She wanted to give Batista room to work. His tough guy portrayal was worthy of Shakespeare.

The fat slob followed the old adage that the better part of valor is caving in completely. Batista backed him into the living room and motioned for him to have a seat on the sofa.

"Silvia Purcell," Batista shouted. "We need you in here, please."

Owens remained outside looking in, too entertained by Batista's performance to interrupt.

Silvia walked timidly into the living room and sat next to her husband on the sofa.

"I called you a wife-beating shitbag before, but can I call you by your given name?"

The fat slob nodded meekly.

"My name's George."

"George, do you know how many times your wife's called for help in this disaster of a marriage?"

George shook his head.

"Twenty-three times. Twenty-three. This means the Philadelphia Police Department has been obligated to respond to this address twenty-three times because you're a fucking violent, wife-beating piece of shit."

The wife-beater sat in silence.

"You think Philly cops got nothing better to do than to clean up after your fat, pathetic ass?"

George was about to respond when he was abruptly cut off.

"No, the answer is a resounding 'we definitely have better fucking things to do,' lots of better things."

Owens moved into the living room but stood against a wall.

"Do you know what happens when your wife makes her twenty-seventh call to the police?"

No answer.

"That's the last call. That's when we just come over and split your skull open with a nightstick and say you had a knife, or whatever we need to say."

Batista definitely had George's full attention.

"We don't take you to the station. No, that's when the ambulance crew works on you desperately as they speed to the emergency room."

Batista squatted down and looked the wife-beater directly in the eyes.

"You think this violates your rights, George? Sorry, after twenty-seven calls you'll have used up all your rights."

Batista stood up.

"Got it, George?"

George nodded. He got it. For now, at least.

"You ever want to see me again, George?"

George shook his head.

"I need you to say it, George."

George stammered a bit.

"I never want to see you again, officer."

"It's Detective Batista," Batista said.

"Detective Batista," George repeated. "I never want to see you again, Detective Batista."

As the two cops got into their car, Owens burst into laughter.

"And scene. Cut," Owens said. "Brilliant performance."

"File that under bad cop."

"You definitely nail that role," Owens said. "Your 'good cop' could use some work."

Owens drove back to the district.

"I wanted to kick him in his fat gut," Owens said, her anger pouring into her words.

"You have to wonder how many times he's punched her around. I'm beginning to lose my patience with guys like George. If we have to go back here, my 'bad cop' routine won't be an act."

Batista sat back in his seat as they cruised slowly down the depressing street, past decaying townhomes and boarded up businesses, another of Philadelphia's forgotten neighborhoods.

"I need a new job," he said. "Definitely a transfer out of this unit. I'm taking this shit too personally."

Owens just let out a sigh in agreement.

"I just wish we could pull the same thing you just pulled on McMillan. I want to push him until he's scared shitless, like George was just now."

"George doesn't have a team of lawyers walking point for him," Batista said.

"Why can't we talk to McMillan when he's alone, no lawyers, no bodyguards, and no financial curtain to shield him. I want to see him as afraid as those girls were before he murdered them."

"At this point, I'd walk into his office and pistol-whip him, if I knew where his office was, if he even has an office. We don't have a work address, home address, or phone number. Let's face it, we're shitty detectives," Batista said.

***

She hated the fact James insisted on having a maid clean her apartment five days a week. She would've welcomed the work, as she had trouble keeping herself busy with no job and very few friends in Philadelphia. She was lucky to see him once a week, and he was in a foul mood most of the time. He hardly ever took her anywhere, not even to a restaurant. The sex was OK when they had it. She'd only been with three other guys in her life, and one was her long-time boyfriend from high school until she decided she couldn't live in Lima, Kentucky, for another second.

She begged Nate to come with her. Her girlfriends said he was more afraid of leaving Kentucky than he was of losing her. After she moved to Philadelphia, he never called and never answered his phone when she reached out to him. She hooked up with two guys she worked with at the restaurant, but they were both losers more interested in smoking weed than doing anything else, and they were broke as hell.

James was old, but she thought he was totally hot the first time she saw him. He was a total gentleman, at least at first. He made her feel important. How could she not feel important when this super-rich businessman was interested in her? The two pretty-boy stoners she dated from the restaurant always acted like they were doing her a favor by going out with her.

Her manager introduced them one night at the bar as the restaurant was closing. James asked her to go out for a drink after work. She was embarrassed because he was wearing a beautiful dark suit and she only had jeans and a t-shirt to change into after she clocked out. He told her she looked "stunning."

The rest was history, as they say. She'd heard that before and it described everything that had ever happened since the beginning of time. She decided it was a stupid saying and she'd never use it again. Caroline was an intelligent young woman who'd simply gotten off to a slow start in life. She came from a broken home, had a mother who was a complete loser, who'd never read to her, had never helped her with homework, and had never asked, "How was school today?"

Caroline didn't want children of her own, but if she ever had kids, she'd hound them about what they did in school. She'd show an interest in their well-being. She'd read to them at night and encourage them to read.

Caroline had no interest in being a prostitute, but there was no other way to describe her current situation. It seemed exciting at first that this insanely successful man was attracted to her. He was impressed by her intelligence, or so she thought, at least at first. He said he had an empty apartment where she could live rent-free, something about the owner of the penthouse spending a year in Dubai on business. She never thought of herself as materialistic, and she definitely wasn't a gold digger, but the apartment took the air out of her lungs when James brought her there for the first time. It was late at night on a perfect early summer evening, and she could see the whole city below her. It was like something out of a movie.

She soon experienced his horrible temper. The slightest disagreement would throw him into a paroxysm of rage that terrified her. She never knew what would send him into one of these fits. It was like walking in a minefield. She could see he got excited by her fear of him.

They never talked about anything concerning his personal life. She knew he was married, or at least she assumed he was. There was never any mention of a family. She was just trying to get by and have a little fun. She had fun, at least in the beginning. Then he started hitting her.

The violent episodes had only begun a month earlier, after they'd been together three months. She couldn't even remember what they were talking about, it wasn't even an argument. She'd said something and James had slapped her violently across the face, knocking her off her feet. She was terrified and furious at the same time. This was at her apartment, where they spent almost all of their time together. After he hit her, he left without a word, leaving her sprawled out on the floor bleeding at the mouth.

The next time they met, there was no mention of the incident, no apology, no explanation, no bouquet of flowers. Her loser deadbeat father had abused her mother, something Caroline blamed her mother for as a child—a typical response for victims. As she grew older, she began to harbor fantasies of murdering her father for what he did to her mother and to his children. She had no respect for her mother, but she stopped blaming her for her father's violence against them. She wasn't comfortable in the role of victim and vowed she'd never be like her mother.

She was getting a quick education and wasn't about to blame herself for the behavior of this rich asshole. She wanted to hurt him, to strike back with everything she had. She knew she needed to be patient.

Women always needed to be patient; they needed to watch for their moment. Their aggression usually had to be masked, a feint, like Owens targeting the feet in her judo moves when the opponent was slightly off-balance. Find the weakest point and strike with precision and surprise.

Caroline was living like one of the richest women in the city, yet she had very little money of her own. James paid for everything, and she had a credit card he'd given her, but he monitored it carefully. She wasn't working and relied on her lover for cash, but he kept her on a short financial leash. She'd always been good with money and still had quite a bit in her savings account she earned before moving into the penthouse. She started buying clothes for two of her girlfriends and taking cash from them—James wouldn't argue about clothing purchases, no matter how ridiculously expensive she found them to be. She needed to be ready to go if things with James got intolerable. She knew there was no future in the relationship, but she wanted to leave when it best suited her needs.

She'd already sold her crappy car because he didn't want her to be seen in it. He replaced it with a luxury sedan he leased through one of his corporate shell companies. If it came down to it, she could skip town in the leased car, drive it for a while, and then simply leave it somewhere. She had two large suitcases packed with new clothes which she kept in a small storage unit, just in case he decided to lock her out of the apartment. She could already see he was the type of man who'd do something sinister for no reason, more sinister than hitting her.

There was another incident with James after she complained they never went anywhere. This time he didn't strike her, but he was screaming at the top of his lungs. She kept her cool and played the part of the cowering handmaiden, bursting into tears and begging his forgiveness. He was thoroughly turned on by this role.

Jesus, what a total fucking creep, she thought.

A week later there was another violent incident over nothing at all, or at least in her opinion. She was going to leave him soon, but she wanted to injure him in some way. She considered trashing the apartment and crashing the rental car, but she knew this would mean nothing to him. He'd just have someone else clean up the mess and find another young girl to abuse. There was no way she could hurt him financially.

The next morning, as was her routine over coffee, she read the entire *Philadelphia Inquirer*. She loved living in a city with a real newspaper. There was a story about a police detective who'd nearly been run down in a hit-and-run incident on her bike. The photo of the damaged car was terrifying, and the young detective looked like a superhero, all muscles and beauty in the photograph of her next to the ruined vehicle. How had she managed to survive? The article gave her name and reported she worked in the Domestic Violence Unit. It was like some sort of divine message, a revelation.

Caroline made the call to the police department from a coffee shop near her apartment. It took almost thirty minutes for the call to connect her to Detective Elizabeth Owens.

"Hi, Detective Owens," Caroline said, giving her name.

279

"How can I help you?" Owens asked.

"I'm in an abusive relationship and I want him to pay for hurting me."

"Testify against him and we can put him away, at least for a bit."

The young woman hesitated.

"You there, Caroline?"

"The problem is he's really rich and powerful. I'm afraid of him."

"No one's above the law, Caroline."

Another pause from the young woman.

"I think he really is above the law. Ever heard of James McMillan?"

# CHAPTER 23 – JAMES HAWTHORNE MCMILLAN (1958 – 2020)

Caroline picked up Owens a few blocks away from their precinct district. Batista followed in a white panel van. Owens wanted to do a final bit of coaching with her new accomplice. The two vehicles drove into the basement parking garage of Caroline's building. Owens was on the floor as they passed through the entrance with two video cameras. Batista wore a ball cap and sunglasses.

Caroline parked and Batista pulled beside her car in one of her assigned spaces. She had three.

"Who the hell can afford three parking spots in Philly? Three!"

Batista was continually dumbfounded by the ways of the rich.

A box strapped down with bungee cords on top of the van blocked Caroline's car from the video camera in this corner of the garage. The plates on the van were stolen from a similar van. Batista got out and joined Owens in the camera blind spot. Caroline stood by the trunk of her car while the two police officers moved behind a load-supporting concrete pillar.

McMillan was scheduled to meet Caroline in five minutes.

There was the outside possibility McMillan wouldn't be alone, he could have a bodyguard with him, although according to Caroline, he never came by to see her with an escort. If he did have someone with him, they'd just deal with it, even if it had to get ugly right from the start…or they'd call it off.

Caroline had two bags in the trunk she'd use as props when McMillan pulled in. She texted McMillan that she'd run a little late on her shopping trip to explain why she'd be in the garage when he arrived.

Owens saw the sedan coming down the ramp.

"Go," she said, giving the word it was on.

McMillan pulled into the spot next to Caroline as she lifted the bags out of her trunk. He got out of his car and closed the door.

"I just got here," Caroline said calmly.

The girl was a natural, Owens thought, she'd make a great cop.

McMillan walked up to the young woman and kissed her cheek, making no effort to help her with the bags or even to close the trunk.

Owens and Batista walked out from behind the pillar, both in a mild form of disguise: hats, glasses and baggy clothes that didn't give away body types. McMillan looked at them without being startled or even surprised. This was his building, and he knew security was very good. He didn't recognize the couple.

"James McMillan," Owens said. "You're under arrest for the murder of Rhonda Perry. Place your hands behind your back."

Now they definitely had the man's full attention. He was surprised and frightened, at least initially. He soon recovered the arrogance he felt was his birthright.

"Ridiculous," he began. "You have no right to…"

Owens punched him about as hard as she could in the stomach. McMillan doubled over.

"Put your fucking hands behind your back," Owens said as she grabbed his right wrist and twisted his arm around his back.

McMillan gave a weak attempt at resisting. Batista hammered him again, deflating the older man completely. Owens cuffed his hands behind his back, then reached into his pocket and took his car keys and phone. She gave these to Caroline who then drove away in McMillan's sedan. Owens shoved her prisoner into the cargo door of the panel van while Batista jumped behind the wheel. Owens closed the door, and they pulled out of the parking spot.

Owens put a nylon zip-tie around McMillan's neck and cinched it down so it was just pressing on his skin.

"I'm right behind you as we drive out of here. You make any noise at all, and I pull on this tie. You won't be able to make noise, and you'll suffocate in a few seconds. Nod if you understand."

He nodded. Batista drove out of the building.

Owens knew if Caroline were stopped driving McMillan's car by the police for any reason, she could tell them the truth, she was his girlfriend. She was young and very beautiful, and White, which meant she was unlikely to be pulled over in Philadelphia.

She'd leave the sedan in Sebastian's territory where one of his people would "steal" it and abuse it like a rented mule until they got bored. Then they'd take it to New York and leave it for some other gangbangers to play with. The best scenario was the car was never recovered, but it didn't matter much what happened to it; there'd be no evidence linking those responsible for the theft.

Caroline thought she'd try California for a while, or maybe Seattle. She'd travel by bus, the most anonymous way to travel if you chose public transportation. She'd made quite a tidy sum as McMillan's mistress, at least enough to live for a year or even longer. She'd always been frugal by necessity, and she'd never found herself too broke not to save money somehow.

283

There was absolutely nothing linking her to McMillan. Nothing was in her name and few people had even seen the two of them together. McMillan's desire to date young, completely anonymous women was now working in her favor and against his. Her fingerprints weren't on record. She was coached by Owens to remove as much physical evidence as possible of her stay in the apartment. Days earlier, she'd thrown out everything in the apartment implicating her through DNA and wiped down every single surface for fingerprints. She doubted McMillan bothered to learn her last name.

Of course, her DNA profile wasn't on record either, but Owens just wanted to be thorough. Even if investigators tracked her down somehow in a week or a month, she'd have nothing to tell them. Gottlieb had coached her on what to say to the police if they came asking questions. It was a simple bit of advice: keep your mouth shut and ask for a lawyer. Ask for Noah Gottlieb. She had his number.

Batista pulled into a large commercial garage of a car detailing service, closed on this day. They switched plates once again on the white panel van, then pulled out again, Batista still at the wheel. Owens covered their prisoner with a canvas drop cloth.

Batista drove carefully, blaring salsa music from a local station. At one point, McMillan had said he needed to urinate. He was ignored.

The only other words spoken in the car during the drive were when they came to a final stop and Owens discovered McMillan had pissed himself.

"Don't worry, James. That's the least of your fucking problems."

They drove inside a large commercial space, some sort of garage or warehouse. It was a big open area with a wooden workbench running along the back wall. A row of windows ran around the space, but they were three meters off the ground reaching the roof. They let in plenty of light, but they couldn't be broken accidentally by an errant machinist's tool or a piece of lumber shooting off of a lathe. They were also high enough they didn't allow anyone outside to see inside unless they were standing on a ladder.

Owens and Batista hauled McMillan out of the van and sat him down on a wood armchair like from an old schoolhouse. They cinched his arms and feet to the chair with more nylon zip ties. Owens removed the zip tie from around his neck, then held a bottle of water to his mouth and told him to drink.

"Get comfortable; this is gonna to take a while," she said.

She pulled up a chair and sat directly in front of the prisoner.

"Do you even know who I am?" Owens asked.

"You're the cop," he answered.

"The cop you punched in the face; the cop you paid someone to kill…"

"I didn't do that…"

Owens stood up and slapped him violently across the face.

"Let me explain the rules for what's going on here today. You just lied to me. If you want to make it out of here alive, you won't lie to me again. If I ask you a question, you need to understand if you lie to me, this morning is going to be the last time you'll ever wake up. There won't be a tomorrow for you. Got it?"

McMillan didn't respond.

"Do you understand what I just said?"

McMillan remained silent.

She struck him in the stomach.

"I understand," McMillan whimpered.

Owens sat back down in her chair.

"It looked like your man Logan—your ex-man Logan—didn't do a very good job vetting your new possession. Caroline is what we call a warrior; she's got spirit. I hope you enjoyed the few times you slapped her around, because she really seemed to enjoy handing you over to me gift-wrapped."

"You're going to spend the rest of your fucking lives in prison. You know that, right?" McMillan said.

McMillan was starting to feel hopeful for the first time in the abduction. He figured if they wanted him dead, he wouldn't have made it this far.

Owens laughed a bit at this remark.

"I'm glad you're concerned for my future, but, as I said earlier, you got bigger problems, much bigger."

Batista placed two more chairs facing McMillan, a couple of arms-lengths away. Owens moved her chair back to line up with the other two.

A few moments later, two hooded people were led into the garage by Sebastian. He put them on chairs in front of McMillan and removed their hoods to reveal Noah Gottlieb and Dr. O'Neill. Both of them were impeccably dressed, as if they were attending an important business meeting.

Or a trial.

The hearing had begun.

Owens stood up.

"Allow me to introduce everyone. This is James Hawthorne McMillan, real estate multi-millionaire and someone I believe is responsible for murdering at least three women."

She motioned toward Gottlieb and O'Neill.

"This is Noah Gottlieb, attorney at law, who'll be representing Mr. McMillan on this day. And this is Doctor Madeleine O'Neill, sociologist, and renowned author on domestic violence issues. She's serving as the prosecutor in this procedure. They are both here against their will."

Gottlieb thought the charade unnecessary, but Owens insisted, saying it was for their protection in case it came down to an investigation.

McMillan looked at Gottlieb.

"What the fuck is this?" McMillan demanded.

"What is this? This is the opposite of a normal criminal court procedure. Instead of proving your innocence, you need to prove, beyond a shadow of a doubt, your guilt."

"What the fuck does that mean?"

McMillan's contempt was audible. He was feeling hope once again, with some of his usual arrogance returning.

"It means I've already condemned you to death. You deserve to die. I can do that right now. I can end your life right here," Owens said.

McMillan's arrogance faded quickly back into terror.

"I need you to implicate yourself so deeply in your many crimes that even the sorriest prosecutor in the Philly D.A. office could put you away for life. I need you to admit to every crime you've ever committed, in front of these people who are here against their will. If you don't, this shitty garage or whatever the fuck it is, will be the last place you'll ever see in your miserable life."

She looked him in the eye.

"Tell me, James. Do you want to die here?" she asked. "The truth is I don't much give a fuck. You tried to kill me, and you failed. Now it's my turn. I think you'd admit I've got a much stronger hand than you did when you had some lowlife try to run me down on my bike."

"I don't know what you're..." he started to say and stopped, remembering the rules.

Owens stepped directly in front of him.

"I don't think you understand what's going on here. I've already condemned you to die. I know the horrible things you've done; I just can't prove anything. You need to give me the proof so we can convict you in a court of law, put you away for a long time. You don't give me a case against you right now, your sentence will be served here today."

Dr. O'Neill raised her hand to speak.

"Mr. McMillan, she needs proof of your crimes in addition to your confessions, which won't be admissible in court since..."

She looked around at the garage.

"Since you're giving your testimony under duress," she finished.

"I'm not giving anything. You're all guilty of kidnapping and assault."

Owens cut him off.

"These two are here against their will," she said, pointing to Gottlieb and O'Neill.

"But we're not here to talk about our crimes. You're the star of this show if you haven't figured it out already," Batista said.

"Let's start with an easy one. Tell us what happened to Rhonda Perry," Owens said.

"Who?" was McMillan's answer.

Batista stood up and picked up a hefty framing hammer from a workbench along with a few nails.

"You tell me another lie and I'm going to start pounding nails into your knee," Batista said, raising the hammer in his right hand and the nails in his left.

"Now tell me what the fuck happened to Rhonda Perry. We know she lived at the same apartment where you had the other girl, the time I split your skull open."

McMillan didn't say anything.

Batista walked over and looked McMillan in the eye, then knelt in front of him and positioned the sharp end of one of the nails on the top of McMillan's knee.

"What happened to her, James. You're going to tell us, sooner or later, so you may as well save yourself a very painful injury," Batista said.

"Not answering is the same as lying here, McMillan. What happened to Rhonda Perry?" Owens asked again.

Batista raised the hammer.

"I swear I don't know. Logan handled the situation."

"What situation?" O'Neill asked.

"I beat her up pretty bad one night. I told Logan to take care of it."

"What does that mean?" O'Neill asked.

"I told him to make her disappear."

"So, you paid this man to kill Rhonda Perry and dispose of the body?" Gottlieb asked.

"Yes."

"Where is she?"

"I don't know. Logan didn't tell me, and I didn't want to know."

"You're getting the hang of this, James. You do know Pennsylvania has the death penalty, right? We haven't executed anyone since 1999, but they'll put you in the front of the line for a murder for hire," Owens said.

"The problem is there's no proof, only his word. Logan's dead, there's no body, so you have nothing," Gottlieb said.

"The way this works, James, is you gotta give us something that'll condemn you in court. If not, you don't leave this place," Owens said.

"I don't know what I can give you," McMillan said.

"Then you'd better start thinking real hard," Batista said.

"Let's go way back, to the girl you killed in high school, the maid. You didn't have a Logan back then to clean up after you. Tell us about that one," Owens said.

McMillan sat in silence.

"You have to be incredibly specific, Mr. McMillan. We need an exact location of where you put the body, and how you killed her. We have people on stand-by to check out any information you give us," Gottlieb said.

This was an idle threat as they weren't prepared to investigate McMillan's confessions. They knew it would be difficult, if not impossible, to fact-check anything McMillan said in his current state of duress. Owens was capable of torturing McMillan simply because he deserved it, but she'd seen first-hand in Iraq torture was a terrible way to get people to talk. Once you started to inflict pain, people would say absolutely anything to make it stop. McMillan would confess to the JFK assassination if they drove a nail into his knee.

What they wanted was for McMillan to think they were going to drive nails into his body. Neither of the cops were comfortable with even slapping McMillan while he was bound to the chair, preferring to meet him face-to-face. He wouldn't have survived one minute if Batista came at him, and he'd already come close to dying when Owens slammed his head into the door frame in their first encounter. This was all a show to thoroughly intimidate their prisoner with the

291

double threats of torture if he lied, and death if he didn't completely implicate himself in his many crimes.

Police interrogations were conducted under completely different circumstances, obviously, but they usually had the luxury of time with a suspect in lockup, and although they couldn't threaten a prisoner with physical abuse, they could force confessions by promising to shave years off of prison sentences. They didn't have enough on McMillan to arrest him at this point, but they had an incredibly strong hand to play if he thought he'd be murdered here for not cooperating.

"I didn't kill anyone when I was in high school. I've never killed anyone."

McMillan was getting his second wind of courage.

Owens shot up from her chair.

"Cut this motherfucker loose," she said to Batista.

He cut the nylon ties. McMillan remained seated.

"Stand the fuck up, mother fucker," she shouted.

McMillan looked away from her.

"I said stand the fuck up!"

She grabbed him by his hair and pulled him out of the chair.

"You like to hurt women? Hurt me, tough guy. Fuck me He wouldn't tolerate the smallest act of insubordination among his employees like you did to Rhonda and Caroline and who the fuck knows how many other women."

McMillan stood in front of her with his hands at his sides.

Owens punched him viciously in the stomach two times. He started to bend over at the waist. She kneed him in the face.

"Fight, asshole. Show me how you beat the hell out of Rhonda and Tanya Jenkins."

He didn't defend himself and held his bleeding nose with both hands.

"And Caroline? Boy, did you ever pick the wrong woman to fuck with. That girl has a real hard-on for you. Seems she doesn't like having a total piece of shit like you slap her around."

McMillan started to respond, then reconsidered.

"Do I really need to explain this to you again? Either confess to your crimes or we kill you right here in this shitty garage. That how you wanna go out?"

McMillan straightened up after gasping with his hands on his knees.

Owens stepped up and struck him again in the stomach sending him to his knees on the filthy concrete floor. She pulled him up by the collar and sat him back in his chair, tying him down again, this time cinching the nylon ties to where they were at the point of cutting off circulation.

"Like I said, either talk your way out of this or die right here, James."

McMillan seemed to think it was all a bluff and remained silent.

"Maybe this will convince you to cooperate," Batista said.

Batista and Sebastian picked up the prisoner bound securely to the wood chair and carried him outside. The truck with the tree shredder was parked a few steps away from the door beside a pile of tree limbs. There was a platform made of stacked pallets in front of the shredder device. They hoisted McMillan up on the platform facing over the mouth of the shredder.

Owens escorted Gottlieb and Dr. O'Neill outside.

Batista fired up the machine.

Sebastian tipped the chair forward to illustrate to the prisoner he'd fall directly into the maw. Batista fed a tree limb into the machine. The noise was deafening, exponentially louder than the machine itself.

Batista shut off the shredder.

"Are you getting this, James?" Owens asked. "We aren't fucking around, not even a little."

"You need to confess your sins, James McMillan. Tell us in great detail what you've done or the next time I turn on this horrible machine, you're going in it," Batista said.

"You can't do this. I have rights."

Owens laughed at this.

"Motherfucker, you need to come clean or you're going into this tree shredder," Owens said.

"Give us enough information to convict you in court, and they won't kill you. They've given me their word," Dr. O'Neill said.

"Take your chances in court, James," Gottlieb said. "Otherwise, you'll never make it out of here. I'm afraid for my safety, but you're in much deeper shit."

McMillan sat in defiance.

"Whatever you say here can't be used in court. None of it would be admissible," Gottlieb continued. "I'm convinced they'll kill you if you don't confess."

"Fuck this," Batista said.

He turned the shredder on again, then stood up on the pallets and tipped the chair forward with McMillan leaning just over the machine. If Batista released his grip on the back of the chair, McMilliam would've fallen into the maw.

"Stop!" he screamed out, begging for mercy.

The shredder wound down.

"Ready to talk?"

McMillan nodded.

"Here's how it plays out. You stop talking, you don't answer a question to our liking, this goes on and you go in," Batista said.

James Hawthorne McMillan confessed to four murders, four women he'd been involved with in one way or another. He talked for thirty minutes giving precise details of the crimes.

Nothing McMillan said wouldn't hold up in a court case against him, but they had a lot of details about the victims, one of whom they didn't know anything about. He gave them the name of the Romanian housekeeper, which was more than they had at this point. At least now they had a name which was all McMillan knew about her along with an approximate location where he'd buried her some forty-six years ago. Owens made him point to the spot on an internet map.

There was nothing more they needed to get out of the prisoner. Gottlieb and Dr. O'Neill were blindfolded and led away by Sebastian, keeping up the fiction. If they were ever implicated in this crime, they'd say they were taken against their will and were threatened with death if they reported their kidnapping.

The closer the lie is to the truth, the easier it is to remember.

There was only a single matter to attend to at this point.

"You didn't really think you were gonna make it out alive from this, did you?" Owens asked as she pushed the chair even closer to the shredder.

"You'd never be convicted unless you actually confessed, like legally confess, and we all know that ain't ever gonna happen," Batista said.

"We cut you loose, you lawyer up, and we'll both end up in jail. We're cops, but we aren't completely stupid," Owens said.

Sebastian stepped up.

"Do you even know who I am?" he asked the prisoner.

McMillan was too terrified to answer.

"I was the guy who said he wasn't going to kill this cop for you," Sebastian said, pointing at Beth Owens.

This sparked McMillan's memory.

"Then you went after my mother and my mother's friends." Sebastian said. "My mother!"

Sebastian had to pause to reel in his fury.

"Now do you remember me?"

Batista pushed the button starting the tree shredder.

"You killed four women, that you admitted to. You tried to kill me, and you had Logan killed. This is it for you, James McMillan," Owens said. "I doubt you gave those girls this opportunity, but you got any last words? Not that anyone gives a shit."

"My lawyers will have you all in prison. Are you out of your fucking minds? You'll never get away with this," McMillan shouted over the din of the machine.

"Maybe not, but you most definitely aren't getting away with your sins, not in this life," Owens said.

Batista and Sebastian pushed hard on the back of the chair. It fell off the platform and fell into the shredder which came to life again with a roar. They ran the pile of limbs though the machine, then switched it off. For the two former soldiers, the silence was like after the last round was fired in an artillery barrage, something they called an "eargasm."

"To the end, the motherfucker thought his money and lawyers were going to come to the rescue," Batista said.

Batista drove the van out while Owens walked over, closed the gate to the compound behind her, and locked it.

*Hermanos Hernandez - Hernandez Brothers*

*Landscaping and Tree Service*

She hopped in and they drove away.

# EPILOGUE

McMillan's disappearance wasn't reported to the police for a full six days after the abduction. The people at his real estate headquarters didn't suspect he was off the grid until four days after his last contact. They waited another two days, still agonizing over whether or not to inform the police of their concerns. James McMillan had been such a tyrant over his staff they were terrified to tell the police or anyone else anything about him. Their boss had always made it abundantly clear to everyone that his private life was no one's business but his.

Finally, Drew Rice, McMillan's chief counsel, decided he needed to cover his own ass. This was a problem that wasn't going to fix itself. James McMillan was off everyone's radar. All Rice was able to learn on his own was McMillan hadn't been seen or heard from in six days. He called the Philadelphia Police.

"What do you think happened to him?" a detective asked Rice during their interview at PPD headquarters.

"In all honesty, I have no idea," Rice said.

"Is there anything to suggest something may have happened to him?"

Rice fumbled with this question and the detective couldn't decide if he had something to hide or it simply took McMillan's executive officer off guard.

"You mean like foul play?" Rice asked.

"Is that completely unthinkable? Does McMillan have enemies?"

Rice almost choked on this one. McMillan? Enemies? Where could he possibly begin? But murder? The real estate scion's enemies in the business world would have viewed violence as a poor weapon in their battles over whatever the rich fought over. As a former lawyer, he understood this better than most people in the McMillan organization.

"All wealthy men have enemies, but I don't believe any of them would resort to murder," Rice said. "It never even occurred to me James may be dead."

"Then let's not jump to conclusions," the detective said. "The first thing we need to determine is whether or not he's even missing. How many homes does he keep around the world?"

Rice didn't have the exact number.

"I don't know for sure. I know of at least six…"

"Six?"

The detective almost spit out his coffee, thinking how he was struggling to maintain one home in a ratty South Philly area.

"Two in Philadelphia, at least one place in New York City, another on Martha's Vineyard, Palm Beach, and the Caymans. He goes to London a few times a year, but I don't know where he stays."

"Maybe he's shacked up somewhere? Is that possible?"

It was very possible, Rice knew.

"Possible, but six days without any word from him is unprecedented."

"Maybe the woman is unprecedented?" the detective said.

There were no suspects and no motives, while at the same time, there were also dozens and dozens of individuals who had countless motives to do him harm. However, there was absolutely no evidence a crime had been committed. PPD had no idea how to even begin an inquiry into the disappearance of the enigmatic billionaire.

Six days without a police report would be something out of the wildest dreams of anyone committing a crime. Investigators would have to backtrack over a week, an eternity which would present countless dead-ends and faulty memories. In many cases, closed circuit security videos would already have been deleted, evidence destroyed, and confusion would increase regarding the facts.

The least favorite question a police detective wants to ask a potential witness is, "Do you remember what you were doing six days ago?"

It took several days just to determine the whereabouts of McMillan's private jet which was undergoing routine maintenance at a facility in Ontario, Canada, and had been there for almost two weeks. The police had no way to track down the manifest of the jet, nor did they have the authority to demand it from the maintenance company who reminded the police it wasn't their aircraft. In any case, private aircraft are only required to submit a passenger manifest when crossing international borders.

To put it lightly, the trail for James McMillan was extremely cold before the PPD was even informed he could be missing. This was good news for quite a few senior members of the department who'd been the beneficiaries of his corruption. No one in the department who ever dealt with the man wanted to see McMillan again. If McMillan had simply vanished into thin air, those high-ranking officers who'd benefited from his real estate deals would have much less to worry about if their property purchases ever came under investigation.

James McMillan had made a lot of contacts in the Philadelphia Police Department with his huge payouts and sweetheart deals on apartments, but he hadn't made a single friend. The truth was that many of the recipients of his bribes would've welcomed nothing more than for him to disappear without a trace. Forever. Now that they'd reaped the rewards of doing his bidding, there was no James McMillan to threaten them if they didn't jump when he ordered them to, nor could he testify against them if he ever went to trial and wanted to sell them out to make a deal for himself. To say the PPD wasn't very motivated to investigate the matter of James Hawthorne McMillan would have been a tremendous understatement.

Twelve days after the abduction, the disappearance of James McMillan had become news, although the story didn't exactly make national headlines and only rated less than a minute on a local network news broadcast. About the only thing remarkable about the man was his net worth was often referred to in a figure with ten digits. He was no industry pioneer, or inventor, or anything other than a highly successful speculator who'd been born into a very wealthy family.

His wife had almost no input in the case and stated through an intermediary from her compound in Palm Beach, Florida, that she hadn't seen him in months. His children couldn't be reached for comment.

James McMillan may or may not have been missing, but it seemed certain no one missed him.

PPD was completely unconvinced it was their problem. There was no evidence suggesting he'd gone missing in their jurisdiction. There was no evidence of foul play. Of course, no body was discovered, nor would there ever be a body. There were no leads in the mystery of the vanishing billionaire. The habits of the James McMillan, of traveling anonymously, of leaving no word of his whereabouts were now working heavily in favor of anyone who may have wanted him dead.

Because there was no evidence of a crime, no one even considered Owens to be a suspect. She had recently reported that McMillan had paid someone to kill her, and there was an attempt on her life. The police inspector handling her statement warned her that she needed to be more circumspect in her accusations against such a prominent local businessman, all but telling her McMillan couldn't possibly be out to murder a policewoman. PPD had not only buried her complaint against McMillan, but it was also completely deleted from the record.

This was well before he vanished into thin air, something that infuriated Detective Owens when she discovered her complaint against McMillan had been erased from the system. Now Owens had one less thing to worry about. There was no longer a single record in the Philadelphia Police Department linking her with McMillan.

Abducting McMillan had been Dr. O'Neill's idea, and she'd insisted on being there at his mock trial—also her idea. Noah Gottlieb was also anxious to face McMillan and question him. Owens had insisted on the charade of bringing the two of them in wearing hoods, simply to make it easier for them to stick to their stories if it ever came down to an investigation. If asked why they didn't come forward before, they'd say their lives had been threatened if they talked about the kidnapping.

James McMillan became something along the lines of Amelia Earhart in the media, and like the female aviator, he was the subject of a lot of wild speculation on television talk shows. Everything from murder to kidnapping to the real estate tycoon running away to join a cult were considered with equal enthusiasm, all with the same complete lack of proof. Batista had suggested at one point they should call in a phony ransom request to throw off investigators, until they realized there were no investigators to throw off.

Even his wife and children didn't care enough to pay for a private inquiry into his whereabouts. Mrs. McMillan had complete control over most of her husband's finances, at least those she knew about. She and her children didn't miss a beat as far as their economic interests were concerned. She wasn't interested in having any more than she already had. Her attorneys informed her that in seven years, he could be declared legally dead. She didn't care enough to even think that far into the future. Whatever had happened to James, it meant almost nothing to her.

Caroline was never contacted by the police. No one would ever learn she'd spent a couple of months as the missing billionaire's girlfriend. Gottlieb had coached her on the value of never telling this secret to anyone, ever. No one worried she would. Owens didn't even know her last name, never asked. Owens always thought this was a pity because she would've loved to hear from the strong-willed young woman.

Three months after the abduction, the group met at yet another Center City pub, the first time they'd all been together since that day.

"He definitely picked the wrong women to mess with when he pissed off you and Caroline," Dr. O'Neill said.

The Temple University professor was careful to avoid names; she'd been coached well by Gottlieb and her two police friends.

"That girl would have made a great cop," Owens said, referring to Caroline.

Noah Gottlieb hadn't uttered a word during the conversation, quietly sipping his pint and listening.

"I have to say, in all my years working in the annals of the criminal justice system, this has been my most rewarding endeavor."

"God damn, Noah. Do you always talk like that? Like you expect someone to write down what you say?" Owens asked. "Cops never even speak in complete sentences."

"If you'll allow me to continue to speak in complete sentences, I'd just like to say I think we're all free and clear on the matter," Gottlieb said.

The four of them raised glasses.

"This wasn't about revenge, or even justice. It's about saving lives," Owens said in way of a toast.

Owens was finally able to contact Schmitt. He was teaching at a university in San Diego, California. He remembered her and seemed excited she'd emailed him.

"War hero college professor. You must have to fight off the coeds with a baseball bat," Owens wrote to him.

"Are you joking? They'd use a baseball bat on my ass if I so much as met a student's gaze. That student-fucking ship sailed. I have to meet age-appropriate women the old-fashioned way: I beg them to go out with me and lie about my income," Schmitt answered.

They'd been corresponding for a couple of weeks before Owens invited him to visit Philadelphia. He accepted the offer mentioning he was making plans for an East Coast tour for some academic conferences.

"I can return your copy of *Memoirs of an Invisible Man* you lent me," Owens said in a phone call to Schmitt to talk about his visit.

"I wondered who had my copy. My memory was sort of interrupted after getting blown-the-fuck-up," he said. "Did you like it?"

305

"I've read it cover to cover three times already. About time for the fourth."

"I can't wait to read it again," Schmitt said, wanting to make a joke about the late fee he wanted to exact from Owens, hoping she was still as hot as he remembered.

I'd like to read it to you in the bath, Owens thought. She didn't have any expectations about the two of them, but there was always something about that boy Owens had never found in anyone else.

Requests for transfers into homicide had been approved for both Batista and Owens. She'd start with homicide in five weeks and Batista at the end of the fiscal year.

Meanwhile in the Domestic Violence Unit, the two detectives still had a job to do. There was a message a woman had logged her twenty-seventh call.

www.ingramcontent.com/pod-product-compliance
Lightning Source LLC
Chambersburg PA
CBHW070737180626
46818CB00007B/2887